Flowers of Tartarus

by

Michele Leech

Copyright Notice
This is a work of fiction. Names, characters, places, and incidents are either the product of the author's imagination or are used fictitiously, and any resemblance to actual persons living or dead, business establishments, events, or locales, is entirely coincidental.

Flowers of Tartarus

COPYRIGHT © 2023 by Caitlin Mullowney

All rights reserved. No part of this book may be used or reproduced in any manner whatsoever without written permission of the author or The Wild Rose Press, Inc. except in the case of brief quotations embodied in critical articles or reviews.
Contact Information: info@thewildrosepress.com

Cover Art by *The Wild Rose Press, Inc.*

The Wild Rose Press, Inc.
PO Box 708
Adams Basin, NY 14410-0708
Visit us at www.thewildrosepress.com

Publishing History
First Edition, 2024
Trade Paperback ISBN 978-1-5092-5502-3
Digital ISBN 978-1-5092-5503-0

Published in the United States of America

Dedication

To my mom.
(Please skip the sex scenes)

Chapter 1

This wasn't how she wanted to find him.

Lily Nehme cracked her knuckles beneath her arms conveniently crossed to hide the faint popping sound. No one in the chattering crowd paid her any mind. They were too distracted by the body on the ground that only recently had been covered with a tarp.

But Lily had seen the tattoo on his arm, the easily identifiable marking she'd studied.

The yellow police tape kept the masses back, but as she nudged her way to the front, her elbows brushed the resilient plastic. Now she stood near the coroner's van, half hidden behind the door and eavesdropping.

"…guess seems to be an overdose," one of the ME's people said.

"Another one?" A heavy sigh echoed against the walls of the van, loud enough for Lily to hear clearly. "We've gotta find this dealer. Whatever they're spreading is laced with something nasty."

"I thought Jersey was the one with the fucked-up shit," a third voice said.

"Welcome to the SPD," the first said. "The origin of fucked up."

A clearing of a throat ended the conversation, and an authoritative voice spoke up. "Clear this place out and get the body back to the morgue. As there are no statements to take, start knocking on doors."

"Captain—"

"Now, Officer Hughes."

A strong looking, tall man with broad shoulders and a week of scruff stepped out from behind the truck. He wore the blue uniform and angry scowl of an officer on door duty. His sullen grey eyes searched the crowd; Lily slipped back into the masses to avoid his gaze. If he spotted her, that would be the end of her day.

Besides, she couldn't do anything more here.

Stepping away from the crowd, Lily pulled her phone out from her purse and typed a quick text.

—You gotta give me something.—

The response came at once.

—Not again. You promised last time would be the LAST.—

—He's dead. Give me something.—

She could almost hear the sigh before the next text came. Not a message, but a picture.

A stamp of some kind in glow-in-the-dark ink showed on the victim's wrist. An ornate T between two lines with a small triangle above it, and two wavy lines below.

A club stamp, she recognized. Recent enough to have been the last place he'd been seen alive. She'd seen the symbol before but couldn't place the venue.

A second image flashed on the phone screen. This one showed a small plastic bag marked with a bisected O and filled with a hint of blue powder. Must have been what he overdosed on.

—Thanks— she sent.

—Don't mention it. Seriously. Not ever.—

Lily put the phone back into her purse, tugging the leather strap over her shoulder before stepping onto the sidewalk. As she walked, she took a moment to breathe deeply before she pulled out the phone and sent out another message.

—I have information. Meet me at my place at 7.—

There was no response, but she didn't think there would be.

The sidewalks grew more and more empty; trash piles heaped higher the further she walked into the former glory part of Southton, New York. After living here for two years, she could nearly pinpoint the street where the financial section ended, and the dangerous section began. Once a thriving factory district, the companies moved out as costs rose, leaving empty warehouses in their wake. With so many empty spaces and hiding spots, the area became a hotbed of criminal activity. Most people avoided it once the gangs and criminal kingpins assumed the control the police had relinquished. It was also where Lily lived and worked.

She used a key to unlock a rusty door into an alleyway. The front door hung open, but she preferred sneaking in the back and getting ready before meeting with her students. She hung her coat up in a locker and pulled out her gym bag. The dress and tights were replaced with a tank top and leggings, the heels by worn sneakers. Her flowing brown locks were pulled back into a tight bun at the base of her neck. She yanked on a pair of gloves over her manicured nails and stepped out onto the mat of Jed's Gym. She grinned on seeing several of her students ready to go.

"Let's get started," Lily said.

****

"No, but I'm seriously seeing a real difference," Reva Hall said, her dark eyes dancing along with the smile on her russet-colored face.

Lily grinned, pulling on her heels again. "Good."

"I'm not," said the third girl in the room, her light brown hair tumbling over her shoulders as she flipped the ends out from her collar. "I don't think I'll ever get the hang of this stuff."

"You will, El," Lily said. "You've got good instincts; you just have to trust them."

"Instincts aren't exactly my specialty," she retorted, zipping up her bag.

Reva stood, buttoning her jeans and slipping her feet back into her boots. "You couldn't land a punch to save your life when we started. Now, not only do you hit, but you hurt. You're getting it."

"Maybe." Eliza smiled. "So, what's the plan now?"

"I've got a meeting," Lily answered, combing her hair into place with her fingers.

"Did you find him?" Reva asked, falling into step as the three of them left the gym.

She nodded, her mouth a thin line—a familiar expression to the others.

"I'm sorry," Eliza said quietly. "Do they know what killed him?"

"They're saying it's an overdose, but weird. It's laced with something."

Reva's eyes narrowed. "That's been going around. Police have been trying to track this dealer down for months. Drug-related deaths have spiked 26% since this shit hit the streets."

"And how would you know that?" Eliza asked, leaning past to glare at her.

She grinned, unrepentant. "I have my sources."

"Yeah and tell your source thanks for me. He sent

me a couple of pictures. Speaking of—" She reached into her purse and pulled out her phone. "—do either of you recognize this club stamp?"

Eliza shook her head, but Reva hissed out a breath. "That's Tartarus. The club off Brookfield. Super classy, super nice. I tried to get you to go there last month."

"Want to go tonight?" Lily asked.

Reva stuck her tongue out at her. "Of course, you would. I have dinner tonight with Jason, and we're not rescheduling again."

"How about you, El?"

"Sure. I could use a little music." Eliza's smile faded somewhat, "But Lily...if he's already dead—"

"Then my job is just prolonged. I found him, but now I need to know why he died. And if this drug is as bad as they say, it's just going to keep becoming a problem."

"And of course, how dare we expect the police to handle it," Reva said, cutting her eyes at Lily.

Ignoring that, Lily paused at Reva's bus stop, her arms crossed over her chest. "With idiots like Doyle Hughes on the case, I doubt it'll be investigated properly."

Reva shrugged. "That's fair. Alright, you ladies have fun and be careful."

"Always," Eliza said, at the same time Lily said, "Never."

"Seriously. Tartarus may be the shit for adult entertainment, but everyone who works there has a criminal history. Arson, robbery, identity theft, hacking, or something," she said with a choppy wave of her hand. "Plus, the place is run by Sebastian Galani."

"Who?" The name sounded familiar to Lily, but

****

Tartarus was only about a half-hour walk from their apartment, through some rather rough areas of town, but Lily didn't carry the knives in her boot and in her purse just for show. Besides, she had a bit of a reputation.

When she first started her PI business, no one of importance came knocking on her door for help. So, she had made her name by starting in the low-income areas, looking for the people the police had given up on. Most of the stories had ended poorly, but a lot of families were grateful for knowing anything at all, even if it was bad news. Though most of her jobs had been missing persons, there'd been a few security-style jobs. Protection. Those all ended happily for her clients. Less so for her targets, and frustratingly for the police. Her reputation enjoyed two sides. The hero who found those whom no one else looked for. The delinquent who'd been picked up several times for assault, bloodied knives doing her talking for her. Either way, even if they didn't know her name, there were few areas in town where her face wasn't recognized by sight.

Whichever reputation they'd heard, everyone left her alone, and she arrived at the side door to Tartarus ten minutes early. A key card entry sat off to the side, but a cinder block shoved between the door and the wall kept it ajar. Behind the club, she could see a truck unloading a bunch of kegs and bottles. Possibly restocking the bar. She eyed them for a minute, noting the shaved head of a large man who seemed to be in charge. As far as she could tell, just alcohol being unloaded, but she noted the name of the distributor to check out later.

She knocked on the door and waited a minute, then pushed through, and stepped into a plain hallway. Off to the right, an open door led to a small lounge, better lit than the club. Likely meant for the employees. A coffee pot percolated on a simple white counter along the back, where a sink and a small dish rack sat, filled with mugs and a bowl. A row of beat-up lockers lined the door, some empty and some holding coats and purses. A table sat in the middle, with an array of chairs, and cards splayed on the surface in an abandoned game of solitaire. Another door off to the back of the room hid a bathroom, and a couch occupied most of one corner, with a couple of pillows and a blanket along the back. The room looked homey. Comfortable.

The door to the left lay propped open, and Lily heard shouting and orders from the men outside. That must be their back room and storage. A staircase went up on the right but curved so she couldn't see the top.

In front of her was a heavy metal door. When she stepped through, she recognized the dance floor of the club. She looked at the other side of the door, seeing another key card entry and a sign that read "Employees Only" on the door.

The club looked much the same in the daylight, just better lit and much quieter. Music played, but mellow and soft, and she recognized Marley at the DJ table, her headphones in place as she worked on her computer. She looked up as she walked in and pulled them around her neck. "Hey! Good to see you again. Teegan was talking with Ellis, she'll be back in a mo'."

"No problem," Lily said, going up to the bar. This close, and this empty, she could see that the floor behind the bar was lifted slightly, giving the bartender access to the shelves up top and able to pass and take items from beyond the bar top easier. A simple lifted top made up the entrance, and she ran her hand over the dark wood with a smile.

At first, bartending at Diamond had been a distraction after her mother's death. Since she didn't think she could handle anything meaningful at that time, the sounds of the bar kept her mind busy, and she could chat with tons of people and not have to worry about forming meaningful connections. Music had always been a wonderful diversion from the anger, forcing her to work out her energy in dance as opposed to something more destructive.

And if she'd had to function as a bouncer a few times, well, a little violence was still fun.

At first, she'd worked there to keep the depression at bay, but Lily found she enjoyed bartending. She liked meeting people, she loved the vibe of the loud music and dancing, she loved making drinks and trying new things. An escape became fun. Something she enjoyed.

"Sorry to keep you waiting."

Lily turned from the bar to see Teegan entering with two men. One, in dark jeans and flannel shirt, was the man from outside. The other was a tall, dark-haired man with a smile that seemed a little too bright and wide for the reputation this place and its people enjoyed. He wore jeans and a black sweater, but of higher quality than the others.

"No problem."

"This is Ellis Ortiz," Teegan waved to the larger man. "He's security, loading, muscle when we need it."

She held out her hand, noticing the tattoos that crawled up his arms. "Nice to meet you, I'm Lily."

"Heard you think my bartending's shit," he growled.

She couldn't help her smile. "Yup."

He glared at her, then snorted. "Might be right, but anyone who wants anythin' other than a beer is an idiot."

"And this is Darcy Richards." Teegan jerked her head at the guy with the too bright smile on her other side. "He manages the tech and security."

Lily shook his hand as well. "Hi."

"Great to meet you," he said, that wide smile somehow still completely honest.

Teegan waved at her. "So, go behind the bar. We'll order some drinks and run you through the paces."

"Sounds good," Lily said, heading back. She took a moment to get familiarized behind the counter. The space was very organized, so it was simple.

When she was ready, she looked at Teegan, who said, "I'll have a Long Island Iced Tea. So, what brought you to Southton?"

Lily filled a shaker with ice from the bucket beneath. "Looking for a fresh start. Once my mom died, I didn't have any family left, and I've been bouncing around. I came out here and started teaching some classes at Jed's Gym." She poured out equal amounts of rum, vodka, gin, and triple sec, just eyeballing the pours. She looked up at Darcy while she put the alcohol back.

"I will have a…Mojito," he said, with the same big smile. "Why do you want to work here?"

Getting the muddler from beneath the counter, she grabbed a sprig of mint from the neatly labeled bucket and mashed sugar and lime juice together. As she finished and put the lime juice and sugar back, she grabbed the sour mix and added that to the Long Island. "I like the vibe here. Like the music. I live in the area, so it's convenient. And I prefer night shifts."

None of that was a lie, even if there were more

reasons to work here. But she did like the place. She looked at Ellis.

"Beer. You got an issue with criminals?" he asked.

Lily popped off the cap of a bottle with her palm — no small feat, but one she had perfected — and placed the bottle in front of Ellis. She reached up to grab the white rum and added that to the mojito, again eyeballing her pours. She didn't meet their eyes as she added a dash of cola and soda water to the respective drinks. "Depends on crime. But I've got enough of a record to know that crime doesn't necessarily mean evil. And no crime sure as hell doesn't mean good. I do what I can to be a good person, and sometimes that means breaking the law."

She put the finished drink down in front of Teegan and Darcy. "Long Island. Mojito. Beer." She shrugged. "Don't know your prices, but I'm good with numbers once I see them."

She looked over and met Ellis's eyes. He didn't smile, but the blue seemed a little gentler. "What's your record?"

Lily quickly gauged her options. Getting caught in a lie would ruin any chance she had, but if she told the truth, they might not hire her. Even though she ran a risk, she found that she didn't want to lie to him. "Assault. Twice with a deadly weapon." When he merely stared, no obvious judgment, she elaborated. "I knew a girl who was having a hard time with an ex. He wouldn't back off, so I made him. Word got around, and I helped a few others. Some of their abusers were easy to convince. Some took more effort."

She glanced at Teegan, who didn't seem to write her off, and added, for full disclosure, "I regret going so far with a few, but I don't regret stepping in. I'd do it again."

Ellis nodded, drawing her gaze again. "You're alright," he said, before slamming his beer back and pushing away from the bar.

Darcy sipped his drink and made a, "Mmm," sound. She nearly laughed. Teegan passed her drink to Marley, who took a big sip and gave her a thumbs up.

"She's good," Marley said, putting her headphones back on.

Teegan smiled, crossing her arms. "Job's yours, if you still want it. Hours are shit. Pay isn't great. The people are assholes. But we have fun."

Lily wiped her hands off on one of the bar towels, "Sounds like my kind of place."

"Can you start Friday?"

"Can you start now?" Darcy added.

Lily smiled. "Friday sounds great."

"Let's go sign some paperwork."

Chapter 3

Sebastian Galani watched the sun set behind Southton's financial district, the tumbler at his side empty, save for a few melting ice cubes. Below him, the floor vibrated faintly as Marley got ready for tonight's set. His apartments above Tartarus could be inconvenient, but he'd trade a few hours of trying to sleep for convenience and security any day.

Pressing a button in on the wall, he watched the curtains come out then automatically slide across to hide his west-facing windows. The room was dark—he hadn't bothered with lights while he got ready—but such was his routine. Turning, he strode between the low, dark leather couches and placed the glass on his counter. Usually, he cleaned up after himself, but he'd lost a little too much time in thought this evening. Besides, Michelle would be in tomorrow morning to clean.

The dark couches were accented by the grey-white marble of his walls and floors, black and dark blue the only spots of color on the couches and little artwork he had. The door to his place opened directly into the living room, intended to be overwhelming. Off to his left lay an open office, the bookshelves reaching the vaulted ceiling and his desk overlooking the view of the city. Off on the other side sat an all-black, marble kitchen, with black stainless-steel appliances, and beyond that, his bedroom door.

Shutting the front door, he heard the lock click behind him, and he started down the steps to his club, taking the right instead of the left fork at the landing. His polished shoes reflected the faint light, the black trousers and shirt matching perfectly. His jacket lapels had a slight sheen to them, giving his suit some depth, as did the tie around his neck. All black, all meticulously cleaned and fitted to him precisely.

He would never be able to rid himself entirely of his family's name or reputation, and there were advantages to leaning into that fear from time to time.

His first stop, as always, was the back room, where Ellis organized the boxes they might need for the evening, and to check on the shipments. "Ellis," he said as he entered, his low voice cutting through the louder thump of the music. "How're things?"

"S'all good," Ellis said, the second he came into view. "Need to get some more soap, Ward says. But we'll last until the next order."

He straightened his cufflinks, his eyes casting over everything. "Good. Everything else?"

"Quiet. Haven't heard anything new lately, and they're laying low for the moment. New bartender passed muster. See how she does tonight."

"Nehme, right?" Sebastian recalled from the papers Teegan had him sign.

"Yeah. Lily Nehme."

"And your opinion?" He trusted Ellis's instincts on almost everything. His read on people relied not on empirical evidence but was usually spot on.

Ellis opened up another box, folding the lid back with a sigh. "Not entirely sure. I think she's on the level, but…" He shrugged. "I'll keep an eye on her."

"I'll have to go say hello."

Ellis snorted, "Good luck."

Not knowing entirely what to make of that, he nodded at Ellis and left the room, checking the empty staff lounge first. Making a mental note to buy more coffee, he stepped out onto the club floor, letting the heavy door separating the lounge and his stairwell swing and close.

Teegan was on her tablet at one of the couches and he nodded at her. He was familiar enough with the security to recognize a diagnostic check. She wore her usual all-black ensemble, her hair down. She would cover for the bar during Nehme's breaks and was far more capable than Ellis. She waved her fingers at him and turned back to her work.

Marley bounced at the DJ's booth, the music already pumping, but turned down as she finished her setlist for the evening. She'd adjust as necessary, but she had her go-to music prepared and organized. Her clothes were mostly black, with the usual shocks of red or dark purple, and her hair in a short faux hawk. She didn't acknowledge him, but he didn't expect her to. He was just checking in on things.

In the center of his club, he saw the new bartender, and his critical eye found several flaws already. Ellis hadn't mentioned her age. She looked to be a little older than Marley, but definitely younger than anyone else.

She dried some shakers, stacking them within easy reach on the side. Her dark brown hair was pulled back into a ponytail, and the black jeans were fine, like the black tank top. But over that, she wore a sheer, brightly patterned wrap covered with flowers in greens, blues, reds, oranges, and yellows. Vibrant and colorful—and not in keeping with his club.

His phone buzzed with one of the many notifications he received throughout the day, and he glanced down as he approached the bar. Even with the lifted floor, she stood an inch or two shorter than his six feet and one inch. She glanced up as he approached, the twist of her lips almost a smile. The amber eyes were clear—no hint of drugs or drinking on the job—and ran over him as surely as his had over her.

"You must be Lily Nehme," he said, placing his phone face down on the bar top.

Her brow quirked slightly at his words, either at the knowledge or the tone he didn't know. Regardless, she grabbed and dried the next shaker. "That's me. And you must be the mysterious Sebastian Galani."

"Correct. Welcome to the team."

"Thanks," she said. Her voice was low, raspy. Sebastian noted the calloused knuckles of a fighter, familiar enough with the injuries at this point in his life.

There was something about this Lily Nehme that he couldn't quite put his finger on. He didn't know if it was the way she spoke or dressed or moved, but something wasn't quite typical about her. His phone vibrated again, and he checked the message.

"You understand," he drawled, tapping through his phone with one hand and gesturing to her outfit with the other, "we maintain a certain…aesthetic, here."

He didn't look up, but he saw her smile in his peripherals just the same, another glass going into the clean pile.

"In my experience, having a bartender who's easy to spot is worth more than ambiance."

That made him look up at her, his brow rising

slowly. "And how many years of experience is that, exactly?"

"Enough to know how to read a job application. And there was approximately fuck all in terms of a dress code."

That made him put his phone back into his pocket and meet her eyes directly. She'd dropped the towel, both hands braced on the bar top. "Look here, Ms. Nehme—"

"Lily," she interrupted.

No one interrupted him, save for Ellis, and the novelty threw him off for a moment. She leaned forward slightly, smiling at him with a few too many teeth showing. "How about a deal?" she suggested. "I make you a drink. If you don't love it, I'll change into something more. . . *appropriate*."

Sebastian considered for a breath, weighing the pros and cons. Worst case, he'd have to put up with flowers. Best case, she'd change. Little risk involved and less of a chance for lingering frustrations on her part. He sat down at the bar with a nod. "I'll have a—"

"No," she interrupted him again. "I'll figure it out."

She grabbed a short tumbler and turned away from him mixing a few things together and turning back once she muddled them together. "So, how long has this place been open?"

"Five years," Sebastian said, watching her carefully. She moved with confidence, despite this being her first night here.

"It's nice," she said. "I don't know why I didn't come here before." She grabbed a bottle of his higher-end whiskey—his favorite, not that she knew that. "Guess I didn't expect something this nice in this part of town." She glanced up at him briefly, from beneath her lashes.

Noting the intention, he kept his face passive. "Do you live around here?"

"About a half hour's walk." She added a splash of water.

He couldn't help the twist of his mouth at that, and she saw, smiling.

"Smooths the alcohol," she said.

"Waters down the alcohol, actually."

Lily grinned. "Trust me, boss."

"Not yet, I won't."

"But you might soon?" she countered with another one of those looks at him.

He almost smiled at that. She was flirting with him, casual, nothing serious that might complicate her working here, but a little levity. He had to admit, after years of honing his reputation, a little levity was refreshing.

She reached down and grabbed an orange garnish which she added to the glass. Plucking a napkin off the tall stack just below the bar top, she placed the drink in front of him, her brow arched and her grin confident enough to worry him.

"Go on," she challenged.

He picked up the glass and took a sip. The whiskey tasted…better than usual, and that irritated him. The water really did smooth out the whiskey. The obvious tastes—the bitters and sugar—made this an old fashioned, but there was something else. Some tart taste that accentuated the whiskey.

He put the glass down. "Trust is earned," he said. "Not given."

"Good thing I'm dedicated."

With a faint chuckle, he stood, taking the glass with him. "Good luck this evening."

"Thanks, boss."

He turned and walked away, taking another sip. He wasn't surprised in the slightest when she called after him. "So?"

Sebastian didn't turn around, but called back, "Keep the flowers."

****

Lily smiled as she placed another round on the bar top, taking the cash patrons gave her and ringing them up just as efficiently. She passed them their change as she checked on the others at the bar, seeing that everyone seemed satiated for the time being. Taking a breath, she grabbed the glass of water she hid beneath the bar and downed the entire thing, her voice hoarse from shouting over the music. She'd have to pilfer Eliza's stash of tea to keep behind the bar.

Over the course of the evening, she'd caught glimpses of the others. Marley was the most obvious, dancing away on the stage behind her music setup. The girl rarely took a break, just a few seconds in the middle of songs. Lily had sent a few drinks her way courtesy of Darcy, who moved through the crowd to check on speakers and lights all night. She hadn't seen Ellis since earlier in the evening—his job as the bouncer out front kept him busy, and there'd been no need to call him in. Not yet at least. Teegan had been back and forth a dozen times already, and Lily saw her slipping beneath the bar now.

"Hey, you ready to take a break?"

"If you don't mind."

"Not at all. I'll see you back here in half an hour. Get something to eat." Teegan slipped her ever-present tablet beneath the counter and rinsed her hands in the sink before turning to take an order. Lily left her glass there, leaving the bar and heading to the employee's door.

"Hey, baby, you come here often?"

"Blonde is my favorite color."

"You'd look better in my—"

Avoiding the catcalls, Lily tapped her card against the door and vanished, leaning against the cool metal for a moment and relishing the quiet. She enjoyed the club scene, but acclimating once again to the high-energy demands exhausted her.

The employee lounge was empty, but the coffee urn was full. She poured herself a massive cup and used the restroom while her dinner heated up in the microwave. Eating took just a few minutes, leaving her a good fifteen to kill before her break finished. Rinsing her cup, she decided a little exploration would be best.

She went back to the hallway and started up the stairs. At the fork at the landing, she took the left side, finding herself at a locked door. She knew from her studying of the blueprints that Galani had a massive apartment above the club. She contemplated trying to get in but saved that idea for another time. Going back and taking the right fork instead, she went through an unlocked door.

The music from the club surrounded her at once as she found herself on the catwalk around the edge. From up here, the drop looked much higher, and she could see every inch of the club, save directly behind the bar. She saw Marley at the table, and Teegan seemed to be doing well at the bar, Darcy danced poorly in a corner, out of sight of Marley. Lily let her eyes drift, enjoying being up here, part of the crowd, but still distant, for a few minutes.

Against the wall by the door, she saw Ellis, not really visible from her usual station at the bar, but from up here, she could see the door on the upper floor. The bouncer leaned against the wall, looking at Galani, who spoke to him. She let her eyes linger a little on her new boss. He'd stopped by the bar twice to check in on her, as he did his other employees, but she'd been a bit distracted.

After Reva had mentioned his name, she had done her research both on the bar and the owner. He was…complicated, to say the least.

Born into the famous Galani crime family, Sebastian Galani apparently had no desire to be involved. His father, Antonio, had put a chokehold on the city even before the factories shut down. She'd seen his rap sheet: money laundering, assault, drugs, even murder. He died in prison eight years ago, and Sebastian's younger brother took over. Daniel was just as bad as his father, though without the level of decorum that Antonio had faked. Daniel was violent and brash; as a result, the Galani family had steadily lost their bloody influence.

Sebastian, though, was different. He had himself emancipated at sixteen, worked his way through college with scholarships and part-time jobs, kept his hands clean and head down, though he stayed in Southton. After his father's arrest, Sebastian began to make some waves—through entirely legal means.

He opened Tartarus, after paying for the building in cash, receiving a liquor license, and renovating the building to comply perfectly with all building codes. The cops had been in and out of the club almost daily for five months after opening day and found nothing out of place. General consensus seemed that Sebastian Galani would have nothing to do with his family name or business, and truly meant to become an upstanding member of society. Sure, the people he hired were criminals, but that seemed like an afterthought.

Except, it wasn't an afterthought at all.

Lily had gone through everything about Tartarus carefully. She'd learned Marley grew up in the foster system and had more name changes than people had hairstyles as she tried to figure out who she was. Having seen the system from the inside, the DJ's later convictions for identity theft seemed almost natural. Teegan's parents and brother had been killed by extremists in their home country, and when she escaped to America, her illegal alien status had conveniently disappeared right after being given access to computers. Darcy had been engaged, until his fiancé had been gunned down during a car jacking eight blocks away from here. Nothing more than the wrong place, wrong time. He'd broken into the police department to retrieve her belongings and get the names of the men who'd killed her. What he did with that information, she didn't know.

Ellis had grown up with Sebastian from the beginning, and she'd read about the jobs he'd pulled for the Galani family as a young kid. When Sebastian got emancipated, Ellis stopped his work with them, getting a job as a mechanic close to Sebastian's school and staying out of the family business. He did, however, have several pops on his record, things that occurred during

Sebastian's college years, mostly assault and battery, and Sebastian was usually present, though not involved.

All these misfits, all gathered by Sebastian Galani, who appeared to be the most enigmatic of them all. She didn't know what to make of him, not really. Other than he was inconveniently attractive.

She had seen the photos from his youth, but he had to be in his forties now. She hadn't expected him to age so well. Gray shaded his dark hair, but that was the only discernible difference. The jawline was strong beneath the close-cut beard, the eyes bright and clever, his movements assured. She caught the play of muscles beneath the expensive suit, and the lean form drew many eyes from the crowd, including hers.

His attitude with her had been brisk, but she had seen how he'd relaxed a bit when she started to joke with him. The flirting had just been good fun, as well as giving her the reputation of easy-going flirt and making most people not think twice about her. But she hadn't found smiling at him to be all that difficult.

Ellis said something and Galani smiled, his eyes dancing even from this distance. Lily exhaled slowly, letting herself indulge for another few moments. He really was handsome as hell. Then a smaller man approached Galani, taking quietly enough that he had to lean down to hear him. With a nod, Galani and the shorter man approached the employee's door, and she caught Ellis's faint frown before she darted back to the stairwell.

She went as quickly as she could down the stairs but kept her silence. She heard the heavy metal door shut and froze, half hidden in the shadows of the stairwell just out of sight of the door.

"Quiet week," the other man said.

"Appeared so," Galani said, his voice cooler than with her earlier. "Do you have my usual?"

"'Course, Mr. Galani."

A shuffle of plastic sounded. Lily frowned in the dark, wishing she could see. Her gut said he was buying drugs, but Galani wasn't like his family, he—

"This is some good shit, too. Fresh."

Lily closed her eyes, exhaling silently and slowly. He was buying drugs. And she'd been stupid enough to have thought he was above that, if the disappointment in her stomach was any sign. Idiot.

"And this?" Galani asked. A moment of silence.

"That's not mine. It's not—"

"I'm aware of that," Galani interrupted. "Find out who's responsible for this and there's an extra bonus in there for you." Another sound of shuffling, like something being passed between them. "Your usual cut."

Any explanation that didn't paint Galani as the villain in her story seemed more and more unlikely. She chewed her lip in silence and listened to the rest.

"Thank you, Mr. Galani. Hey, was gonna mention, I'm loving your new bartender. She's better than Ellis, and a hell of a lot hotter. And she's got a great fuckin'—"

Galani's voice was icy as he interrupted again. "She's an employee. I'll thank you to remember the usual rules."

"Y—yes, Mr. Galani," the man stuttered, obvious fear in his voice. "Thank you."

"Good evening."

"G'night."

The man passed the stairwell below her, heading out

the side door. Blond hair and squirrely looking, but that was all Lily caught before he walked past. The door opened and closed with a squeak, before shutting with a loud click.

There was a small sigh from below, then Galani walked past the stairs, one hand in his pocket and the other rubbing the back of his neck. He walked into the employee's lounge and Lily heard the bathroom door close.

Quickly, Lily climbed down the last few steps and slipped back into the club. She returned to her position at the bar, letting Teegan head back out and doing her best to put her smile back on her face as she fell into the rhythm of the work.

She did, however, see Galani return to the club via the employee's door. She couldn't see his eyes, and his hands looked steady, but Lily looked away as his gaze drifted over the bar, her focus on making the drink in front of her. She had forgotten herself for a moment, but she wouldn't forget again.

Sebastian Galani may be good looking, but he was also her number one suspect.

Chapter 4

"You saw him actually taking the drugs?" Reva asked.

Eliza ducked beneath Lily's punch, coming up too close for her to get a good swing in. She shoved her shoulder into Lily's chest, knocking her back. The blonde grinned at her.

"Good," Lily said, slightly out of breath. "And I heard it."

"Maybe it wasn't what you thought." Eliza blocked Lily's punch to her side, her abs burning as she twisted out of reach. She glanced at her legs, suspicious. "You do have a tendency to jump to the wrong conclusion."

Lily's brows snapped together. "I know what I heard."

Eliza shrugged, blocking Lily's punch, but missing the sweep of her foot. She hit the mat hard, her air knocked out of her lungs.

Before she could catch her breath, Lily was already apologizing. "El—"

"It's fine," she wheezed, getting to her feet. "That's what I get for getting overconfident."

Reva stepped over, giving her a hand up, and they stepped off the mat.

"I'm sorry," Lily said, coming over.

Eliza smiled, knowing that Lily was truly sorry. The PI sometimes lost her temper, and Eliza knew she would never intentionally hurt her. "I'm fine."

"Nehme!" Jed, the owner of the gym called. "I need a minute."

Lily waved at him, not looking away from Eliza. "I'm really sorry."

"I know. It's okay." She nodded to Jed. "Go on."

Reva and Eliza grabbed the bags, heading back to the locker room.

"You sure you're okay?" Reva asked.

"I'm fine, honestly. She just winded me. I'm okay."

Reva and Eliza had stayed to help Lily blow off some much-needed steam after their usual class. Eliza's many text messages had kept Reva in the loop about Lily's new job, and both women were concerned. Though she hadn't said anything to the contrary, something about this case clearly had their friend off-kilter. And, considering what Lily did for a living, she needed to be on her game.

The girls washed up and changed before Lily joined them. Her frown vanished the second she saw Eliza observing her face.

"Everything okay?" Eliza asked her cautiously.

"Yeah," Lily responded, grabbing her bag and heading into the shower.

Reva gave Eliza a look and they both got up, leaning against the tiled wall of the shower. "What's going on?" she called through the steam.

"Nothing."

"Is it Jed?" Reva asked. "Because I can just get my dad to shut this place down."

A faint laugh had Eliza relaxing slightly. "I'll keep that in mind."

"So, you heard Galani taking drugs?" Reva said,

going back to what had riled Lily up in the first place. "Didn't you say he was your suspect?"

"Yeah."

"Sooo..." Reva trailed off, frowning at Eliza, who merely shrugged. "He's a criminal and your suspect. What's the big deal?"

"Because he..." Lily cursed under her breath. "He's not a criminal. His whole family's a bunch of assholes, but he stayed out of it and opened up this club in spite of everything, and he's kept his nose clean. He helps people, but now he's dealing? Getting people killed? I...expected more from him."

Eliza cocked her head, as Lily explained, the hurt surprise in her voice so uncharacteristic for her painfully realistic friend. "Do you like him?"

"Don't be stupid."

But Reva nodded. "No, that makes sense."

"I barely know him!" Lily argued, turning off the water and grabbing a towel. "We've had one conversation."

"Love at first sight," Reva responded.

"Doesn't exist," Lily said, walking past them towards her things in the locker.

Reva opened her mouth, but Eliza shook her head, ending the conversation. She followed Lily, sitting on the bench and smiling, trying to get her hackles down.

Lily hung up her towel, then met Eliza's eyes, still wary.

"You respect him. What he's done," Eliza said gently. "And he disappointed you."

Without a hint of any affection beyond professional courtesy, Lily relaxed further. She nodded after a moment. "I do. Did. It just doesn't make sense for him to do all of this, to climb so far, only to take a risk on something this stupid," she said, zipping up her bag. "He's smarter than that."

"Then," Eliza said slowly, gently. "Don't you think you should give him the benefit of the doubt?" Lily opened her mouth to argue, but Eliza continued steadily, not letting her get a word in. "If he is as smart as you say he is, then this doesn't make sense. He wouldn't take this risk, not after everything. Could there be another explanation?"

Lily shrugged. "Maybe."

"Then you owe it to him and yourself to find out. You don't want to accuse him of something he didn't do. If he's worked so hard to overcome his past, you should give him the opportunity to explain himself." When Lily remained quiet, she added gently, "Like we did for you."

Lily's eyes darted up, and Eliza arched a brow. Lily could beat her into the mat day after day, but she listened when Eliza spoke.

"I hate it when you do that," Lily said, a faint smile appearing and letting Eliza know they were still good.

"I know, which is why I only do it rarely." Eliza stood, grabbing her bag. "I'm going to be late for work if I don't leave now. Have a good night."

Reva waved, but Lily stopped her.

"Hey. You guessed I was going for your legs. That was a good instinct. You should trust yourself more."

Eliza smiled gently and left. Hoping Reva didn't rile up Lily again, Eliza walked down to the bus stop and hopped on, her building several blocks away and the ride second nature to her.

She loved her job at the low-cost, general clinic, even if the more terrible parts of living in town were on display. Her work mattered here, unlike in more affluent areas, and she could see the difference they made. The clinic was small, with only three actual doctors on staff, but they did the best they could, and the community respected them, for the most part. They weren't bothered or held up by any of the many protection rackets, usually, though they weren't entirely safe. Just safer.

Despite the comfort that settled over her shoulders as she pulled her doctor's coat on, Eliza couldn't keep her thoughts from drifting to Lily's dilemma. Even if she refused to admit it, Mr. Galani's apparent indulgence in crime had hit Lily harder than the PI had expected. And to have to see him every day at work…working so closely with someone she liked and respected, without understanding why he was doing what he did must be difficult.

"Hello, Clark."

Eliza turned in her seat to smile at her boss. "Hey, Will."

He looked down at her, leaning against the wall. "Thank god you're here, I thought it was just going to be Ramirez and me, and I would have killed myself had that been the case."

Several years her senior and several degrees her superior, William Lintz rarely acted as such. His gray eyes constantly danced with sarcasm and humor, though she'd seen him in the midst of a few memorable brainstorms and sat in awe of him. She respected him and appreciated any time she could spend here, even if the rest of the city looked down their noses at them.

"Thank goodness I'm here to save you," Eliza retorted with a grin.

The corner of his mouth tilted up. "My hero." He

cleared his throat, looking over her shoulder after a moment. "Did you finish those diagnostics?"

"Of course." Eliza grabbed them out of her bag. "Explain to me again what you're doing? Research into hallucinogenic substances? You aren't going MK Ultra on me, are you?"

"If I tell you, it'll ruin the surprise."

"Will—"

"Don't you trust me?" William asked.

Eliza met his gaze, the challenge in his eyes as he stared at her. She might not understand entirely, but she knew the answer to his question was simple. "Of course, I do."

****

Lily placed one of her unique Old Fashioneds in front of Galani as he sat at the bar, going over a few papers and checking something on his phone. She looked over the bar, adjusting small items to suit her needs and finishing her final touches before they opened for the evening.

"Thank you," he said, without looking at her.

"Sure, boss."

He stayed quiet and she looked away from him to finish counting up her till. In the past two weeks, there hadn't been much of a change. She came in for work every day but Tuesdays and enjoyed herself. Despite her reservations about the owner, Galani hadn't done anything to increase her suspicions. In fact, everything about him seemed to be above board and disproved her original theories. Now, if only she had something to replace her theories with.

Fitting in at Tartarus had been startlingly easy. Her schedule was great, the pay decent, and the company wonderful.

She loved Eliza and Reva so very much, but this particular group of people made Lily feel like she belonged. All of them struggled and overcame what life had thrown at them, all of them felt like outcasts, and all of them had their own issues and problems they were trying to work through. Lily felt closer to home than she had in a long, long time. She got along with everyone here, which was also a source of some guilt. Doing her best to justify it, she told herself she may have started working here under false pretenses, but she'd been honest with them. And she did enjoy being here.

"You don't need to call me that."

Lily dried her hands—cash was low-key disgusting—and glanced over at Galani. "Huh?"

"You can use my name."

She leaned against the bar top with a wry grin. "It's what Ellis calls you. Besides, you don't use mine."

He avoided addressing her by name, and when he absolutely had to, he always said 'Ms. Nehme'. But she'd noticed.

Placing his phone face down again, he gave her his full attention. She appreciated that about him. Despite how constantly busy he always seemed, he made it clear he listened when you needed to be heard. Lily's grin widened as she saw the faint lift at the corner of his mouth. He wasn't a smiling kind of man, and it filled her with a weird sense of accomplishment when she managed to draw one out. Suspect or not.

"Ellis calls me boss because of the old days. No one else here has to."

"Teegan does."

"Because she knows it annoys me."

"Another reason for me, then." Lily grinned, folding her towel and grabbing her glass of water from beneath the bar. A small part of her, the cynical part that sounded like Reva, warned her about flirting so much with her number one suspect. She ignored that voice, watching Galani try and fail to look annoyed with her.

"Wonderful. Remind me why we hired you again?"

"Because Ellis was shit at tending bar."

"Are you ever gonna let that go?" Ellis called from the other side of the club, helping Darcy replace a lightbulb.

"Not likely," she retorted, causing Ellis to flip her off. She returned the gesture, and the big man hid a smile as he turned away.

Galani chuckled, taking a sip from his drink. He looked at the glass for a moment. "What do you put in this again?"

"If I tell you, I'd have to kill you."

He smiled, turning back to his phone and she watched him for a moment. He wasn't a bad guy, right? He had some sort of angle. He had to.

Her own phone buzzed and broke her contemplation. Jed's name appeared on the screen, and she answered. "Hey, Jed. What's up?"

"Nehme." From just that one word, Lily prepared herself for unwelcome news. The gym's owner never called, and his tone filled her with dread. *"Look, I hate to do this, but time's up."*

She went to the other end of the bar, dropping her voice even as her temper rose. "You said I had until the end of the month."

"He came back with a better offer, what was I supposed to do? You know these guys are connected."

"You're supposed to have a backbone and not screw over your regulars," she hissed. "What the hell am I supposed to tell my class?"

"You can find a new place."

"You know that I—" She caught her voice rising and forced herself to remain calm. "You know it's not that easy for me."

"Sorry, but that's not my problem."

Lily's spine straightened at the casual dismissal of the years of rent she'd been paying alone to use the gym three times a week for years. The disregard he had for the self-defense classes she taught. How much he just didn't care. "You screwed me over. I'm not going to forget," she spat into the phone.

She heard him swallow through the earpiece. *"They own the gym as of Sunday. I'd suggest you grab your shit before then. Nothing I can do. I'm sor—"*

She hung up, cutting off his insincere apology. She glared at the phone as the call ended. "Motherfu—"

"Everything okay?"

She turned back, seeing Galani had put his phone back down, his forearms resting on the bar as he looked at her. His eyes narrowed slightly as he looked over her.

"It's fine. Nothing," she said, a little sharper than she intended. "Do you want another drink—"

"What happened?"

From the stage, Marley laughed at something on her phone, calling Teegan over. Lily rubbed her forehead, pissed that Jed had managed to upset her so much. She knew this had been coming, but she thought the weasel would actually let her have a chance before pulling the rug out from beneath her. She dropped her hand, ready to spill out some sort of trifle to placate Galani into leaving her alone and—

"Lily." The name sounded strange coming out of his mouth as if it made him uncomfortable.

She met Galani's eyes, the blue narrowing further, as if he knew the lie on her lips. She took a breath and, to the shock of both, the truth came out. "I rent space in Jed's Gym to teach a class three times a week. Two weeks ago, he told me someone had made him an offer to buy up the place, and that I had a month to come up with a shit-ton of cash if I wanted to keep him, and me, in business." He knew she didn't have it, but she'd been working long hours at the club and pulling small cases to make extra cash. There had been a chance. A small one, but she had been trying so hard. "He's apparently done waiting. He just sold it and told me I'm shit out of luck."

Galani's face stayed carefully still. "He extorted you."

"What else is new in this town?" she muttered, refilling her glass.

"Can you go to another gym?"

She sipped her water, trying to get a rein on her temper. "I teach self-defense to the kids in the area. There isn't a lot of money in that. Less so, since I don't charge them." She put the glass down. "Gyms in the nicer areas won't let me do that, and the shittier ones charge too much." She pushed her straw around, not meeting his eyes. "Besides, it's difficult for me to rent anything with my…history."

"Why didn't you say something?"

She looked up at that, slightly confused. "Teegan gave me more hours to try and make up the difference, but it was a long shot."

"If you had asked—"

Oh, she understood now. She interrupted, gentle but firm. "I don't do handouts, boss." Certainly not from mob connections. "Thanks anyway."

"I don't give handouts," he said. "I meant using the club."

Lily frowned. "What?"

"Use the club for your class during off hours," he said. When she continued to just frown, he elaborated, "We don't use much of it before opening. You can store whatever you need in the back, clean up after yourself, and no rent necessary."

Lily shook her head. "I can't, I…the kids might make a mess."

"Then you can clean it up."

"I have my class three days a week."

"I own the building every day of the week," he countered.

"I won't have time to go home to shower and change before work."

"There's a full bathroom upstairs. You can use it on the days you teach."

Lily scoffed, trying to think of an argument he couldn't tear apart, and wondering why she hadn't already accepted this generous and amazing offer. Then she remembered Marcus and her suspicions of Galani. How could he deal drugs, when he clearly cared about the club and everyone around him? She didn't want to believe it.

So, she wouldn't.

She met his challenging gaze as he waited for her final attempt. "I don't like to owe people."

"Nobody does. And you won't owe me anything."

"Why are you bothering?"

He drained the rest of his drink, placing it back down on the table as he spoke, not looking right at her. "My family is…" His mouth twisted. "Complicated. Ellis wasn't always there to back me up, and I had to learn how to get out of trouble. No one should ever be in that position." He pushed away from the bar, taking his papers with him. "You can start tomorrow here. I'll let Ellis know and he'll have a key for you before we close tonight. Don't do anything stupid."

He left, leaving Lily reeling behind the bar just moments before opening. She found her voice before he got too far. "Thank you, Sebastian."

Chapter 5

Sebastian hung up his phone, ignored the sounds of the shower running, and made another note on his computer. This entire business was completely unnecessary, as his advisor had told him multiple times in the past week, but Sebastian wasn't about to stop now.

It had been over a week since he'd told Nehme—Lily—that she could hold her class in the club; he hadn't seen much of her since then. He'd been busy with his investment advisor, Alex Harris, and when Lily hadn't been working, she'd been busy moving her supplies into the loading bay. Ellis said she'd only brought a pile of old mats that didn't take up much room. He'd given Sebastian a funny look when he explained that he was allowing Lily to teach at Tartarus but hadn't said anything else.

Sebastian didn't need to hear any pithy comments from Ellis; they ran through his head almost constantly. The shower stopped, and Sebastian stood, ready to head down to the club, but his phone rang, Harris's name lighting up the display. Sebastian answered, one-half of his mind on the conversation, the other on his failed attempt to renege on his agreement with Lily.

The first day, he'd made sure to be present at the club, to observe the class and find a way to cancel the arrangement. He should have thought before he spoke, but the unfairness with which Lily and her students had been treated was unacceptable. He hated it when people took advantage of others and couldn't help his knee-jerk reaction to make it right. With time, however, he realized that he'd been foolish to offer the club for her class. He didn't need another complication, especially not now.

Then the students came in. They seemed uncomfortable as he sat at the bar, pretending to do work, but Lily had told them to ignore him and jumped into her lesson.

He snuck a few glances once they got more comfortable and forgot about him. They ranged from young teens to mid-thirties, mostly girls, but a few boys, too. Lily's focus seemed to be on escaping grasps. A review for some of them, and Lily encouraged those who were familiar with the movements to help one another, correcting positioning and movements. She worked with the group as a whole as they paired up, taking turns being the attacker and defender.

"Swing your hands down as you push your hips back," she told a pair, demonstrating what she meant. "Then as always, what do you do next?"

"Run," half the group chorused.

"Run. Scream your head off and *run*." Lily adjusted one student's hold and kept talking. "Predators go after people who are weak and won't make a fuss. So, make a hell of a fuss. Give the bad guy a reason to rethink going after you."

He watched them go through a few more holds and paces. The hour and a half flew by as the students mastered the moves and helped the ones who were struggling. They packed up with some chatter; a few of them smiled at him when they remembered his presence. Lily instructed a couple to put the mats away, and another two mopped the floor clean and collected any trash. She approached Sebastian when one of the older girls stopped her.

"Gerald showed up again when I was taking the trash out. I used some of your stuff and sent him on his way." She had a faint lisp that made her seem young, but Sebastian saw the marks on her wrists and arms.

"Good," Lily said quietly. "Remember, you have my number. If you see him again—"

"Thank you."

Sebastian kept his eyes on his phone, doing his best to keep his face calm. Lily walked the class to the side door, letting them all out before returning to the bar.

"Thanks again for the use of the club," she said. "Are you sure that wasn't an inconvenience?"

Here was his opportunity to end it all. To maintain the distance and demeanor he had. Instead, he just kept seeing the faces of Lily's students. The diligence with which they practiced the moves. The ease with which they executed them. The apathy as they mentioned using the moves effectively.

"Not at all," he said instead.

He led her up to his apartment door. The key code in the handle was easy to use, and he'd given her a personal code to get in. His security system would track and note when she went in and came out. He didn't tell her that.

"Holy shit," she muttered when she walked in.

Sebastian agreed silently, the sunset lighting up his apartment in the best way. His living room was directly in front of them, and she took a step towards the couch before remembering her sweaty leggings and t-shirt.

"Living room," he said unnecessarily. "That way,"

Bookshelves lined half-open walls, surrounding the open archway. His desk sat in the middle of the room, with a view of the city on his right. He loved the smell of the classics he'd collected, and though a lot of them were business-related, there were a fair number of his favorites interspersed within. An armchair and a small side table were the only other pieces of furniture, situated right next to the window to enjoy the view. She'd stopped in a couple of times in the past week, to let him know she was leaving, but he found her gaze lingering on the books and knew she didn't come in just to talk to him.

"Hello."

"So, out of curiosity, when you're not lurking around in the club," she said, leaning against the frame, "what do you do?"

He sat back in his chair. "Keeping this place in business is a full-time job."

"Yeah, but you're always working, so you have time for three more full-time jobs."

He nearly smiled. "I have a few other investments I keep track of."

"Like what?"

"Currently, I've been buying up real estate." He gestured to the papers and blueprints on his desk. She edged in, and when he didn't say anything to stop her, reached out to look over the papers. Her brows drew together as she compared the pages.

"You're buying gyms?" she asked, looking at him. "Why?"

Sebastian kept his face calm. "Karma."

She stared at him, her eyes widening when it clicked. "You're outbidding Jed."

He merely lifted a brow.

She tried to shake her head, but the smile on her face grew wider with every second. "That is so petty. I didn't expect it of you."

"What's the point in being rich if I can't be vindictive every once in a while?"

She laughed, and Sebastian's own smile escaped. Dangerous, his head whispered, but he ignored it as she rubbed her face and laughter away.

"What the hell are you going to do with five gyms?"

"Six, as of a minute ago. Some I'll sell in a few months. But I'm thinking of keeping a couple. Getting a few people on staff to run them for no membership fees. Try to make your kinds of classes more available to people." Since he'd seen her class, he couldn't stop thinking about doing something good for his community. His little efforts wouldn't help balance out the terror of his name, but they helped him sleep better at night.

She looked incredulously at him. "You...aren't what I expected."

"The feeling is mutual."

Her smile turned soft, her eyes on him and not on the papers in her hand. He felt his expression mirroring hers, and another dangerous thought entered his head before he could silence it. His phone rang again, and though there was no name, he recognized the number.

All of his reservations came hurtling back and he picked up the phone, not answering yet. He didn't look at her as he said, "Teegan said she's going to be a little late, so have Darcy do the normal checks on security before we open."

She frowned, but he ignored her, clearly waiting to answer the phone until she left.

"I should get down there, then," she said quietly.

He nodded, waiting for her to shut the door behind her, and suppressing the faint burn of guilt. It was his fault to begin with. He never should have allowed her to have her class here.

Bringing the phone to his ear, he stared straight ahead, his voice losing any warmth. "Hello, Oren."

****

Lily leaned over, trying for the third time to hear the brunette's order. The idiot kept looking down at the bar top, making it impossible for Lily to even read her lips to take a guess. "You've gotta speak up!" she shouted, losing her temper.

The girl finally did, grabbing her drink and left Lily without a tip, unsurprisingly. Lily gritted her teeth, chugging half of her water and refusing to let her eyes wander up to the catwalk. After her less-than-polite dismissal this afternoon, she hadn't been inclined to be all that pleasant to anyone, least of all her ass of a boss.

She'd finally believed that he really didn't have anything to do with the drugs. That she'd misinterpreted the whole exchange her first night here. She hadn't seen him speaking with the dealer since then, or the dealer himself. Galani had been straightforward, and despite his statements to the otherwise, she knew she owed him big for allowing her to have her classes here.

But his dismissal of her today brought back all of her suspicions.

She'd already texted Jason and asked if he knew anyone connected to the case with the name of Oren. She didn't expect an answer anytime soon, but knew he'd come through for her.

Sebastian hadn't come to the bar like he normally

did, and she told herself it didn't bother her. But a half hour later, she poured one of her special Old Fashioneds down the drain and frowned.

Said frown had yet to leave her face, reflecting in her tips.

When Teegan came to relieve her for her break, she swore to get her head on straight. She ate the leftovers Eliza had made the night before, then sipped a cup of coffee slowly, trying to let go of her irritation.

"Hey."

She looked up, seeing Ellis in the doorway. "Hey." She jerked her chin to the coffee pot. "I just made that. Should be done."

"Thanks." He grabbed Darcy's cup, removed the sticky note with his name, then filled it to the brim and slouched down on the couch. "How's it going?"

"Fine."

"Yeah? And how's the new look working out for you?"

Lily cut her eyes at him.

"Yeah, that look," he rumbled, snorting and closing his eyes.

Ignoring him, she tried to chug her coffee, but it was still scalding, and she needed the caffeine to survive the night.

"Boss told me about your class." Ellis's eyes were still closed. "Good thing you're doing."

"Thanks," she said shortly, pushing through the pain and finishing half of the cup.

"You ever had to use that kind of shit yourself?"

She lowered the mug, glancing at Ellis again. "Couple times."

"That sucks."

"Suck more if I didn't know how."

"True. How'd you end up teaching?"

His eyes were still closed, but Lily felt oddly judged by him. She turned in her chair to see his face but could read no sign of his thoughts. "I was coming home one night and saw a guy harassing a girl. Turns out it was her ex, and he'd followed her out. I scared him off, and she asked me to teach her a few moves." She remembered Anna's smile when she'd reluctantly agreed. "I met her at her place the next day, and she'd invited a couple of her friends, who wanted to know how to do protect themselves. I was already going to Jed's, so I just booked enough space for everyone who wanted to come. Been doing it for a couple of years now."

"I know the boss already said, but if you ever need a hand, I'm always up for a fight." He chuckled to himself, a joke only he knew, and added, "Catch him on a bad night and Galani'll be there, too."

"Right," she muttered, turning back to her coffee.

When Ellis sank into silence for a minute, she assumed he fell asleep, but a quick glance showed her that he was very awake and staring at her.

"Boss does a lot of shit I don't agree with. But he does everything for a reason, and it's usually a damn good one. You don't have to like him, I don't half the time, but you gotta know that."

"Why?" she asked, the anger shaded with curiosity.

Ellis drained the coffee that was still too hot for her, getting to his feet and leaving his mug on the counter. "'Cause people like us, we gotta look out for one another. No one else is gonna do it." With a final nod, he left the room, leaving her staring after him.

She scoffed after a minute, shaking her head at the

strangeness of criminals. Finishing her coffee, she cleaned her mug and, after a minute, Ellis's, too.

Stepping into the bathroom, she checked her makeup and fixed her hair, all the while eyeing her expression. The frown was gone, and the smile she tried on didn't feel so uncomfortable. Rolling her neck, she smoothed her skirt down and pushed open the heavy door to head back to the bar.

Or she would have, had a blood-curdling scream not echoed from the women's bathroom.

Lily didn't hesitate, she bolted to the john, shoving past patrons, most of whom hadn't realized what had happened. Marley still danced at the table, but Lily saw Ellis approaching from near the bar, and Teegan's face drew into a concerned frown.

Shoving the bathroom door open, Lily saw the brunette from earlier crouched over a small Asian girl who lay on the ground, her eyes open, but her chest eerily still. "What happened?" she asked.

The brunette babbled for a moment, nothing coherent came through, so Lily stomped forward. "What happened?" she asked again, grabbing the brunette's shoulder hard enough to bruise.

"She—she took something, I don't know!"

Next to the girl, Lily saw several dime bags, all with the same bisected O. Two were full, but three were empty. "Did you take one?" Lily asked, kneeling next to the girl and trying to find a pulse. She couldn't find one.

"No, I didn't, I just—I was about to, but then she collapsed and—"

"Call 911," Lily ordered. The brunette tried to say something else, but Lily cut her off. "Call 911, now!"

Getting into position, Lily began chest

compressions, trying to keep the blood flowing to her brain, but the girl got steadily cooler. Still, Lily tried.

She didn't know how long she stayed there, but she felt a hand on her shoulder a lifetime later. "Lily," Sebastian said gently, shaking her a little. "You can stop."

When she looked up, he stood behind her, and emergency services entered the room, taking her place. She stumbled as she got up, her legs asleep and her arms too weak to support her. Sebastian helped her up, steadying her with a hand under her elbow when she winced as the blood came flowing back.

She swallowed, her throat dry from numbering the counts between breaths, and her shoulders and arms aching from the repetitive movements. She watched as one of the EMTs shook her head, looking at her watch and calling the time of death.

Her breath blew out slowly, and she tried to stem the feeling of guilt that she hadn't gotten there quickly enough. That she hadn't found the dealer quickly enough. That she'd been too distracted to discover what she needed, and this girl paid the price. She stared at the girl for a long moment, until Sebastian tugged her arm gently.

"Come on," he said. "The cops are here."

Chapter 6

Another cup of coffee landed in front of Sebastian. He looked up at Teegan to thank her, but her focus wasn't on him—but moving between the cops still at the door and Lily huddled on the couch.

Sebastian followed Teegan's gaze and with some restraint, managed not to rub his temples.

The EMT's hadn't been able to save that girl, and the cops had been right on their heels. A small, sinister part of him wished they hadn't called 911 at all, knowing the cops would blame him. He buried that, knowing they'd all done the best they could.

In the confusion between the discovery of the girl and the arrival of the cops, most of the crowd had left. Tartarus shutting down their Wednesday night early. His employees, ranging from nervous to pissed, stayed in place once the door closed, waiting for the inevitable questioning and all the comments.

Sebastian had stood at the door of the bathroom, Ellis right behind him, watching Lily perform compressions long after they all knew it was pointless. She seemed completely unaware of their presence, her entire focus on the body beneath her.

Looking between them, Sebastian realized they could have been the same age.

It wasn't until emergency services had arrived and she had shown no sign of stopping, that he stepped in, and tugged her away from the body. She had been shaking, and he didn't drop the hand on her elbow until they made their way back to the employee's lounge, where the cops waited. Lily took a seat on the couch, her mouth shut in a thin line, eyes staring into the ground and hadn't said a word since.

That had been three hours ago.

One by one, his employees had been called out and questioned by the police, who took detailed pictures of everything in the club, save behind his locked door. As his private residence within his place of business, the search laws were shaky, but he knew enough to know that if they didn't have a warrant, he didn't have to let them upstairs.

He did, however, show them security footage from the evening, where they all saw the girl walking into the bathroom alone, followed by the brunette they'd questioned for an hour before releasing, then Lily walked in. He had opened the door moments after and stayed there, and though the cameras couldn't see everything inside the bathroom, the reflection of the mirrors showed Lily performing compressions. No one else had been close to the bathroom and his employees were all innocent.

Of course, that meant next to nothing.

Ellis came back in from his inquisition, muttering under his breath. Marley grabbed his arm and pulled him over to the coffee pot, talking quietly to him. Eventually, he relaxed enough that she let go of him, but kept close, the two of them whispering back and forth what Sebastian knew were unsavory jokes about cops.

Trusting Marley to keep Ellis occupied, knowing Teegan would die before losing her calm, and knowing that Darcy couldn't say anything to get himself into trouble unless he actively tried—which wasn't completely out of character for him—Sebastian kept his eyes on Lily, the only person who had yet to be questioned. He had been taken back first, invited to sit at the bar as if he didn't own it, and had to talk to Officer Hughes, a complete waste of brain cells if he'd ever seen one.

After humoring the officer for a good thirty minutes, Sebastian had gone back to the lounge to sit with the others, making the coffee that kept them going. But his patience waned, and nearly snapped when Doyle Hughes came back. He took off his police hat, tossing it carelessly onto the table and nearly knocking over Sebastian's mug of coffee.

"Alright, all of you but Nehme can go. Don't leave town, we may have more questions," Hughes announced, crossing his arms. "Tartarus is shut down until we finish our investigation."

"If I didn't already know the city doesn't give a damn about this part of town," Marley said, getting to her feet, "I'd know now, considering they put an idiot like you in charge of the case."

"You want to be arrested for harassing an officer?" Hughes retorted.

Marley grinned viciously, her eyes glimmering, but Teegan stepped between them. "No, we're all just tired. Thank you."

Hughes narrowed his eyes but gestured for them to leave. She pulled Marley out, followed by Darcy and Ellis, who glanced back at Sebastian. He nodded, staying in his seat. Ellis shut the door behind him, leaving Sebastian and Lily with Officer Hughes.

Hughes made good cops look bad. The type criminals used to justify their own terrible actions. He constantly hung around Tartarus, looking for a code violation or minor infraction to bust Sebastian on. He was the worst example of law enforcement, and Sebastian wouldn't leave any of his staff alone with him.

"I don't need you to stay," Hughes said to him. "Me and Nehme are old friends, right?"

Lily moved for the first time in a few hours, lifting her eyes to meet Hughes's. She leaned forward, resting her elbows on her knees. "Right."

Sebastian definitely wouldn't leave now. "Appreciate the thought, but this is my club, Nehme is my employee, and this is also technically my house, I'm not going anywhere." He sipped his coffee, completely unrepentant as Hughes glared at him. "You want to question her privately, you'll have to actually press charges. Which you don't have evidence for."

"You'd better tread carefully, Galani." Hughes remained standing, looking down at Sebastian. "This is the second body we've found connected with your club. And the second to die of an OD of the same new drug. We found a packet on both bodies. One might call that a pattern."

"Drugs and clubs usually go hand in hand." Sebastian kept his tone level. "I do my best to keep them out, but I can't control what people bring in. I seem to remember Ghostbar having a rash of similar deaths—eight over the course of a month."

"You know your numbers," Hughes said.

"One of you has to," Lily muttered.

Officer Hughes cut his eyes at her. "You've got something to say? You aren't out of the woods either,

Nehme. You've been indicted in several assaults, and now I find you with a dead body?"

Lily stood, facing Hughes despite their six-inch difference. "I tried to save her."

"That makes one in—how many? Seven?"

"Those men were attacking people. Girls. Kids."

"You killed two of them!" Hughes shouted, his fists clenching. "One lost an eye and the others—"

"And if you'd helped those girls when they asked you," she interrupted, "I wouldn't have had to step in and do your fucking job."

"Killing people isn't my job, Nehme. That's the difference between us. I'm a cop, and you're a glorified murderer."

Sebastian kept his mouth shut, watching the exchange. He couldn't get involved; he was on thin ice with law enforcement, and they were just looking for a reason to shut him down permanently. Besides, Lily could handle herself.

"Figures you'd be working here, now," Hughes said, gesturing around the room. "Galani's a criminal, too. Guess you all eventually find one another, right?"

Sebastian arched a brow, unfazed. He'd heard far worse than that. But Lily's jaw jumped, and he saw a flush start in her cheeks.

"You know," Hughes continued. "Your mom used to think you'd be worth something. Too bad you disappointed her. Repeatedly. What a disgrace to the Nehme name you are."

He waited for Lily's sharp tongue to make an appearance. For her to cut him down like he knew she could, like she'd done to him, and laugh in his face. Instead, her eyes lowered, and she remained silent.

"It's a good thing she's dead," Hughes continued in that same sneering taunt, "because you would have killed her yourself by now, slumming with criminals and—"

"Enough."

Hughes choked, nearly swallowing his tongue as Sebastian interrupted him, getting to his feet and stepping between Hughes and Lily. A stupid, stupid move, but he was already committed. "I don't think you understand the situation you're in, asshole—"

"That would be Mr. Galani to you," Sebastian interrupted again. "And I understand that you're harassing my staff."

"There's been a murder—"

"Which all of my staff have alibis for, and you've corroborated. You aren't asking questions, so I have to assume your attack on Ms. Nehme is personal, which has no place on the police force." Sebastian refused to let Hughes look away, unblinking, his voice dropping in temperature. "Next time the department would like to interview my employees, they can make an official arrest, or I'll be filing a complaint with your supervisors."

Hughes started to scoff, but Sebastian took a step forward, noting with pleasure that Hughes stood just a bit shorter than him. He raised his chin, looking down his nose at Hughes with a cold glare. "If not, I'm they'll be very interested to hear about the payments you've been getting courtesy of the Mazrani family."

All the color went out of his face as he took two steps back from Sebastian. "How did you—I mean, I'm not!"

Sebastian smiled without humor. "Of course, you aren't. Then I guess an investigation won't reveal anything."

Hughes glared at him, but his mouth remained shut. Grabbing his hat, he stomped his way towards the door.

"Officer Hughes," Sebastian called after him.

Hughes turned slightly and Sebastian was sure he would have spat on the ground if he had the nerve. "You owe Ms. Nehme an apology." He gestured to Lily but didn't tear his eyes away from the cop.

A dozen expressions crossed Hughes's face, until he choked out, "My apologies, Ms. Nehme," without looking at her. He turned on his heel and left, slamming the door behind him.

Sebastian stared at the door for a long moment, confirming he had control over his temper before he turned to look at Lily.

She stared back at him, her expression skeptical at best. The confusion started to slip in. "Why did you do that?"

"I don't like people harassing my staff."

"They want to shut you down. You've given them an excuse."

"They've been trying for years," Sebastian said, grabbing his mug and dumping it out. "They'll fail. Hughes's too much of a coward to push. My concern is how long the crime scene is going to take. They've taken weeks before."

In his head, he could see the decline in numbers and profits, and what he would have to do to support the club until they reopened. He rubbed his temples now, giving into the headache he'd had for hours, ignoring Lily's presence as he tried to figure out how to make this work.

"I know someone who might help," she said quietly.

He turned, leaning on the sink and crossing his arms.

"He works at the precinct. He's an evidence technician and a friend. I'll ask him to step in. They won't be able to keep you closed for long. Jason's famous for working through scenes quickly."

"How do you know him?"

"He's engaged to my friend," she said, grabbing her bag from next to the couch and fiddling with the strap. "But I met him through my mom, first."

Sebastian remained quiet, and Lily kept talking, not looking at him. "She was a detective. A good one. The only reason she wasn't promoted to commissioner was because she hated paperwork. She died a few years ago and never wanted me to be a cop, but when I started to get into trouble, she was...disappointed." She cleared her throat and looked up at him. "I'm sorry if I got you into trouble."

"It's nothing new. And if it hadn't been you, it would be Ellis or Marley. I'm more concerned about this drug." He had about a dozen phone calls to make and more footage to review. Which meant he wouldn't be getting to sleep tonight—today—what time was it? He saw his watch inching along to four a.m. and suppressed a sigh.

"I'll text Jason and get him on the case," Lily said, noticing his movement and headed toward the door. "He'll have it done in less than twelve hours."

"I appreciate it."

Still, she lingered, confusion on her face. "Thank you, for looking out for me. All of us. If there's anything I can do, let me know."

He nodded, still not entirely certain he'd made the right choice. But he felt responsible for his staff, and even when it went against his best interests, he couldn't ignore them. That was part of the reason his staff was so small—fewer opportunities to make these kinds of mistakes. But he'd made two very big ones for Lily Nehme in less than a month. He also found that he didn't regret them.

Not yet at least.

"Everyone has something in their past they'd rather not," he said, cleaning out his mug to avoid looking at her, his own name his biggest problem. "Own it. Don't let them use it against you."

"Thank you," she repeated.

"Enjoy your day off," he said as she went towards the door. He followed, to lock up behind her.

"You, too." She put her hand on his arm and squeezed gently before slipping out into the glow of early morning.

Sebastian stood in the door and watched until she vanished around the corner, then he shut and locked the heavy metal door. He confirmed that the rest of the club was locked down and empty, then trudged up the stairs to his apartment, and slumped on the couch. He loosened his tie and scrolled through his contacts on his phone.

It was going to be a long day.

****

While Will washed his hands in the sink, Eliza sat at the small table behind him sipping her coffee. Miguel was handling a small cut on a walk-in patient, resulting in a quiet morning thus far. She relished the downtime.

"Mazrani contacted us again," Will said quietly.

Eliza put her cup down, her foot swinging anxiously. The Mazranis were an organized crime family, and they had some idea of honor, but not much of one. They'd been coming by for months, strongly suggesting that Will start paying them to make sure nothing bad happened to the clinic. "And?"

"I told him we weren't interested in his protection services," he said as he dried his hands then turned around to lean on the sink.

"Good."

"But," Will continued, his voice heavy, "we may have to reconsider. They're all circling, Mazrani, the regular dealers in the area…we don't have the security to do it on our own. Even Galani—"

"If we give in to any of them, no one will come to our clinic," she argued. "They'll all be too scared of owing a crime lord, or whoever else tries to take over. And you know they'll take over."

"I know, but if it'll keep the clinic safe—if it'll keep you—"

She stood, cutting him off and narrowing her eyes at him. "Don't use me as an excuse. I've lived here my whole life, and I know what this town is like. I don't want us to give in to them. We can't."

He didn't move for a second, then nodded half-heartedly. "You're right."

Miguel walked in with a sigh. "Seven stitches, done."

"Congratulations on doing your job," Will shot at him.

"More than what you're doing." Miguel grabbed one of the cups Eliza had prepared for her coworkers. "Thanks, El. What else is on the board today?"

"We've got a few x-rays scheduled, and a cast removal for Ms. Dawson."

"Dibs on x-rays," Eliza said, just a half-second faster than Miguel.

"Oh, come on," he whined. "I hate cast removals!"

"Be a little quicker," Will said, marking Eliza name down on the incoming appointments.

"You're just biased. You like her more than me."

"Obviously."

Eliza grinned, sipping her coffee. "What do you have, Will?"

"I get to do interviews for another receptionist and on-call nurse." He sighed. "Rather have the cast, honestly."

"That's what you get for being the boss," Miguel said in a sing-song tone.

"Eternal torment?"

"Pretty much, yeah." Miguel nudged her shoulder gently, "Hey, you and I should do that Thai place for lunch since—"

He trailed off, looking behind her.

Eliza spun in her chair to look behind at who stood in the doorway of the lounge. "Lily? Oh my god…"

Her roommate gave a tight and forced smile, but that didn't catch Eliza's eye.

Her left eye was almost swollen shut, her lip cut and bleeding in a steady stream down her chin. She held her arm away from her side at a strange angle and the slice in her sweater right at rib level looked like a knife wound. Her knuckles were split and bruised, every last one, and various bruises dotted her arms and face. And there were undoubtedly more, Eliza guessed, where she couldn't see just yet.

"Sorry to bother you," Lily said, her voice scratchy. "Hey, Dr. Lintz. Miguel. Becca let me back here, hope you don't mind."

William took a step nearer, "What happened?"

"Fight," she said weakly, trying to smile and only managing to split her lip open wider. She winced and Eliza finally reacted, getting to her feet to take Lily by the arm and lead her to one of the exam rooms.

"What the hell happened?" she asked as she pulled out her ophthalmoscope to start a basic neuro exam and look for signs of a concussion.

"I always forget how cute Lintz is," Lily said, trying to smile again.

She wasn't distracted. "What happened?"

"Told you. A fight."

"Lily, as your doctor and your friend, you have to tell me." She held up three fingers. "You know the drill. How many?"

"Three," Lily said, clenching and releasing both fists in a rhythm Eliza had seen before. "Someone died at Tartarus Wednesday night. She overdosed on that new drug. I tried to…but they called time of death at the club."

"I'm so sorry," Eliza said, "follow the light, using only your eyes."

After completing the routine exam, she then checked Lily's shoulder for range of motion. He roommate hissed in pain but managed to move it all the same. No sign of a concussion, which seemed about right, considering how thick-headed Lily could be. Her shoulder was sprained though. "But what about all this?"

She lifted raised Lily's shirt and found a shallow knife wound across her ribs. It needed to be cleaned, but she could avoid stitches.

"I needed answers," Lily said, her words starting to lisp together. She must be exhausted. "I checked the usual haunts for dealers and tried to get information.

Most of them didn't want to cooperate. I had to…persuade them."

"Lily…" Concern and worry quieted Eliza's tone. "You could have been seriously injured."

She shrugged, then winced. "I had to do something. The cops have no idea. Even if they did, they aren't moving quickly enough. Tartarus was shut down as they work the crime scene, but Hughes is in charge and…" She sighed, rubbing her eyes and leaving a red smear in place of eyeshadow. "Sebastian's trying, but the cops don't care. They just want to shut him down, and he can't stop this, but I owe him, you know?"

Eliza tried to make sense of her friend's babbling. "Because of the classes?" She hadn't been able to attend one at Tartarus yet, but they'd been looking forward to doing so. Reva had a plan to expose Jed's extortion, but after he was unable to find a place he liked here in Southton, he'd left town. Eliza said good riddance.

"Hughes was giving me a hard time; Sebastian stepped in. He shouldn't have, but he did, and he might lose the club if I can't figure this out."

Knowing her past with Detective Hughes, Eliza said a silent thank you to Galani as she finished cleaning Lily's cuts and cruises, bandaging the worst of them. "You sprained your shoulder, and you need to sleep," she said. "I'll call an Uber and we'll go home."

Lily shook her head. "I've got work. You've got work."

"It will be fine," Eliza said firmly. "Call out sick from work."

Lily squeezed her eyes shut for a moment. When she opened them, Eliza caught her breath when she saw tears gathering.

"Lily—"

"I have to do something."

Taking her by the good shoulder, she ducked her head to catch Lily's attention. "You *are* doing something. A lot more than you should, but first, you need to rest. You need to keep yourself safe. They'll understand."

Lily scoffed, but didn't argue, her hand going into her pocket as she considered. Eliza waited in silence, until Lily finally nodded, pulling out her phone. "I'll stay home."

Eliza stepped out of the room to call for a car, then walked into the staff lounge. Will was still there, replacing her name with his on the board. "Everything okay?" he asked.

"No, but it will be. I'm going to leave a little early and take her home. I'm sorry. I'll call Reva and see if she can come over for a bit, then I can finish up that paperwork—"

"Don't worry, Clark. You do what you need to do." He lifted his hand like he was going to touch her shoulder, then stopped. "If you need anything, don't hesitate to call."

"Thanks. It'll be fine. Just…roommate stuff," she finished lamely.

"And that's why I live alone," he said, humoring her bad attempt at lightening the mood.

"You live alone because you can't stand people."

"Only some people. Others aren't so bad."

"I knew you loved Miguel," she said, half focusing on the banter as she grabbed her bag and coat. She looked up as Lily joined them, her mind already on how she could keep her roommate quiet and still and missed

Will's muttered comment as she left.
   "Not what I meant."

Chapter 7

Much to Sebastian's relief, the club remained closed only for Thursday night. Lily's contact stayed true to his word and had gotten everything cleaned up and recorded in record time, even if he'd done so amid mindless chatter and an excessively exuberant smile. The crime scene investigator, Jason Ortega, seemed to exist purely on optimism, and though irritating, he powered through the investigation. Sebastian almost wished he could have seen the look on Hughes's face when he found out Tartarus reopened.

However, he knew that his luck with Hughes and the rest of the SPD was running out. They were going to continue looking for any reason to shut him down permanently; he didn't want to give them an inch. So, with more than a little irritation, he read Lily's text a few hours before opening on Friday.

Finding Teegan on the floor, he spoke a little harsher than he meant to. "You'll need to cover the bar. Lily called out sick."

Looking unsurprised, she merely shrugged. "I kind of figured she would."

He frowned, unsure what she meant.

"Come on, boss. Show a little heart. She tried to save that girl who died despite all her efforts. That's gotta be hard. Then she's read the riot act by Hughes, living proof that sometimes it's neither brain nor brawn, and we all know he's a piece of work. You said she seemed shaken when she left," Teegan reminded him. "She lost her gym a few weeks ago. Give her a break. She's had a shit month."

When put like that, Sebastian could see the point.

"I'll have Darcy cover my break," she said. "He'll mess up all the drinks, but he's cute enough that people might tip anyway."

Sebastian snorted quietly and finished his rounds in a lighter mood. A few minutes before opening, as he sat at the bar reviewing the orders for next week, Teegan placed a drink at his elbow. She was comfortable behind the bar but didn't have Lily's particular brand of flair. Still, he appreciated the help and nodded at her as he sipped his drink—

And nearly spit it out.

Teegan had turned away, luckily, and missed his reaction. He quickly regained control and forced himself to finish, staring at the glass. It was an Old Fashioned. Why in the world…?

He had gotten too used to Lily's unique version, apparently. His former usual suddenly disappointed him.

Pulling out his phone, he scrolled through his messages. His phone calls over the past few days had been fruitless. No one came forward. Not yet, at least. He'd gotten a rumor that there was dissension among the dealers, but no one said why, other than a hazard to the job. He hoped that would bring some of the unattached ones forward, looking for his help and protection.

Unfortunately, the only person he had been able to get in touch with was Oren, who steadily denied everything, though they both knew better. Sebastian didn't believe him for a second, but he couldn't push him just yet. Not until Oren gave him what he needed. He still pushed for a face-to-face conversation, and though Sebastian didn't want to oblige him, he knew he would have to, and soon. Stifling his annoyance and making a mental note to put out a few more feelers, he scrolled back up.

Lily's name fell a few from the top of the most recent texts. The messages that came in prior to her calling out were updates of when her classes were, or that she was coming into the building and giving him a head's up. As he generally found texting to be an exercise in irritation, he usually didn't respond, other than an occasional acknowledgment when necessary.

He considered and reconsidered, then sent her a short message.

—*You'll be missed. Feel better.*—

Midway through the evening, after he'd turned down another Old Fashioned from Teegan and watched Darcy fumble his way through the simplest of orders, he made his way up to the catwalk and saw an answering message.

—*Thanks, boss. Sorry to disappoint.*—

He quickly wrote a response, and maybe if he'd been down there among the others he would have reconsidered. Up here, alone, he sent back:

–*You don't. Get some rest. Goodnight.*—

—*Goodnight, Sebastian.*—

He put his phone away long after he'd received and read the message and remained on the catwalk for the rest of the night.

He was in trouble.

****

Lily fumbled through the door, her bad shoulder

complaining when she forgot and used it to push open the side door. With a muffled curse, she turned, using her good arm and checking the hallway. No one as far as she could see.

Hurrying to the employee lounge, she checked and sighed in relief when that too was empty. Her bruises were turning all sorts of colors and though she owned a decent supply of makeup, she needed the high-caliber kind of cover-up to deal with her eye and swollen lip. The black shirt under her flowered shawl hid the bandage that still encompassed her middle and the icy-hot patch on her shoulder. The jeans covered the other various bruising on her knees and shins, and her boots helped hold the ankle brace in place. Her knuckles were bruised and scabbing, but she hoped the dark lights would hide that. The only saving grace for her dignity was that she'd received most of this from her fourth shakedown of the night, and she'd been ridiculously outnumbered. She'd still won, but it had taken a little longer than expected, and she still hadn't gotten any answers about who was in charge of this drug.

In order to hide her activities, she'd stopped at a convenience store and picked up the makeup, planning on getting to Tartarus early to hide what she could before the rest of them arrived.

She shut the door behind her and dumped her spoils on the table, taking off the wrappers as quickly as she could. Not a big deal; she could make herself presentable in five minutes and no one else arrived this early.

The door opened and Lily froze, her back to the hall. She leaned her head forward slightly, her hair falling around her face as she swore silently for forgetting the one person who would always arrived earlier than her.

"Welcome back, Nehme."

She stood, still keeping her back to Sebastian as she heard him step into the room. She grabbed the makeup off the table. "Hey, boss."

"Feeling better?" He put something down on the counter and turned toward her. She tried to keep her face averted, but it was getting weird now, and he was going to notice—

"I am, thanks." She turned to the bathroom. "I just have to use the—"

"Everything okay?" he asked, pushing away from the counter and stepping forward to block the bathroom door.

Gritting her teeth, and wincing at the pain, she looked at the floor, trying to find a suitable response, but coming up with nothing.

"Nehme."

Lifting her chin and biting back a sigh, Lily looked him in the eye, her hair falling back from her face.

Sebastian didn't react, and that was a reaction in and of itself, that careful and sudden stillness that revealed nothing—and so much. His hand lifted, taking her chin gently and turning her face up to the light. His fingers were cool, and she clenched her jaw to keep from shivering. "Who?" he asked quietly.

"A bunch of assholes. I sent them on their way." After searching for them specifically.

"Undoubtedly. How many?"

"Four or five." A dozen.

"When? Where?"

"Thursday morning," she said. "On my way home." Not a lie. That's when the first fight began.

After he let go of her, Lily took a deep breath,

suddenly feeling like she'd sprinted a mile. She took a step back from him, but he didn't move to open her way to the bathroom.

"Are you okay?" His voice stayed calm, but his brows were starting to draw together.

"A sprained shoulder. Some bumps and bruises. I'm fine." He didn't look at all convinced, and she smiled. "I'm fine, really."

"You should have called."

Lily shrugged again, regretting the motion as pain flared. "I texted—"

"No, I meant during. Or right after."

"I don't have Ellis's number."

"You have mine."

If she had called Sebastian, what would have happened? He would have pulled up in his fancy car, loosened his fancy tie, and thrown punches? She recalled the times Ellis had been arrested for assault when Sebastian was present, and she'd suspected that he'd been involved, but the last incident had been years ago.

Looking at him now, cold fury burning behind his eyes and the white tightness of his knuckles, Lily wasn't certain those days were all that long ago for him. Her answer, though, wasn't a lie. "I didn't want you to get into more trouble."

"Wouldn't that be my decision?" he asked her, arching a brow and some of his anger seeping through, though not aimed at her.

"I can take care of myself," she retorted, unsure if she should be offended or not.

"I'm aware of that. That doesn't exclude asking for help to make your life easier." When she didn't answer, he sighed, running a hand over his mouth before speaking again. "If it had been Darcy or Teegan, you would have thrown yourself in after them."

She didn't need to answer. Obviously, she would. Without hesitation.

"We look out for one another," he said.

Lily looked at the ground, feeling oddly like she'd disappointed him. Not that she could tell him the truth—that she had been looking out for him, and Ellis and Teegan and Darcy and Marley, all of them. She'd been trying to find answers as to who dealt this crap and risking everything they cared about. Because she did care, and that's what made her failure all the more painful. She loved Tartarus and her new, loser friends with their records and bad habits and poor taste in drinks. She needed to protect them, and she only knew how to go at it alone. Somehow, she'd still messed up.

"Sebastian," she began quietly.

He took a step forward, but they heard the side door open, and Teegan and Marley's chatter as they came in. With a short, indecipherable look, Sebastian stepped aside and intercepted the others with a few banal questions, keeping them distracted enough that Lily could cover up the worst of the marks, masking the rest with shadows and curled hair.

When she came out, he was gone.

****

Numbers were down.

Sebastian worked at the bar. The spreadsheets in front of him showed cover charges, alcohol purchases, and tips. He didn't need to look at them to know the truth. He merely looked through the crowd on this Saturday night, seeing the gaps between people, the space still available on the dance floor, and the lack of action at the bar.

Profits were still in the black but declining quickly. With the first body, overall income dropped, but had started to head back to the high point, especially with Lily's bartending skills bringing back some of the earlier patrons who'd left. But the second body had gutted them. They were barely at forty percent capacity and that was unacceptable.

A drink landed at his arm. He looked up to see Lily standing near him, a hesitant smile on her lips as she looked at him.

"Thanks," he said, picking up the Old Fashioned and sipping slowly. That unique taste was back, and he savored it, looking at Lily only once before she'd turned to take another order.

Had he not seen her without makeup, he might not have realized. He could still see the faint shadow of a bruise around her eye, and the strange stiffness at a few of her movements, but he already knew where to look. Had he not seen her earlier, would he have been able to identify the smell of the icy-hot patch somewhere on her arm? The bruises around her knuckles? The care with which she moved her shoulder? He wanted to think so, but he wasn't sure. The others didn't comment, though he caught Marley watching Lily a little closer than usual.

He'd thought she was sick and had still been annoyed when she called out. Instead, she'd been attacked, and he barely had the decency to wish her a goodnight. She certainly hadn't said anything, but that didn't excuse his obliviousness.

Sebastian told himself that this was necessary, that this had to be maintained to protect those who and what mattered to him. But if he couldn't even do that, what was the point? He was losing Tartarus, one low-attendance night at a time. He was losing his footing with the cops, one overdose at a time. He was losing the trust of his staff—his friends—one lie at a time.

He might be able to put an end to this, but if he lost everything else in the process, would it even matter?

Placing his glass over the folder of papers, he rubbed his eyes for a moment, ignoring the glances of various singles at the bar, all looking to catch his attention. He was infamous, but nowhere more so than here. Letting his eyes drift across his club, he could clearly see his employees doing their best to keep the crowd excited, and safe, dancing, and drinking—

And a man who had his hand around Lily's wrist.

She didn't look amused or encouraging, she was trying to pull her arm away, but Sebastian caught the flare of pain in her eye. He saw her lips moving, and though too far to hear, the words were clear. *"I said no, let go."*

Sebastian moved before he thought, coming up behind the man who leaned forward on his stool so he could reach Lily. "...promise it'll be fun," he slurred, too focused with his moves to notice Sebastian coming up behind him.

Resting his forearms on the bar next to the man, Sebastian glanced at him, waiting for his full attention before speaking. "She said let go."

The man smirked, flipping him off with his free hand, and turning back to Lily. She didn't look concerned, her expression clearly warning Sebastian not to get involved.

He'd learned long ago he wasn't great at that.

With one leg, he hooked the stool the man sat on,

yanking it out from beneath him. The man hit the bar with his chest, his air bursting out of him in a gust of tequila fumes, letting go of Lily as he tried and failed to catch himself before sliding onto the floor. Or, he would have, had Sebastian not grabbed the back of his too-tight T-shirt and kept him mostly upright.

"Let go!" the man said, his neck and voice scrunched in the awkward position and coming out in a nasally whine.

Sebastian ignored him, arching a brow at Lily and unfazed the flailing arms below him.

She shook her head, but he saw the smile at the corner of her mouth, growing wider as she looked at him.

Glancing back down at his captive, Sebastian shook him slightly. "I'm waiting."

"I'm sorry, okay! I'm sorry!" the stunted voice squeaked out.

Sebastian released him and the man sprawled on his ass amidst laughter from the crowd around them. With red cheeks and shame, he stomped off to the corner of the club. Sebastian watched Ellis separate from the wall and stay close to the man in case he tried the same move with another clubber.

A few people congratulated Sebastian as he returned to his seat, his drink already refreshed and waiting for him, along with his bartender.

He opened his mouth, but she smiled. "I'm fine. Thanks."

"Sure."

Lily watched him for a moment, and then rested her elbows on the bar, leaning over the wood to speak as close to Sebastian's ear as she could. "You were right. I should have called you. I'll remember next time."

Her tone was low, barely audible among Marley's oppressive bass and the loud hum of conversation around him. He didn't miss a word, though, so focused on her voice. Her breath brushed his ear, like a current down his spine. Turning his head to look her in the eye, he was still somehow surprised at how close she was, mere inches away. He could see the faint hint of red in one of her eyes, leftover swelling that she'd managed to hide from everyone else.

"Good," he managed to say in response.

Her fingers brushed over the back of his hand as Lily smiled again, pulling away to get more drinks moving.

He shouldn't be encouraging this. He played a dangerous game and had managed to keep the others away for years. They'd gotten close but never close enough to complicate things. Lily was too close. Too complicated. If he was smart, he'd cut her loose now, before it was too late.

Instead, he drank her Old Fashioneds and stayed at the bar for the rest of the night.

****

They were cleaning up after closing, loading the dishwashers and putting things away when Teegan broached the subject. "Numbers are down," she announced from her seat at the bar, where she tapped through her tablet, double-checking all the doors and cameras.

Lily wiped down the bar and glanced at Sebastian, who still sat in the same spot he had been all night, save his short adventure with the handsy frat boy. She wasn't certain if he stayed to look out for her, but his presence helped all the same.

At Teegan's comment, he looked up. She half

expected him to deny or pacify them with some half-truth about certain seasons being slower than others. Instead, he nodded. "They are. We've been declining for a while now."

Marley hopped up to sit on the bar top. Lily flicked her with a towel, but she just grinned and winked, her tongue between her teeth. "People don't want to party with corpses, despite what their clothing choices might say."

"How bad is it?" Darcy asked.

"If it follows the same pattern," Sebastian said, "there's a good chance we won't make it through the year."

Ellis took the seat next to Darcy. "Shit."

Sebastian sighed, and leaned back, looking at all of them. "Suggestions?"

Lily put the towel away, wondering if all their staff meetings were like this.

"Raise prices?" Teegan said half-heartedly.

Darcy shook his head. "We stole Cameo and Ghostbar's clientele by being cheaper. If we raise, we might lose them anyway."

"Our area means we have to keep it cheap," Ellis added. "We're in the slums, in case anyone forgot."

"Not likely, considering how polite our guest was tonight," Teegan said, looking at Lily. "How many times has that guy been here?"

"Six that I can remember. He's not normally that bad. I usually cut him off after three, but he stole a friend's tequila."

"Fucker," Ellis muttered, cracking his knuckles.

"If we can't raise prices, what can we do?" Darcy said, refocusing the group.

"Get rid of the bodies," Marley said, only half joking. "They're scarin' folks away."

"We can't stop them from taking drugs if we don't see them," Teegan reminded her. "They take this shit before they get here, or in the bathrooms. Ellis's kicked out a half dozen the past two nights with some new stuff."

"What stuff?" Lily asked, trying not to sound too interested.

Her eyes still on the tablet, Teegan said, "Some green pill, I don't know."

Sebastian's eyes narrowed. "Are they getting it from here?"

"I don't know. I've been looking for anything, but if the dealer's here, he's good."

Lily kept her eyes on the bar until Darcy cleared his throat. "We could change up the club…"

"You're not touching my club," Marley said at once. "We're not conforming to whatever those assholes in upper-Southton call a club."

"Maybe just a temporary—" Teegan started.

"No," Marley interrupted.

"What about a theme night?" Lily suggested.

Marley complained, "Theme nights are for karaoke bars and old folks' homes."

Lily threw the towel at her. "Theme nights upped Diamond's attendance by a third with little overhead."

Sebastian turned his gaze onto her. "Elaborate."

"Your den of sin thing here is cool, but you've pulled all your regulars in already. Theme nights give you a varied clientele who are more likely to come back on a regular night and keep your regulars from wandering after a bad night," she said. "Gives the impression of a revamp of the club without actually doing anything permanent. Start off easy. Keep with the vibe…a masquerade or vampire night or something."

"You're not serious."

She grinned at Marley. "Vampires make bank for a reason. Halloween just passed, so everyone's got costumes or cheap options, it's a perfect time to try."

The others looked at Sebastian, who seemed to be considering. He stared at her until she raised her brows at him. "Trust me."

Sebastian finally nodded. "Fine. Wednesdays are our slowest nights. Take the next one. If you can up attendance, we'll make it a regular thing. And if you can't—"

"No more flowers, I know," she interrupted, getting a laugh from Ellis and Marley and a smile from the others.

They finished cleaning up, helping Ellis take out the trash before they congregated in the lounge, grabbing their things and chatting. Lily found her mind running at a mile a minute with ideas for Tartarus. Potential themes and how to get the information out there. She ended up chatting with Teegan for a while after the others had left.

They walked to the side door and out to the front of the club where Lily saw two cars waiting. The first one Teegan had apparently called because she hopped in the backseat with a wave.

The other car rolled down the passenger side window and Lily got just close enough to look inside. "What are you doing?" Lily asked Sebastian, leaning on the open window.

The console was dim, and though she could barely see his face, she heard the smile in his voice. "Driving you home."

"Why?"

"Should I answer alphabetically?"

With a roll of her eyes that she didn't entirely mean, Lily got in the car, putting her bag between her feet and buckling her seatbelt. "This is a one-time thing."

"I believe the phrase you're looking for is thank you."

Lily scoffed and smiled. "Head north. Take a left on 5th."

Sebastian pulled away from the curb, the car nearly silent. It was a nice ride, probably worth ten times what she made in a year. She rested her head against the back of the seat, refusing to admit she appreciated this. Her ankle throbbed and she felt a headache coming on.

The quiet between them comforted her. Neither one of them needed to talk, save for Lily's quiet directions. She felt like she could relax for the first time in a while.

Not until they pulled up outside of Lily's building did she ask, "Are you doing okay?"

"I'm fine," he said immediately, and almost convinced her.

She unbuckled her seatbelt but turned to face him. The streetlight cast an orange glow on his face, not that she could read him well, but she didn't believe him. The silence stretched on for a minute before he spoke, his hands still on the steering wheel. "I don't want Tartarus to fail."

A lot rode on that statement, only some of which she understood. She reached across the seat and touched his arm. "We're going to do everything we can to make sure that doesn't happen." She didn't promise, because she couldn't, but she'd give him her best effort and hope that was enough.

He nodded, covering her hand with his for a moment before she remembered herself and pulled away gently. "Why'd you call it Tartarus?"

With a tired smile, he said, "It's what the deepest, darkest part of the underworld is called in Greek mythology. Where the worst of the worst end up."

"Is that what you think about the people who go there?" She felt like she already knew the answer, but she asked anyway.

"I think," he said quietly, with a brief glance at her, "a lot of the world sees us that way."

To be grouped with him and the rest of Tartarus, after dealing with people like Detective Hughes and Jed for so much of her life, was validating in a way she hadn't experienced before. Even Eliza's friends looked at her differently when she showed up with a black eye at the clinic, but Sebastian hadn't. He looked at her just the same.

She swallowed, just saying, "Thanks for the unwelcome ride."

Sebastian chuckled, and Lily got out of the car. Before she shut the door, he said, "Goodnight, Lily."

"Goodnight, Seb." The nickname slipped out instinctively. She thought maybe she shouldn't have, as he stilled, his eyes moving to her. Then he smiled, and she shut the door. He didn't pull away until she unlocked the main door and waved.

She stood in the entryway until his taillights were out of sight. Catching herself, she shook her head, blaming exhaustion, and trudged upstairs.

She had work to do.

Chapter 8

Tartarus looked just as imposing during the day as during the night. Eliza saw a few familiar faces from the class and followed them down an alley to a side door, hitching her bag higher on her shoulder. The short hallway led to a metal door, which hung propped open, and Eliza heard Reva's voice from somewhere inside.

Eliza entered and had to pause, making sure she had the right place. For the past two weeks, Lily had been going on about the theme night she was putting on—a masquerade—but Eliza hadn't expected her to go all out.

Fake candles, lit with flickering plastic tea lights ranged over the top of the bar, gold and black streamers and chains hung in loops around the entryway and along the walls. They weren't on yet, but Eliza could see floor lights along the wall, red and gold and dark purple. The entire effect would be striking.

Eliza and Reva had already promised several times that they would be there. After class, they would go back to Reva's place to clean up and get some dinner, then come back out to help celebrate Lily's big night.

"El!"

Refocusing, Eliza saw Reva and Lily at the bar next to a man she could only assume was the mysterious Sebastian Galani. Eliza approached, trying not to be too obvious as she looked over the club's owner.

Every time they talked about Lily's job, Galani's

name came into the conversation. What he'd said or done, how he helped Lily scare off the few creeps that made it past Ellis, how he'd been driving her home regularly, which Eliza appreciated, despite Lily's complaints. She didn't know if Lily was aware of how much she talked about him.

Eliza hadn't said anything, despite her suspicions, because she thought this life was good for her. Being a PI was wonderful and selfless, but dangerous and thankless, too. Plus, her friend had been en route to being arrested again if she continued with this mission of hers. Sure, the bruises from her beating a couple of weeks ago had only just faded, but Eliza hadn't heard Marcus's name in a while. She knew Lily still worried about it, and that she wanted to help everyone, but Eliza was thankful she had a safe—safer—job with people who genuinely seemed to care about her. Just like Eliza had with Will and Miguel. And if Lily solved her mystery in the meantime, that would be nice. Eliza had silent hopes that this job would be permanent regardless.

And looking at Sebastian Galani, she figured Lily had another motivation to stay, too.

He was older than she expected, but the sharp dark eyes were quick, the tilt of his head devilishly charming, and his faint smile enticing.

"This is my roommate," Lily said, her elbows on the bar as she leaned back, waiting for the others to arrive. Reva perched on a stool on her left and the topic of Eliza's interest stood to the right of Lily.

He took a step forward to take her hand.

"I'm Eliza Clark. It's nice to meet you."

"Sebastian Galani," he said, his voice lower than she thought, his words slow and deliberate. "Pleasure."

She took her hand back, her palm tingling and her knees pathetically weak for a moment. "I've heard a lot about you."

"Is that so?" He turned that intense gaze to Lily, who merely rolled her eyes.

She already knew that Lily was a very strong person, both physically and emotionally. Now, she hypothesized that she must be a superhuman to have been working with Galani for over a month and not jumped him by now. He wasn't even Eliza's type and she felt half in love with him right now.

"What do you do, Miss Clark?" Sebastian asked, turning his attention back to her.

"It's Dr. Clark," Reva said, smiling a little too widely. At least Eliza wasn't the only one affected.

"My apologies, Doctor."

"It's fine," Eliza said, tucking her hair behind her ear. "I work at the clinic on Passeo."

"Dangerous spot for such important work." He spoke without any hint of sarcasm.

"That's what makes it important," she said, lifting her chin.

"I have no doubts." His expression seemed sincere enough, so she decided to take his words at face value.

Taking a breath, she tore her gaze away from him and looked at Lily. "I thought you might have canceled class, what with your big night and all."

She grinned, looking around. "I've been here since noon setting up. If I don't burn off some of these nerves, I'm gonna lose my shit. So," she said, raising her voice. "Let's get started!"

They jumped into their lesson with vigor. They were reviewing one of the few moves Eliza had actually perfected, so she felt confident enough to let her attention wander somewhat, glancing back at the bar periodically.

At first look, Sebastian seemed to be occupied in his work, recording something in a classic paper ledger, checking things on his phone, writing out lists, and whatever else club owners had to do. But she kept checking, unconvinced. Why would he feel the need to stay down here the entire time, when she knew he had a comfy office just upstairs, according to Lily? Maybe he felt he needed to keep an eye on the class, but he kept looking when he thought no one else saw, and not at the class.

His attention seemed to follow Lily constantly, though he rarely looked directly at her. But as she shifted around the room, Sebastian would turn in his seat, just slightly, but enough so that if he glanced up, he would see her. He seemed conscious of where she was at all times, his head tilting just slightly whenever she spoke, his hand pausing briefly to listen.

They were subtle moves, but Eliza had spent enough time around classic recluse and introvert William Lintz to see some of the same movements. Will was much the same, very conscious of those he worked with and shifting appropriately. He may do it more often to her than to Miguel, but that was part of his whole game to pretend he hated Ramirez. She knew better.

Only once did he look directly at Lily. She had been showing how to flip a larger person over her hip, and as Julian's body hit the mat, Lily grinned, her ponytail clinging to her shoulders.

Sebastian watched her with a smile, then his eyes moved to catch Eliza staring. He arched a brow, the smile gone.

She cocked her head with a grin. She expected him to look away, or glare, or somehow ignore her.

Instead, he slowly lifted one finger to his lips in a shush motion, then turned back to his work.

****

Sebastian stepped back from the main doors and resigned himself to the fact that he'd have to let Lily keep her flowers yet again.

The line outside Tartarus extended down two blocks—unheard of for a Wednesday night. People in full costumes and masks, colorful and vivid outfits, dark and ethereal, all were pressing for admittance. Marley's music thumped out through the open doors and escaped into the street, the colors from the lights inside dancing with the shadows.

He'd been here since before opening, keeping the masses in line with Ellis, taking extra care to check IDs as they took cover charges. Sebastian saw three undercover cops trying to get in with fake IDs, but they were turned away each time. If they kept even a third of this crowd, he wouldn't have to worry about Tartarus for a long time.

And this was just the first night.

None of the other clubs around this area had theme nights, so they had to take advantage before they caught on. He already had a few ideas to continue this on Wednesdays and add a monthly weekend one, too. The decorations had been minimal in cost—a couple hundred, and most of the supplies could be reused.

He recalled the shopping trip with Lily to the party store on her day off, where she'd grabbed the most ridiculous items, trying to justify when they would be used with increasingly absurd explanations until he laughed—full-on laughed—beneath the fluorescent lights of the store. Her smile had hung around for the rest of the day, as they bought and bagged their spoils, unloading them back at the club and chatting over drinks before opening, then hanging around to help out, despite not having to.

Even the marketing hadn't been costly, though he knew Lily had taken the point on that, too, posting on every form of social media under Tartarus's new accounts. She had Darcy design a flyer and had Reva print them out. She gave giant stacks to everyone and taking two for herself, distributing them around town until Sebastian couldn't go anywhere in Southton without seeing one. He'd saved a copy for himself, tucked between a book in his office. Proof of the lengths to which his friends would go in order to keep Tartarus running.

Still, it almost overwhelmed them. They were nearly to capacity, and the night had barely started. Ellis would slow down admittance, keeping the line moving just enough to keep them quiet, but they'd have to stop soon. Darcy moved among the crowd with Teegan's tablet, watching for any signs of danger, but still bopping to the music, the mask he insisted on a little too large and sliding out of place with nearly every other step.

Sebastian shifted between people, seeing Marley surrounded by a heaving crowd, masks and gowns glittering, dresses sparkling with sequins and rhinestones in all colors until their refractions nearly drowned out his stars above. He saw lots of gold masks among the gentlemen in the crowd, shining and eye-catching, their outfits ranging from jeans to a literal knight in armor. Marley was in rare form tonight, the excitement levels constantly rising, never giving anyone a break, until a feverish energy filled the people around him.

Making it to the bar, he had to wait to get to his usual place in the corner, the crowds packing around the edges. He caught one glimpse of Teegan helping out before the people pressed around the bar again. Despite the waves of people, he wouldn't complain.

Eventually, the crowd lulled, and Sebastian got his usual spot. He hadn't seen Lily since she went up to shower after her class, and he owed her a thanks. She turned away from him, the same flowered shawl on her shoulders—a mockery or a testament to how confident she felt about this evening's success, he didn't know.

Then she turned to grab something.

A scandalous black dress, a bustier style bodice that led down to a jagged skirt just above her knees. Black ankle boots lent her a few inches, and a necklace with a blood red pendant, which dangled just above the plunging neckline. In her hair she'd woven red flowers into a makeshift crown, and her lips matched. The mask on her face was a simple red domino, decorated with small flowers.

Because of course.

She smiled when she saw him, and he had to remember to breathe.

He'd mastered himself when she came over a few minutes later, taking a sip of the water she had beneath the bar and already grabbing the ingredients for his drink.

"Nice mask," she said, nodding at the black mask Darcy had dug up for him. Save for the two horns that extended up, the mark was simple. Ellis had snorted when he saw him, but they'd all agreed to participate, some with more excitement than others. "Feeling a little devilish?"

He smirked. "You're the one who called Tartarus a...den of sin? Got to play my part as king."

She laughed, finishing his drink, and grabbing the orange garnish. "Good, 'cause I've seen way too many heroes around here tonight. Nice to see something different."

"I'm certainly no knight in shining armor."

Lily placed his drink down, leaning on the bar in front of him. "And I'm no damsel in distress."

Not letting his gaze wander took a great deal of self-restraint, but he met her eyes, half hidden behind the mask. "No, you're not," he murmured, taking a sip from his glass.

Lily's eyes widened slightly, surprised at his comment, at his playing along when he'd been keeping a line between them. They would chat and laugh, but whenever she started to get too reckless, he pulled back. Not to say they didn't talk about personal things—he'd heard the full story of her mother's death, and he'd given her hints of his childhood—but they both tried to keep to their sides of the invisible line they'd created. But tonight...

He told himself harmless flirting was fine and played into his reputation, meaning nothing. People expected that kind of behavior. No one would read anything into it.

Well, except the doctor, apparently.

Her brow arched up and her tongue darted out to wet her lips, "So is it true there's no rest for the wicked?"

Sebastian leaned over, close enough that she could hear, but far enough away to make it seem like he was talking to an employee. "That's why sinners have more fun."

Before she could answer, he stepped away, feeling her gaze on his back as he wove his way through the crowd, cheering and singing and dancing and drinking in his club. He walked a dangerously thin line, but his lips curved into a smile as he surveyed the crowd, his club, his bar, and his team, and took a deep sip of his drink, feeling invincible.

What was life without a little danger?

****

Lily maneuvered through the crowd, three glasses in her hand as she made her way to a booth along the side. People jostled her left and right, but she couldn't find the energy to be annoyed.

She had done this—she had helped save Tartarus.

The people pouring in were here because of what she had done. And that satisfied in a way that being a PI couldn't.

Saving people felt great but happened so rarely. Too often, she delivered bad news or confirmed someone's worst fears. At Tartarus, she didn't have to tell someone that their son would never come home, or that their wife really betrayed them. And she still saved people.

She saved Teegan, slinging drinks like a pro, giving Lily the rest of the night off before cleaning up to enjoy herself.

She saved Ellis, who had already enthusiastically broken up three fights outside the club, his laughter the only thing louder than the music.

She saved Darcy, who had somehow managed to convince a group of millennials that he danced ironically and was now cheering on his legitimately terrible dance moves.

She saved Marley, who set records for how loudly the crowd cheered for her as she gave them track after upbeat track.

And she'd saved Sebastian, who...

Lily pushed that aside, placing the three drinks down in front of Eliza, Reva, and herself.

"I take back everything I've said about theme nights!" Reva shouted, pounding half her drink in one go. "This is amazing!"

Eliza's grin was wide. "Seriously, Lily. This is unbelievable. I'm so proud of you."

Her cheeks hurt from smiling so broadly. "I'm glad you guys came."

"I'm coming here every theme night," Reva announced. "Or at least, every night Jason cancels on me."

"He get called out on a case?"

"Another overdose." Reva drained her drink and Eliza pushed hers in front of her.

"Really?" Lily asked, some of her joy at the night fading. "Where?"

Eliza opened her mouth to speak but flinched and grabbed at her phone in her purse. "Hello?"

"A few blocks from Jed's," Reva said. "Or what used to be Jed's. Did you hear he left town?"

"Will?" Eliza repeated, plugging her ear with her other hand to hear better. "Is everything okay?"

Lily hadn't heard about Jed, but she grinned. "Good riddance."

Reva agreed. "No shit."

"I can't hear you," Eliza shouted into the phone. "I'm at a club."

Lily arched a brow at Eliza, who seemed oblivious,

then glanced at Reva. Reva rolled her eyes. "I'm going to die of old age before she figures this out," she muttered, draining the rest of Eliza's drink.

"No," Eliza laughed. "No, I'm with Lily and Reva. Hang on a second, let me get somewhere quieter." She mouthed something neither Lily nor Reva understood, then walked away from the table, still shouting into her phone.

Reva watched her go, then slammed her palms on the table. "I think I'm drunk enough to dance. Want to join me?"

"Always," Lily said, taking Reva's extended hand and walking out onto the dance floor. Finding the rhythm was easy, pounding through her bones, and Lily threw her head back and laughed, savoring this moment.

Several songs later, Reva had recognized a few people she worked with and had joined their group for a moment, bragging about how she knew the owner, and Marley finally slowed things down slightly. The music still bordered on deafening, but turned smoother and sultrier, giving everyone a chance to catch their breath or a better reason to lose it.

Lily remained on the dance floor, not needed a partner or a group or a friend to dance with, and closed her eyes, rolling her neck on her shoulders as she worked out whatever tension remained from throwing the biggest party she'd ever hosted in her life. Her face tilted up to the stars above her and she smiled, letting the music wash over her.

She didn't know what prompted her to open her eyes. A feeling, a guess, a hope, but she did. Above her, nearly indistinguishable from the stars above, she saw a figure standing on the catwalk, a drink in hand, and the outline of horns against the starlight.

She couldn't be certain, not really, what he looked at, but she knew, nonetheless. So, she continued to dance, her eyes open and on the stars, as he watched her, only moving to sip from his glass.

When the song faded away into something more upbeat, Lily stopped dancing for the first time since hitting the floor and waited for...something.

Sebastian stared down at her, his face only visible during certain pulses of the lights. During one of those brief visible moments, he jerked his head to the side—toward the catwalk door.

Toward his door.

For a minute or an hour, neither one of them moved. Then they both—impossible to say who moved first—broke their gaze and walked. Lily to the employee door and Sebastian to the catwalk door.

She looked back only once, seeing his smirk before he shut the catwalk door behind him. Hiding her stupid, unintentionally wide smile, she moved as quickly as she could, anticipation buzzing beneath her skin and her stomach doing flips as she weaved between couples and under arms and around drinks and—

Smashed directly into someone.

"Sorry," Lily said, grabbing his arm to steady him.

"It's fine, my bad."

She knew that voice. Lily blinked the lights away from her vision, focusing on the man in front of her.

"Are you alright?" he asked, his brown eyes concerned. The blonde hair had been sprayed with red for the evening, to match the more traditional devil mask on his face. His red suit was garish, though not the worst she'd seen tonight, and Lily cocked her head, recognition tickling up her spine.

"I'm fine," she said, still not letting go. "I know you."

He grinned, mistaking her confusion for something else. "My reputation precedes me, huh? Something I can help you with? Take the edge off? I've got all the good shit."

That phrase. Her first night here, when she'd seen Sebastian meeting with a dealer, he'd sounded like this. He'd said it. *"This is some good shit, too. Fresh."*

Her grip tightened and her smile vanished. "You."

The recognition seemed mutual now, and he tried to pull away. "Oh, fuck, you—you're Galani's bartender. Sorry. I didn't—"

She hauled him to the employee door, most people looking past her and choosing not to notice, and those that did would fail to recognize her anyway with the mask in place.

The door slammed shut behind them, as Lily shoved him into the wall.

"Hey, look—"

"Shut up," she hissed, taking off her mask. "You're going to leave this club and never deal here again, do you understand?"

He found a bit of his backbone, "I have an agreement—"

"I don't care." Lily leaned in, letting him see the fire in her eyes. "I don't want to see your face here ever again. And if I do—"

"Let him go."

She turned her head at the order, coming from the stairs to her left. Sebastian stood on the last step, moving into the hallway. His eyes were on her, the mask in his hand, and she shook her head at him slightly. Asking him to stay out—and not repeat what he just said. Not to prove everything she'd believed about him that first day. Not to be the man she feared and instead be the one she hoped for.

His expression was inscrutable when he repeated, "Let him go, Lily."

Chapter 9

"Let him go, Lily," Sebastian repeated, keeping his face calm.

Thirty seconds previously, he'd been on his way to an ill-advised tryst with no one but himself to blame—and thank. He'd been done with plotting and lying and everything, at least for tonight. At least with Lily.

But then he'd heard her voice. He'd heard Tanner's voice. And his hopes were dashed before even starting.

Her hand still wrapped in Tanner's suit, Lily stared at him. "He's a drug dealer."

"I know."

Lily's eyes narrowed, and he now knew why even the most persistent men and women tended to give up when she told them no. Fire burned behind her eyes and her mouth twisted into a snarl. She shoved Tanner away from her, sending him stumbling towards the side door.

Tanner looked up at Sebastian, who forced himself to shrug carelessly. "I warned you about trying to deal to my staff."

"This is fucked, Galani, if you're out, then Reyes—"

"I am not out," Sebastian said coolly. He completely ignored Lily as he walked past her, ignored her clenched fists and jaw, ignored the confusion and anger in her stance, ignored the way she stared at him like she didn't know him at all. "This is merely a...misunderstanding.

Our arrangement is unchanged."

Tanner's eyes darted to Lily, but Sebastian shifted, putting himself between her and Tanner to ensure her safety. "Take the night off. I'll explain things to her, and this won't happen again."

He hesitated, but Sebastian knew the pull of money was too great for him to leave. "Fine. But if she comes after me again—"

"She won't," Sebastian said, praying she had the presence of mind to be silent.

There was a scoff from behind him but lost in the music and Tanner's panicked breathing. Sebastian held the side door open for him, and the dealer took off, knowing better than to try to push anything right now.

Sebastian shut the door, making sure to lock it before turning around.

Lily shook in her anger as she stood by the stairs. "You knew?"

"Yes."

"You knew?" she repeated, taking a step towards him. "And you allowed him in here?"

"Yes."

Sebastian walked towards her, seeing her raise her chin as he approached, defiance written on every inch of her aspect as she spoke. "Then I quit. I will *not*—"

He walked past her.

Sputtering loudly, she came after him, like he thought she would. "What the hell are you doing?"

He didn't slow his pace. "We can discuss this in my office, or you can quit and go home now. But I'm not having this conversation in the hallway."

She muttered something he missed, but then pressed her mouth shut and followed him upstairs. They were silent all the way up, the only sound the creak of metal beneath his feet. He didn't hear any noise from her, but refused to look back to see if she followed him. Unlocking his door, he stepped aside for her to go first, and she walked past him, her mouth in a thin line and refusing to meet his eyes.

A far sight different than he'd been hoping for just a few minutes ago.

He shut the door behind her and gestured for her to go first. Or, he would have, had she not immediately burst into speech, her temper snapping almost audibly.

"How could you allow him in here?" she hissed. "We're barely keeping open with the bodies they've found, and you just let him deal that shit? I thought you were better than that! You said you wanted Tartarus to survive, but letting people like him in here is what's going to destroy us. I respected you, I thought you were better than what people said you were. Turns out you're not."

Sebastian let her keep going, ignoring the comments that stung until she ran out of speed and crossed her arms. Waiting another moment or two to be certain she was finished, he spoke. "Do you know what happens when you try to keep dealers out of clubs?"

"You don't have drugs?" she spat with a huff.

Sebastian stared at her for a minute, remembering that for all of her experiences and the force of her personality, he was older than her. Nine years, if he had his math right. That rarely seemed important, but right now…those years were a world of difference.

He could lie. Let her believe the worst and quit. Tartarus would be okay, eventually. They could survive, and she'd just be one other person who believed what he presented to them.

But the thought of Tartarus without flowers…didn't sit right with him. So, he decided to do what he thought he wouldn't ever do. He'd tell her the truth.

"Without having a designated dealer for the club, this becomes an area of contention for rival gangs or families, each of them trying to get a foothold in here. Which means fights and casualties. It also means more drugs."

He took a seat on the couch, running his hand over his face. He glanced up at her, pleased to see she had lowered her arms. She still frowned, but not at him. "If I know who's dealing, I can keep an eye on them. No turf wars, one designated dealer. If he brings bad products, he knows he's out. If anyone OD's on the premises, he's out. I know his face, I know his boss. They won't try me." He recalled the first time someone had overdosed at his club, from the dealer assigned to the club. He hated using his last name as leverage, but that had been one of the few exceptions. Had Detective Hughes bothered to investigate that disappearance, he might have been able to shut down Tartarus in its earliest days.

He found his fingers fidgeting with his cufflinks and stopped, lowering his hand. "I can't keep people from buying. But I can control what's offered."

"Greater good," she said quietly.

"I hate that term. But, in a word, yes." He looked up at her.

She had taken a few steps closer to him, still suspicious, obviously. And why wouldn't she be? Everyone believed he was a criminal, still part of the family, and it was in his best interest that they did.

She chewed her lip, thinking over something. "You

bought some. I heard. My first night. I came down from the catwalk and I heard you. You bought from him."

He got to his feet, crossing over to the bar on the side of the living room, and pouring himself a drink and one for her, too. Assumptive, but he poured it anyway. "Dealers don't trust those who don't…indulge. I buy from him, just enough to keep them from getting suspicious. It goes down the drain as soon as he leaves." He glanced over his shoulder, meeting her eyes. "I've never liked drugs."

She still didn't seem convinced, but she stood there, waiting for an explanation, waiting for his answers. If she'd believed since day one the worst people thought of him, the fact that she was still here astonished him. That she gave him an opportunity to explain himself at all. He walked over, handing her the drink. She took the glass but didn't drink.

"You paid him, too," she said, her temper fading. "What for?"

"An added clause his boss doesn't know about. He makes his cut from Antonio Reyes for selling. He makes almost the same from me for not dealing to the drunks, the ones who overdose, the obviously nervous. Teegan and I watch him throughout the evening, and if he's behaved, he makes more."

He saw her jaw jumping slightly as her eyes glanced around the room, putting the pieces together, making sense of what he said and weighing against what she'd seen and heard.

He hoped she didn't find him wanting.

"You said if anyone OD's, he's gone. So, he isn't selling what killed the girl I worked on?"

She was more well-informed than he expected. But

that was his own damn fault, for thinking she wouldn't meticulously shatter every one of his expectations. "No. That's...another issue."

She threw back the scotch without a wince, then walked past him to take a seat on the edge of one couch. "Fuck."

Sebastian's snort of agreement was lost as he sipped from his drink, but he shared in the sentiment. He crossed over to an armchair, close enough to continue the conversation, but separating himself from her. Too little, too late, but he had to try.

Lily stared into the empty glass, and he watched her, uncomfortable with the quiet, but knowing she needed the time. A few flowers from her hair were missing. He'd seen one fall out while she danced but—

Less than ten minutes ago and he'd invited her up here. Foolish, but he hadn't been able to resist, and she seemed amenable to the idea as well. The mood was irrevocably killed now, but the memory remained. The anticipation remained. He'd wanted to feel her dancing beneath his fingers, taste what those smiles were like, see if he could catch her laughter in his room, between his lips.

Swallowing silently, Lily finally looked up. "I'm sorry."

"What?" Whatever he had been expecting her to say, it sure as hell wasn't that. "Why?"

"Because I didn't trust you. I mean, I did, but I thought—"

"You thought exactly what I wanted you to think. I gave you every reason to believe what everyone said I was. I am." He finished his drink, a cold smirk on his face, but he couldn't keep it.

"You're exactly who I hoped you were."

He didn't know what to say to that. She didn't seem to expect a response, though, sighing and breaking eye contact as she shook her head.

"What are we going to do?"

"About what?" he asked.

"This drug. If we don't find the dealer, they're going to get someone killed again. And Tartarus—"

"*We* are going to do nothing. You need to stay away."

The anger appeared again, the glare lighting up her eyes. "I can handle myself."

"This isn't some low-level thug," he said, getting to his feet. "You have no idea—"

"You know who." She matched him, rising as well, interrupting him in that infuriating way that she did. Taking three large steps forward, she got into his personal space, narrowing her eyes as she looked up at him. "Tell me."

He didn't budge, his smirk in place to keep her back, and keep her at arm's length. "As interrogation tactics go, not the best—"

"Oren?"

He blinked.

Fucking hell, how did she know? She couldn't know. He'd been careful, the only time she may have heard something was…the phone call.

Lily's smile was wicked and confident. She turned away, apparently leaving this very second to find Oren and—

Sebastian grabbed her arm as she turned away.

Logically, not the best move he could have made. He'd been present in her classes when she'd shown how to flip, break, and incapacitate anyone from doing exactly what he did now. He knew, as her muscles tensed beneath his fingers and she turned to look at him, that he lived on borrowed time. Doing the only thing he could do, he told her the truth.

"I know that you want to get him now, but he has the slums under his thumb. Everyone reports to him, and no one knows where he makes his base. He's being funded by someone, Mazrani or another gang, which means connections," His voice verged on insistent and, embarrassingly enough, pleading. "I don't know what's in his drug or how it's being dispersed or where it's being stored, and if you somehow manage to get to him, he's got dozens of lieutenants lined up to take his place."

Her muscles were still tense, but she hadn't pulled away yet.

"I've been working this for months and he's ruthless. Do you think it's an accident Tartarus seems to be being targeted? He suspects, despite my efforts, and he's pressuring me to make a move. Then, he can make his." He took a breath, his voice dropping slightly. "If you go after him and fail to wipe out every last piece of his operation, he won't go after you. He'll go after Tartarus. Marley. Your students. Dr. Clark."

The look he got was angry, frustrated because she knew he was right, and she hated him a little for using her friends against her. But he'd been living with this knowledge for half a year. It was the only reason he'd gone to such lengths to keep his temper and reputation.

After he let go of her arm, she took a step away from him, her fists at her side.

"Then what am I supposed to do?"

He clearly couldn't tell her to do nothing. "Play it

smart. We need to know everything before we try to take him down. I have connections, but Oren does, too. If I ask too many questions, or the wrong one—"

"He could hear. What do you need?"

"I need to know what the drug is made of. I need to know where their operation is. I need details on how they distribute, and where the other bodies were found. I need to know Oren's history, his lieutenants and their records, everything." He scoffed, not a laugh, but a humorless noise. "I need a cop."

Lily went still, biting her lip. She seemed to be coming to some sort of decision because she took a breath in, and a step nearer, and said, "Seb, I'm—"

There was a knock on the apartment door.

****

Lily glanced at the door, cutting off her admission before Sebastian threw up his hand. He grabbed his phone and looked at something, then cursed quietly, running his hand over his head. "Fuck, Ellis was supposed to…" He looked up at her, and the expression went blank like when he hid something.

"Oren," he said, by way of explanation, of warning, of…apology. His raised hand became just a finger as he pressed a button on his phone and spoke into it. "Thought I said next week for our face-to-face."

His voice had dropped, that oozing, deliberate choice of words, layered under inches of condescension and pride. The voice he used with Doyle Hughes.

Oren's voice came through phone, but Lily could hear the faint murmur from outside the door. "I came to celebrate your big night, Galani. Wasn't gonna bother you, but when I saw you kicking out Reyes's bitch and taking the brunette upstairs, I figured you could spare a minute for an old friend."

Well, that ruled out her hiding.

"Give me a minute," Sebastian said. He slid his phone back into his pocket and when he met her eyes, regret sat in them. "I need you to do exactly as I say, without question. You keep quiet and play along, or everyone in this club is going to die. Do you understand?"

She didn't, not in the slightest, but she nodded anyway.

Sebastian moved quickly, pouring dark alcohol into their glasses again, and placing them next to the couch. He took a deep sip, and without looking said, "Lose the flowers."

For once, she didn't argue. The tension layered everything, and she didn't want to add to it. He lowered the lights and removed his jacket, unbuttoning the top two buttons of his shirt. Lily realized what he wanted his guests to think. She slipped off the sheer flowered wrap and ran her fingers through her hair, tousling it and sitting on the arm of the couch.

A second knock came at the door; Sebastian took a deep breath and murmured, "I'm sorry."

Then his demeanor changed again, his expression shifted to one of arrogant disdain, his movements smoother and artful, and even his voice lowered as he opened the door. "Oren. I wasn't expecting you."

Lily kept her face mildly bored, her eyes on Sebastian as he sauntered back to her, sitting on the couch. His arm went around her waist and pulled her into his lap, as casually as breathing. Lily turned her gasp of surprise into a breathy giggle and realized why Sebastian had apologized.

As a PI, she'd been a distraction or temptation before. She knew what to do.

She rested on one of his legs, her knees between his, as one of his hands curved over her hip, idly sliding up and down along the fabric of her dress. One of her arms went around his shoulders, the other landing on his chest. His free hand, however, settled on the bare skin of her knee, and he gave every impression of a man caught in the midst of being ready to ravish a woman.

The man who followed Sebastian in would have been at home in Tartarus. A suit jacket half covered his dark red patterned shirt, though not nearly the caliber of Sebastian's clothes. A cluster of silver chains and pendants hung against an emaciated chest. Though clothes were clean, and he seemed to take care in his appearance, Lily saw the bitten nails and ragged skin of an addict. The two men behind him looked like any number of thugs she'd met before, large and violent, eyeing her closely. She'd give anything to take them down, here and now, but Sebastian's warning rang in her ear, and she didn't want someone else to pay the price.

"Most people call me the Orchestrator, now," Oren said, his chin lifting slightly in unearned pride.

The bisected O shot through Lily's mind; the symbol on the baggies of drugs. The Orchestrator.

Sebastian smirked. "That's a bit of a mouthful. You'll always be Cecil Oren to me."

A flicker of anger went through the dealer as Sebastian refused to acknowledge his supposed rise to power. Lily couldn't help but be impressed. In one easy sentence, Sebastian set the stage, off-balanced Oren, and made it clear who had the power here.

Sebastian was fucking good.

"Didn't mean to interrupt," Oren said, his voice smooth, if with a slight edge now.

Sebastian's chuckle verged on cold, his hand still moving up her thigh, down, then back up higher, then down again, repeating the motion. "You aren't. To what do I owe the pleasure?"

Oren glanced at her, but she smiled vapidly at him, then turned back to Sebastian. The seating arrangement put her in close proximity to his face, so she tried to remain focused on that, fingering the buttons on his shirt, undoing a couple more, looking too wrapped up in him to take any part or interest in the conversation.

Honestly, a part of her was. Since she'd never been this close to him before, she inhaled, tasting notes of whiskey and sandalwood on the back of her tongue, and leaned a little closer, the nearness heady.

"I saw you threw out Tanner," Oren said, taking a seat, though Sebastian hadn't offered one. He grinned. "What did that spineless pissant do wrong?"

Sebastian didn't smile. "Tanner dealt to my bartender. He knows no dealing to employees on the clock."

"What did she take?"

Sebastian glanced at Lily, their noses brushing as he met her eyes. "Don't know," he said, uncaring. "We were…working it off when you arrived." The hand on her waist slid up, brushing the swell of her breast, and he looked away from her to meet Oren's gaze again. She kept her eyes on Sebastian, her breathing only slightly ragged.

Oren made a sound that could have been amusement but came out more disgusted. "So, you've reconsidered?"

"Time doesn't change my mind. We can discuss Tartarus's loyalties when your shit doesn't kill my patrons." His hand still moved, separate from the conversation, as a distraction and throwing Oren off guard. Lily herself had to remind herself to focus as Sebastian's fingers edged further beneath the hem of her skirt, cool against her heated skin.

Oren waved his hand, to encompass everything in the room and beyond. "There are always…casualties in the creation of art."

"My club won't be one of them," Sebastian said, his hand ceasing its movement. Oren hadn't noticed yet, but if he did—

Lily shifted slightly, and her hand slipped beneath his shirt to press warningly on his skin, out of Oren's sight. He already knew he cared about Tartarus, but he didn't need to know how much. So, she ignored the warmth of his skin, the feel of his breath against her lips, and focused on keeping her smile flirtatious. Sebastian resumed his journey after a breath, edging higher and higher between her legs.

"Reyes's operation is flawed, as you've seen," Oren said, glancing at Sebastian's movements before looking away quickly, a faint flush rising in his cheeks. His goons, on the other hand, couldn't look anywhere else but at her as she grew warmer by the second, her eyes half-closed and her lips parted. "Throwing your lot in with him—"

"Let's be clear," Sebastian said, that cool detachedness lowering the temperature in the room. "I don't 'throw my lot' in with anyone. Tartarus is a no-man's land, until I say otherwise. I benefit from allowing Reyes to deal here, while you bring the cops to my doors.

I won't have my business suffer because you can't get your product under control."

She caught Oren's cruel smile. "You'll regret that."

"Is that a threat?"

Lily couldn't help herself. She rolled her head slightly to look directly at Oren, keeping the smile on her face, as she shifted in Sebastian's lap. Her movement brushed her against his arousal, and though he didn't react, she felt how much he wasn't acting with her.

Had she not seen Tanner, had she arrived upstairs without interruption, would they still have ended up in this situation? Would they have gone further? With his hands on her, his breath in her ear, she knew the answer would have been a hell yes. She felt half drunk on him right now, even with the other men in the room. Her hand around his shoulders, reached up, tracing the edge of his jaw as he spoke.

"You remember what happened to the last man to threaten me."

Oren hesitated, and she forced herself back to the conversation, even as Sebastian upped the ante with Oren, making him more uncomfortable as he leaned forward slightly, moving her hair to the side before pressing his lips to her bare shoulder. Her eyes slid shut and she leaned into him, her knees sliding open further, not acting at all. Sebastian's hands tightened around her, holding her against him, and she heard a faint breath from him that Oren might not have been able to hear.

She opened her eyes a touch, to see Oren shifting uncomfortably in his seat.

"It's not a threat," Oren backtracked, trying to look anywhere but at Lily and failing. "But I stand to make a lot of money with Opus, money that you'll miss out on."

So that's what he called his drug. Opus.

"From what I've seen," Sebastian's words were muffled against Lily's skin, "you have a drug that kills people, no home base, and no proof of longevity in this game. If you gave me something concrete, I'd reconsider, but at this moment…" He chuckled, the vibration sliding through his lips and fingers to settle beneath her skin. "I think I have everything I need."

His fingers moved up again, as Lily rolled her hips a touch, the action instinctual. The combination meant he moved too far up and brushed against the now damp material keeping her covered.

Sebastian immediately withdrew, but Oren had already stood and turned toward the door, missing the action. "I will keep you updated on our progress, and when there aren't any…negative side effects, I'll let you know. Then you can decide," Oren said, facing them again, tugging his jacket nervously.

"Can't wait," Sebastian said lowly, his tone indicating he was already bored and moving on.

Oren had no response. He grabbed for the door, glancing back at her with a slight frown. They needed a believable finale.

Turning with ease, Lily shifted so she straddled Sebastian, though her neck prickled at putting her back to Oren and his men. She looped her arms around his neck, as if they were immediately picking up where Oren had interrupted them. Lily couldn't help her moan as her eyes closed, his lips against her throat and moving down, his hands hard on her hips as she rolled against him.

"Always a pleasure," he said over Lily's shoulder, a clear dismissal. He placed both his hands on her thighs and slid them up—

Oren slammed the door behind him.

Chapter 10

Lily's alarm went off the next morning, and she didn't move for a long moment, staring up at the ceiling. Last night had been…

Complicated.

After Oren had left, Sebastian had shifted her off of him at once, putting several feet of space between them and doing up his buttons once again. Lily had taken longer to catch her breath, sitting up on the couch and trying to fix her hair into a semblance of control. She'd opened her mouth to speak several times, but the words had died in the silence, remaining unsaid, and things got more uncomfortable with every quiet second.

By the time Sebastian turned around, his demeanor was back in control. Nothing of the flirt who'd invited her up, or the criminal who'd talked down to Oren, or the man who'd told her the truth of what he was doing and why.

"I'm sor—"

"It's fine," she interrupted. "Really, I didn't—"

"—if there had been another option, I—"

"—totally understand if—"

"—never again."

Lily bit her lip, nodding without looking at him. Never again? Maybe his physical reaction had been purely physical. He could feel regret, for a variety of reasons. A sane person would probably regret being felt up as a distraction and in front of killers and drug dealers.

That didn't stop Lily from dreaming. Cool hands on her thighs and lips on her skin and when Oren had left, she'd straddled Sebastian's lean hips, and he'd smirked and hadn't stopped and—

But apparently, the feeling wasn't mutual. They'd gone back downstairs without another word between them, and Lily helped out until closing, feeling no inclination to dance anymore.

As they'd closed the club down and cleaned up, Sebastian had avoided her without ever appearing to. He would only approach her if someone else was there, kept their conversations purely about work, and when she walked outside, a prepaid taxi waited to take her home.

So that was how he wanted to play this.

Though the rejection stung, Lily couldn't bring herself to be angry or upset with him, not really. The avoidance hurt, but…she knew he did everything to protect Tartarus, and all of them, including her. She couldn't be upset with him for that. If she got caught up in the moment, that wasn't his fault. She had to deal with her issues and had to put her…attraction aside and do her job. Jobs. She could still help Tartarus, but she'd have to tread carefully around Sebastian for a while, if she wanted to stay. So, she exhaled and got up out of bed, leaving her moping and regrets behind her.

Lily's shower went a long way in restoring her mood, but a headache still toyed at the back of her eyes and danced along her temples. Coffee was in order, and a visit to Eliza, which she didn't relish.

Still, she had to grab her stuff for class and for work later. She eyed the clothes in her closet, settling on a pair of black pants and a flowing, flowered wrap. She ripped off the tag, remembering Eliza's odd looks when she'd bought a bunch of flowered pieces to add into her predominantly black wardrobe. The club got hot enough to make the tank top appropriate, and even if she had to walk home, she'd manage. Despite the chill of October, November had been unseasonably warm. Besides, she'd dealt with worse discomfort before. Putting her clothes in her bag, she threw on her workout clothes and went out.

As she hit the street, the gray sky keeping her from dawdling, she picked up her phone, clicking on one of her contacts.

"Ugh...what?" Reva didn't sound like her peppy self.

"Aww, did someone party a little too hard last night?"

"I hate you. What do you want?"

Lily hesitated. Though this was definitely the easier request of her day, she still felt guilty. "I need some help."

There was a shuffling noise as Reva apparently shifted and focused. *"I'm intrigued. What's up?"*

"You've been tracking this drug case, right? The one Jason's been called in on?"

"Well, when I have such a great source, how can I resist?"

Deciding to review the ethics of that later, Lily sidestepped a pedestrian. "I need what you have. Where the incidents were, how many, what they were doing prior to being found, suspects. Everything."

"Why?"

Blunt and no nonsense, exactly what Lily has learned to expect from Reva. She didn't want payment, not really, but she dealt in information the way Eliza dealt in medicine and Lily dealt in fists. She knew Reva would tell her either way, but she owed her some truth.

"I think this is a lot bigger than just some new drug. It's a new dealer, and I think he's shaking down big names. If someone doesn't stop him, he's going to hurt a lot of people."

Reva stayed silent for a long moment, and Lily checked to make sure she didn't hang up. A faint tapping, like a keyboard, came through the phone.

"When this blows over, I want an exclusive."

"When it blows over, I will tell you so much more than you want to know."

"Impossible," Reva retorted. *"I've emailed you what I've got now, but my contacts at the PD are holding back a bit more than usual, with Hughes on the case. Everyone knows he's got a temper, and flirting doesn't work, now that I'm engaged to Jason. I've got causes of death, but not official autopsies. If I get something, I'll let you know."*

"You're amazing."

"I know," she said calmly. *"Now, I want to know something."*

"I just told you—"

"Were you planning that little tryst with Galani last night? Or was it spur of the moment?"

Lily had to put a lot of effort into continuing to walk. "I—"

"I saw you dancing, and I saw you leaving. I'm observant, even when drunk."

For a moment, she debated lying. But even if Reva couldn't spot a lie from a thousand feet off, Lily didn't want to. "It's not what you think."

Reva hummed quietly, unconvinced or not, hard to tell. *"Did you want it to be what I thought?"*

"No. Yes. Maybe."

"I'll take it for now. And I know you won't listen to me, because you rarely do, but be careful. There are a lot of bodies dropping. I don't want you to be one."

"I'm always careful."

"No, you're not," Reva said ruefully. *"I'm going back to bed. Text me."*

"Bye."

The walk to the coffee shop closest to the clinic and the long line outside ate up a good part of her afternoon. She made her way through the quiet lobby, passing off a cookie to the receptionist, and continued to the lounge, where raised voices reached her ear. She cocked her head, recognizing Miguel and Dr. Lintz's tones easily, as well as the laughter of her roommate in the background. Gritting her teeth, she forced her expression into a smile.

William Lintz leaned over the table to talk to Miguel, whose smug grin made it clear he was winning whatever argument they were having. "...will never understand how you manage to get dressed in the morning, without two brain cells to rub together."

William conceded defeat, pushing himself away from the console and turned away. Catching sight of Lily in the doorway, he paused, glancing at Eliza.

Her friend got out of her seat, smiling gently. "Hey."

"Hi." Lily lifted the carrier of coffee she'd brought, one for each of them and herself. "I come bearing gifts."

"I knew I liked you better than Reva," Miguel said, grabbing the carrier and passing one to William after an inspection.

"I heard you had a successful evening," William

said, obviously trying to distance them from the way they'd met last time. "Congratulations."

"Thanks," she answered, though her excitement of yesterday diminished with everything else.

"Yup, I heard the party was bumpin'," Miguel said, taking a big sip from his drink.

"No one says 'bumping' anymore," Eliza interjected, knocking her shoulder against his.

"From the look on your face this morning, you closed out that party," Miguel grinned. "You must have had quite the night."

Eliza flushed slightly but couldn't deny anything. Lily had seen her and Reva leaving with the last bit of the crowd, chatting with Reva's coworkers. Regaining a bit of her former energy, Lily's eyes darted to William. "I'm surprised you managed to shake those lawyers who were talking to you all night."

In her peripheral vision she watched William freeze, just for a moment, then very carelessly turn to the whiteboard, like he paid little attention. Lily knew better.

"Did you get some digits, girl?" Miguel laughed.

Eliza's flush was high on her cheeks now. "What century were you born in?"

"That's not a no." Lily glanced over at William again. He stared at the board, but his eyes weren't moving.

"Shut up," Eliza said. "Why are you here, other than to disrupt my day?"

Lily's good mood faded, but she plastered on a smile. "Let's talk in private."

With a slightly suspicious look, but still smiling, Eliza led her back to her tiny office, closing the door. "What's up?"

Lily picked at the edge of her lid of coffee, buying some time. "Does Lintz always get that jealous?"

"Lily."

She chewed her lip, then quietly said, "I need a favor."

She rarely, if ever, asked for favors. Not real favors. She knew what favors were—doing something you felt uncomfortable with for a friend. She hated making Eliza uncomfortable, but she needed information.

"What is it?" If Eliza had one fault, it was unwavering loyalty.

"I need to know where the drug comes from and what it is."

"I can't do much if I don't—"

Lily pulled out a small baggie with green pills. "I took this the night that girl...I needed to know. It's called Opus."

Eliza inhaled slowly, her eyes wide. "...I could lose my job."

"I know," Lily said quietly. "And if I had anything else, I wouldn't have asked. But people are dying, and Hughes isn't doing shit to help them. I shook down every dealer I knew, and I got nothing but bruises. I know who's behind it, but I don't have any proof. If I knew what it was, maybe I could do more."

Eliza stared at the baggie. "Knowing what it is isn't going to stop it from being on the streets."

"I know. That's what I'm working on."

"What are you going to do?"

"Whatever it takes."

Eliza met Lily's eyes. If she said no, she wouldn't ask her again. But she also knew that Eliza had taken the job at this clinic where there were many other, more reputable hospitals that wanted her. She knew that Eliza had kicked gangs out of the clinic without hesitating. She knew that she stitched up bullet wounds and knife wounds without a word, and never ratted on anyone to the cops, unless abuse of a minor was involved.

So, she wasn't shocked when Eliza nodded and took the bag, though the guilt still niggled at her. "Thank you," Lily said.

"Don't thank me until I've got answers."

She put the bag in her pocket.

****

Sebastian wasn't a pacing kind of man.

Pacing meant uncontrolled thoughts. The inability to control oneself. It meant frustration and lack of calculation. Pacing was for those who messed up and found no other way to vent their anger and guilt.

He wasn't pacing. But he wanted to.

Last night had been…disastrous, in so many ways.

He shouldn't have suggested Lily come up, he shouldn't have told her so much, he shouldn't have allowed Oren in, and he definitely should not have…

He ran his hands over his head again, unable to focus on his computer.

Despite his late night, he hadn't slept much. Or at all. Every time he closed his eyes, he saw Lily in his lap, felt her breath against his cheek, smelled the faint scent of the flowers she'd been wearing.

Every time he'd drifted off, he'd picked up where they left off, but every time, Lily got upset, accusing him of taking advantage and he'd snap back into consciousness, sick to his stomach.

Logically, save his first invitation upstairs, the other things he'd done had been the only choice at the time. He couldn't have Lily kill Tanner or have him breaking his contract, not without Oren or another vulture trying to swoop in. He had to tell her the truth because she'd been hellbent on finding the truth and had known more than he'd expected. Enough to know if he'd been lying. And as for Oren coming up…he had done the only thing he could.

That didn't make what he did right.

Oh, she hadn't argued or complained, but he'd just explained that Oren would have killed everyone she cared about. What other choice did she have? They'd been backed into a corner, and though he'd made the best move, the only move that kept them all alive, there had been a cost.

Sebastian went still, the phrase jarring something.

His brother used "backed into a corner" to justify what he did as necessary. The only choice he had. Sebastian absently rubbed his shoulder, the scar tissue from when his brother had stabbed him when Sebastian had called him out for stealing from their parents. That had been one of times his brother had been backed into a corner.

If Sebastian could tell himself anything to make him feel like something more than a criminal, it was that he wasn't like Daniel.

Maybe they were more similar than he thought.

Even if he had, however briefly, hoped his evening would end with Lily up in his apartment, he never wanted to go like last night.

He knew he wasn't a good man. Even without actually committing crimes, he'd manipulated people into deals that benefited him, bullied them into toeing the lines he put in place, relying on his family's dwindling reputation. His name made him the furthest thing from a good man. But there were lines he wouldn't cross. And last night had felt far too much like dancing across that line.

His phone buzzed, and he glanced down instinctively.

—I've got a class today. I'll be there in 10.—

Sebastian picked up the phone, staring for a long moment. He wouldn't cancel her classes, not now. If she could pretend like nothing had happened, he could do the same. That didn't mean things wouldn't be changing. He typed out a calm response he didn't entirely feel.

—I have work to do. Just clean up—.

—Always do.—

A few moments went by, and another text arrived.

—Are we good?—

—We're fine— He didn't entirely believe it but wanted to pretend.

She didn't answer back.

Sebastian busied himself during her class by heading to the garage off the loading dock, out of the way. He had a small, but functional gym Ellis used several times a week in the back, and his car near the front. Giving his car a tune-up wasn't strictly necessary, not with Ellis's near-obsession with engines, but the routine kept him occupied. He and Lily had gotten too close, and even if he wanted to tell her the truth to keep her from doing something stupid, that didn't mean he could let last night happen again. He needed distance. He needed space. He needed the lines drawn between them again if he intended to take down Oren and the rest of his crew without getting anyone else hurt.

His phone buzzed as he finished up, and Sebastian

wiped the grease off his fingers before reading the message from Teegan.

—Don't forget, boss. I need the signed timesheets today.—

He had forgotten. But they were up in his office. Ignoring the voice in his head that called him a coward, he checked the log of his door.

Lily had been in after her class and had left five minutes ago.

Feeling calmer, he proceeded up to his place to shower and grab the paperwork. He wouldn't avoid her forever, he just…took precautions. He'd been stupid enough to break his rules for her several times already. He wouldn't make those mistakes again.

Stripping off the jeans and sweater he'd been wearing, he jumped in the shower, getting rid of the rest of the grease and trying to wake up a bit more to get through the night. He got out, drying off and wrapping a towel around his hips as he strode into his bedroom—

Just in time for Lily to walk through the bedroom door.

She saw him and froze, staring, then wrenched her gaze to the side, "Fuck. Sorry. I just—uh, I forgot my phone."

"It's fine," he said, his voice a lot calmer than he thought it would be.

She grabbed the phone from the bathroom counter, which he'd missed seeing, and hesitated in the door. Her eyes kept wandering back to him as they stood in awkward silence, Sebastian aware of the skin. He didn't look at her, not wanting to test his hastily constructed boundaries, and picked out his suit for the evening, trying to pretend she wasn't there.

He'd only looked briefly, but her tight black pants left little to the imagination. The tank top left her shoulders exposed and if he focused, he could still taste her skin on his tongue, something floral and metallic. He glared into his dresser, cursing his memory.

"I should have knocked," she said finally.

"It's fine, Nehme." Her surname came out, classic Galani self-defense, and she made a tiny sound, drawing his gaze.

She forced a smile, something like regret in her aspect. "I'll see you downstairs, then. Boss." She turned away from him and left, closing the door quietly behind her.

And just like that, the lines were drawn again. The distance established.

He didn't feel relieved.

Chapter 11

The clinic was, oddly enough, quiet.

Eliza leaned back in her chair, stretching her muscles. Though it was a Monday, Miguel had a couple of days off with his family and Will had been out of town visiting his sister for the holidays. He'd be back tomorrow, so Eliza took the opportunity to use the quiet lab to follow through with her favor to Lily. With Christmas just a couple of days away, she wanted to get this done before the new year. Today might be her only chance to be here alone.

Lily kept busy with work, and when she was home, she'd been oddly quiet, which was worrisome for a variety of reasons. Eliza knew Lily was still working on this particular drug, but something else had happened.

At class last week, Eliza noticed Galani's absence. In fact, she realized he hadn't been there for the last three classes. She exchanged a look with Reva, and they'd cornered Lily in the employee lounge as the rest of the students were leaving.

"Everything okay will tall, dark, and criminal?" Reva asked.

Lily's obviously fake smile was almost offensive. "It's fine."

"He hasn't been at the class in a while. Did something happen?"

Taking her hair out of her ponytail, Lily turned her

back on them. "No."

"Lily—"

"Drop it." Lily rarely said no to Reva, and the tone was something new entirely.

Eliza fidgeted by the door. "We're just worried about you."

Lily visibly forced herself to relax. "Everything is fine. There was a…misunderstanding. But it's fine."

Though clearly a lie, they didn't push for the moment. Lily hadn't been talking about work very often when she'd come home, and even when she did, Eliza had noticed Galani's name missing from their conversations. A falling out? Possibly, but Eliza had noticed how her expression would sometimes get a little softer and distant the few times she mentioned the owner. Maybe bad timing. If they got a little push…

Putting aside thoughts of matchmaking for the moment, Eliza refocused. The mass spectrometer in the corner ran an analysis on the Opus sample while Eliza read through the information Lily had given her from Reva on the victims. Definitely not light reading, the vague information still fascinated her, despite the grisly nature.

Though all of them had been determined to have died from an overdose, and all had been found with bags of the same drugs, some had died from serotonin syndrome—high fevers, muscle rigidity, and seizures—while others had died of heart failure, with severe muscle tears. She turned on some music and curled up on the couch with the files on the table.

The spectrometer beeped, but as Eliza unfolded herself from the couch, William entered.

"Will," she said, surprised, anxious. "I thought you

were gone until tomorrow?"

He seemed just as startled to have found her here. "I was, but Julia had…plans."

Eliza gathered her folders, trying to subtly hide some of her research. "What kind of plans?"

"Apparently she met a boy and would rather spend time with him than with me."

Unable to hide her smile, she met his eyes. "She's growing up, Will. You can't be the only man in her life forever."

"I'm sure I could be. Nothing's impossible."

She laughed, holding her files to her chest as she crossed over to her bag, resting on the table.

"I didn't mean to interrupt," he said, putting his bag down. "I was…just coming to pick up some papers I'd left."

"You're fine. I'm done."

He wandered over to the machine, his eyes on the monitors. "If you're done, then, we could get dinner, since I was so unceremoniously thrown out of Julia's place."

"Sure," she said, putting the files in her bag, her back to him. "What were you thinking? Chinese or—"

"Methylenedioxymethamphetamine?"

Eliza froze, then turned slowly, seeing him at the mass spectrometer, reviewing the readouts. He arched a brow at her. "Is there a reason you've put Ecstasy in the spectrometer?"

The danger and implications behind that question were lost as she frowned, her hands pulling out the files. "That can't be right…not entirely. MDMA doesn't affect the thalamus like this. But obviously Opus…"

She felt him come up behind her, reaching over her

shoulder to take the file out of her hand. "What are you up to, Clark?"

Turning, Eliza found herself pinned between the table and William, his gaze suspicious, but not angry. She felt a blush on her cheeks, plucking at the sleeve of her sweatshirt. "I'm…helping Lily with one of her cases."

That got a reaction out of him, and not the one she expected. His brows drew together. "Is that why she was hurt the other month? She should know better than to have involved you—"

Angry on behalf of her friend, and indignant at the thought that anyone knew better than Eliza on what she should do, she glared up at him, ignoring the significant height difference, and snatched the folder back out of his hand. "I will get involved in whatever I want, William Lintz."

"Clark—"

"No. I'm trying to help people. And if it's a little…delinquent," she decided, "it's better than not doing anything."

He raised his hand, but let it drop. "I'm just concerned about you."

"I can take care of myself." She ignored him and turned around, shoving her stuff into her bag.

"I know that," he insisted, coming up behind her, his hands on her elbows. "I'm just—I want you to be safe. Drugs and those they draw are never safe."

"I'm well aware of that, working here," she said, refusing to turn around and still angry. "I don't need a lecture."

William's hands dropped, and he stepped back. "You're right. I'm sorry."

Guilt choked her; he was just trying to look out for her. "Will—"

"It's fine. I should get home," he interrupted gently. "I'll see you tomorrow."

William stepped away from her, picked up his bag, a small pile of folders, and headed out the door.

Eliza stared after him and thought that maybe this was worse than losing her job after all.

****

"Thanks, El," Lily said and hung up the phone.

Though Eliza sounded like she had a lot more on her mind than she admitted to, Lily filed that away for later, focusing instead on what she had discovered about Opus and the victims. Add that to the files Reva had produced and the locations of the bodies, and she had a good chunk of the information Sebastian had been looking for.

Now, if only she could get him to listen to her long enough for her to tell him.

The first couple of days right after the...*incident* had been tense, but they'd found their footing. Lily didn't linger in his apartment, and he seemed to have more than perfect luck in avoiding her before and after class, save that first day. She'd figured his lock had some kind of recording system, but now she knew for certain.

But slowly over the past few weeks, they'd been falling back into their old routine. Sebastian still stayed away when she was alone, but he stopped by before opening to check in and pick up the drinks she still made him. They would still talk about work and laugh about Ellis's stories. They were almost back to what they had been before...whatever almost happened.

The only tense moment, aside from Lily walking in on a half-naked Sebastian—and that image had yet to leave her—was when she stopped him before opening that same day.

"Hey, boss?" she said. "Thanks for the rides home, but I'll take it from here."

He hesitated, just for a moment, then nodded. "Of course."

And that had been that. Sometimes she and Teegan shared an Uber, sometimes Lily called her own, and sometimes, she walked. But no one needed to know.

She still loved Tartarus and had been planning for the next theme night, but the past two weeks, she felt like she'd lost something. Something she hadn't really had, not truly. But the…opportunity for something. A chance.

It felt like something important.

Lily didn't find time to catch Sebastian alone until two days later, as they were cleaning up. She'd been on edge; the crowds had been more riled than usual, and she had to go and breakup a fight between a group of guys on the stage because Ellis was tied up handling a few mouthy assholes at the front doors. As it all went down, the group nearly took out Marley's stage, and knocked Teegan to the ground. At that point, Lily saw red.

She jumped over the bar, sliding across the top to lay two of them out cold with one move, knocking down a third when he didn't take the hint and sucker-punched her. Standing over them, Lily glared at the others, hip cocked, and brow arched. "Make a move or get out."

The others hesitated, glaring at her.

Lily waited.

One of them spat on the ground, and then they turned to leave. As they left, she saw Darcy and Sebastian standing behind them, both tense as they waited for the guys to make a move.

They didn't. Unfortunately for her. The fight had been too quick and too unsatisfying. That might have been part of the reason why she'd decided that Sebastian would listen to her tonight, or she'd make him. No excuses.

When he came up to the bar later, carrying a few discarded glasses, she caught his eye. "We need to talk after."

He nodded, half-heartedly, already moving away.

"Boss," she said firmly, drawing his gaze. "I mean it."

Sebastian met her gaze then, understanding. "After." He glanced at her mouth. "You're bleeding."

Lily wiped her mouth on the back of her hand, rolling her eyes as she cleaned up. By the time she looked up, he was gone.

****

They locked up, and gathered in the lounge, Lily made sure Teegan was okay after her fall. "Maybe I should start coming to your class," Teegan muttered, examining the bruise on her arm.

"I was thinking the same thing." Marley grinned at them, slinging her arms over their shoulders. "Me an' Darcy."

"I don't want to make anyone uncomfortable, though," Darcy said, his eyes wide. "I know a lot of your students have…concerns about men. If I'd upset them—"

"You might," Lily said honestly. "But it's good for them to meet good guys. And you're a good guy." She glanced at Ellis, who had been suspiciously quiet. "Might be helpful to have you there, too."

"Me?"

"They only get to practice on one another, and most guys are bigger than them. If they can throw you or get you to let go—"

Over his snort, Lily saw a speculative look in his eye, so she stayed quiet for the moment. They all filed out, while Lily begged off to use the restroom and told them she'd see them tomorrow. Once the door shut and locked, Lily stepped out of the bathroom and went upstairs to Sebastian's apartment.

She hadn't been in here with him since the day after their…moment. And honestly, she still hadn't shaken the image of shirtless Sebastian. He had more muscle than she expected, and she was beginning to think he had a gym somewhere in the building. His towel hadn't obscured much, and the v of his hips had become a constant in Lily's dreams since then.

The lack of closeness frustrated her. Not just what they might have had, but because she felt like they were friends. They got along. He understood her, even without knowing everything, and vice versa. She enjoyed spending time with him, and now…she missed that companionship. She missed him.

She knocked as she unlocked the door, giving him a heads up. She heard his voice telling her to come in, so she did, shutting the door behind her. He was already sitting down in an armchair, the next closest piece of furniture several feet away. Thoughtful.

Carrying her backpack over, she put it on the floor next to her, taking out the folder she'd been compiling. Sebastian watched her carefully, his eyes half-hooded and distant.

"What's on your mind, Nehme?"

She had thought this over several times, and though

she wasn't the planner he seemed to be, she knew she held the cards. "I have information on Oren."

A spark of interest, and surprise, flickered through his eyes, as if he thought she wanted to talk about something else. "How?"

"You aren't the only one with connections."

That almost got a smile out of him.

"I've got locations of bodies. I've got some info on where they were before. I've got causes of death, and I know what the drug is."

"I'm impressed," he said quietly. "But why do I think there's a catch to this?"

Lily drew in a breath. "Here's the deal: I want Oren and Opus off the streets. You want to save Tartarus. You know Oren, and how he operates, and I can get the other information you need." She didn't mention her occupation, though she'd considered doing so. She stood on shaky enough ground with him, she couldn't risk giving him another reason not to talk to her. "If I give you this, we figure it out together. You don't do anything without me, and vice versa, or no deal."

She was fair. Fairer than she wanted to be. But she would hold to the deal, and for all his posturing, he cared about the club and the employees, and that included her, so—

"No."

"Great, I—" Lily froze, staring at him. "Wait, what?"

"No. I don't want you involved."

He spoke so flippantly. And for some reason, that made her furious. "Are you seriously this stupid?"

His eyes narrowed to slits. "Are you this reckless? I told you what Oren is capable of."

She put the folder back in her bag, zipping up the pouch. "Which is why we need to get him off the streets as soon as possible!"

"I've been working on this for months—"

"And gotten nowhere. I have more information than you managed to get in months."

"I'll manage." He got to his feet. "Have a good evening."

He was dismissing her like he had Oren? *He was dismissing her?*

Hell, no.

Lily stood in a second, fury burning away the sympathy left in her. She was here, trying to make this work for the good of everyone else, but he was so damn stubborn.

"Look here, Galani, I'm tired of this martyr bullshit." She took two steps forward, and he turned, not showing any concern as she approached. "You've done a great job alienating yourself so no one gets hurt, but you've worn that line out and gotten nowhere. So, you're going to have to change up your shit."

His smile was cold, and he walked across the room, Lily on his heels. "You've been here three months and think you know better than me?" he asked, his brow cocked as he glanced over his shoulder. "I've been in this longer than you, and you have no idea—"

"Seems like I have a better idea than you," she interrupted, finally seeing a mark of anger on his face—he must hate people interrupting him. "You've got nothing in terms of information and you're turning away your best source because you think you can get it some other way? How?"

He bent to place his glass on the low table in the

middle of the room, then straightened. "I just did."

Her bag was in his hand.

"Motherfu—" Lily lunged, but he sidestepped her, faster than she expected. She twisted mid-movement, grabbing the strap.

They stared at one another and for a moment, Lily looked in on the situation from the outside:

Sebastian, the calm, collected club owner with a criminal family.

Lily, the PI vigilante turned bartender.

Both adults.

Playing tug-of-war over a backpack.

This was so stupid.

"Don't be ridiculous," Sebastian said, his grip on the bag tight as he stepped back, dragging her with him. "You don't need to be involved."

"I'm already involved, you asshole." She turned, pulling the bag forward, and getting it under her arm. Sebastian still had a hand on the strap that went under her arm, but she had her back to him, the bag tucked against her chest. "Stop being such a jerk and let me help."

"And you stop being so reckless and stay out of things that don't concern you." He pulled the bag slightly, and she tensed, wondering if she'd have to really use force to make him let go.

"Are you really this stupid?" Lily snapped at him.

"Are you going to keep insulting your boss?" he retorted, his voice thin with anger. His free hand landed on her shoulder, pushing her, too gently to do much, but not relinquishing the bag.

"Until you stop being an idiot, yeah," she muttered.

"Oren is dangerous."

"Good thing I'm used to dangerous things," Lily retorted, planting her feet.

Sebastian cursed under his breath, pulling more insistently on the backpack. "If you think the meeting with Oren was the worst that could happen—"

"That was a cakewalk," Lily said, before she remembered that he hadn't felt that way. "I'm sorry if I made you uncomfortable, but isn't that proof that you need me? I can help when you can't—"

Sebastian let go of the strap, and Lily nearly stumbled from the sudden lack of tension against the bag. She shifted the bag behind her as she turned, staring at Sebastian and trying to figure out what game he was playing.

"You thought…" he said quietly, then scoffed, and crossed the living room, completely ignoring the bag and going to the bar in the corner and pouring himself a drink.

Lily's eyes narrowed as she watched him throw back the measure of whiskey and pour another one before turning around. "I was uncomfortable," he said. "But not because of you."

"Oh." She didn't know what to say in response to that. "Well…same goes for me."

The frown started between his eyes again and he leaned against the bar. "I used you."

She shrugged. "I know. But so what? I mean, wasn't ideal, but I still liked…" she trailed off, suddenly awkward. "But after…got so weird, I thought you just wanted to forget about it."

"I didn't. I would have preferred not to have Oren there, but I thought you—"

"I didn't." It didn't matter what he'd thought, he'd

probably been wrong. "I had been on my way up here, before everything, after all."

"And I had invited you up."

Lily inclined her head, acknowledging their mutual misinterpretation. Despite clearing the air, a different type of tension hovered between them. Now that they both knew they hadn't been upset, the potential for something to happen seemed attainable.

Maybe she hadn't lost her chance.

Sebastian stared at her for a long, long moment, and Lily dug deeply to remain still under his gaze. Finally, he blinked and looked out the window. "Oren is dangerous. He uses people against one another. As moles or collateral." He poured out another glass of whiskey, carrying it over to her. "We're fighting an uphill battle, and we can't give him anything else to use against us."

She heard the meaning beneath his words. There was something here, and that something was mutual, but they had to wait until Oren was dealt with.

She could work with that. Probably. "Does that mean you're taking my deal?" she asked, accepting the glass from him.

"Partners, Nehme. That means you tell me what you're up to."

"Right back at you. It's me and you together, or not at all."

"Deal," he said, lifting his glass.

Clinking her glass against his, Lily met his eyes, the dark gaze fixated on her. His slight smile held a lot more than the promise of a partnership, and she realized that if she'd been thinking about that night for weeks, he might have been, too. Maybe he'd been thinking of what would have happened had they not been interrupted, and she'd already seen his ability for…creativity.

They both drank the liquor, eyes never leaving one another's.

As if she needed more motivation to get rid of Oren as fast as possible.

Chapter 12

He couldn't remember how it all happened.

One minute, he'd been sitting at the bar as Lily conducted her class with the rest of his staff present for the first time. The next—

"What about an actual fight?" her student Julian asked. He was a larger kid, and though Sebastian had watched him master all the defensive moves, he clearly attended this class to learn how to keep people from bothering him.

Taking a moment to grab a drink, Lily glanced at Julian. "Gonna end up in a fistfight?"

"Maybe. Can you show me?"

Teegan smiled. "If it's anything like the guys at the club, I don't doubt it."

"Good thing we've got her around," Marley added, winking at Ellis to take the sting out of her tease.

"Me and Galani used to throw punches with the best of 'em," Ellis said, his conscious effort to keep his arms from being crossed and his voice calmer noted by Sebastian, if not the others. "You should've seen him in his prime."

"Bet it's been a while." Marley grinned back at the bar. "Ain't that right, Galani?"

He merely glared at her, which had zero effect.

"Come on." Darcy grinned. "Why don't you show us if you've still got it?"

Sebastian shook his head, ignoring him.

Ellis snorted. "He's just scared he'll lose."

That earned a darker glare, but Sebastian saw Lily smiling behind him, a teasing, impish smile as she cocked her hip to the side. Ellis's comment faded as Lily watched him, and before she even opened her mouth, he knew he was doomed.

"Come on, boss," she taunted. "If you knock me down first, no more flowers."

The staff grinned, far too familiar with every foolish bet that had occurred regarding her attire and knowing he had yet to win. Not that he really minded.

Sebastian stood and removed his jacket.

Amid the hoots and hollers of his former friends, he rolled up the cuffs of his shirt to give him a little more movement, toed off his shoes, and stepped onto the mat. Lily, making sure they were on even footing, kicked off her sneakers, and circled to face him.

"Will this be street rules?" Darcy asked.

"Like you've ever been in a street fight," Marley muttered.

"Hey, I've…seen musicals."

Teegan laughed and started snapping her fingers, and the others joined in. Lily grinned at him. "First one on the mat loses."

He'd seen her fight. He knew he was screwed. "Deal."

Knowing that he'd only have a short amount of time to keep whatever bit of dignity he could, Sebastian moved first, feinting left before going right, his fist coming up towards Lily's ribs. He had a brief thought to pull the punch, but she grinned too widely for him to be that worried.

She knocked his arm aside, much like he thought she would, so he dropped, trying to sweep her feet. Lily jumped and rolled, coming up next to him and grabbing his arm. He twisted away from her grasp, grabbing her wrist. She grabbed his other hand, then twisted, wrapping his arm around her as she put her back to his front.

Sebastian felt her smile—

And then he flew over her shoulder as she knelt and hurled him onto the mat, kneeling next to his head. "Sorry, boss," she said, still grinning.

"No, you're not," he retorted once he got his breath back.

She laughed, and the slight ache in his shoulder vanished. Lily bounced to her feet and stood next to him to help him up.

Sebastian swung his arm out, knocking her legs out from underneath her. Lily landed on the ground next to him in a huff. Turning her head, her glare was ruined by the laughter and clapping around them.

She laughed, and with a shake of her head, got to her feet and, with a narrowing of her eyes, offered a hand to him. He accepted her help, dropping her fingers quickly when he was upright.

Sebastian endured Ellis and Darcy's teasing as Lily slowly showed Julian, Teegan, and Marley how she got out of his grip. That ate up the rest of the class, and everyone began to disperse. Sebastian headed upstairs to change shirts and Lily on his heels.

"So, we've hit a bit of a snag," she said, heading into his bathroom.

"With what?" he asked, laying his jacket on the bed.

The water started, and she shut the door partway,

leaving a crack as she continued talking. "I checked with Reva yesterday, and she said not only will the morgue not release the autopsy reports, but she's also hit a wall with her sources. None of them are going to help us out. Hughes's been threatening everyone left and right about releasing information and they're all scared."

He unbuttoned his shirt, his brows drawing together. Lily had shared Eliza's concerns that—despite what the cops claimed—there were two different drugs on the market, based on the varied causes of death. They couldn't confirm that without an autopsy, nor would they get any hints about what the victims had been doing prior to death. "Can we request the files from the morgue?"

Her voice muffled for a moment. "Not unless you're a close relative, with documented proof of relationship with the deceased, in triplicate. Approval takes weeks, and sometimes denied anyway." Her voice echoed and the water stream was interrupted.

Taking a clean shirt from his closet, he reapplied deodorant before sliding the fabric on over his shoulders. "So, we go look at the files for ourselves."

"The cops are never going to show us."

"Not the cops, the morgue. They have copies."

"We're just going to walk in and ask?"

"I didn't say that," he said, doing up the buttons on his shirt.

She fell silent for a few moments, then the water shut off. "What are you proposing?"

He straightened his cuffs, fixing the buttons on those. "City morgue moved from SPD headquarters three years ago. Nothing more than a few rent-a-cops and a decent security system. I'm proposing a…nighttime visit."

"And looking for what?" Lily asked. He heard the sound of a zipper pulled open as she went into her bag.

He donned his jacket, smoothing the sleeves down over the cuffs of his shirt. "Not sure. But if we take photos, the good doctor might see something."

"It's dangerous."

"Perhaps. But I'm done waiting." He smiled faintly at his reflection, deciding that action looked good on him.

"If you get caught, you'll be in trouble."

He glanced at the door in a reflex, the slight opening revealing a part of the mirror. Lily stood in front, just a grey towel wrapped carelessly around her torso and her hair in tangles around her bare shoulders. She held a brush in her hand as she frowned at her reflection, worry between her eyes.

"They won't catch us."

"What if they do?" she asked, her worry obvious in her voice now.

"They won't," he said, cursing himself as the words came out a little softer than he'd meant. Clearing his throat, he added, "I'm a Galani, remember? Old habits die hard."

She smiled at his voice, looking down and fidgeting with the handle of the brush before using it. "You sure you've still got the moves? It's been a while."

"Not that long," he argued, a little too quickly. "Besides, there's something to be said for…experience."

Lily grinned at that, catching her lip between her teeth. "I'm sure there is," she said, her own voice getting a little softer. "Can't wait."

Putting the brush aside, she grabbed the edge of the towel and—

Sebastian looked away. "I'll see you—"

"I had a question."

He paused in his walk to the door but didn't look. "Yeah?"

"Oren already saw us together. Or so he thought. Why is it still dangerous?"

"There is a chance he already believes that we're...involved," he admitted. But, far more likely, he believes that I was taking advantage of a drugged-out girl," he said that last part bitterly, unsurprised at her follow-up question.

"Why would he think that?"

"Because it's what he does."

"Bastard," Lily muttered.

"Oren is under the impression that his disdain for women is a common feeling. So, when he sees others acting in a way that could be interpreted as what he would do, that's what he tends to believe is fact," Sebastian explained. One of the many, many reasons he hated Oren.

"I can't wait to get rid of him."

"You and me both."

****

On Thursday, Eliza stared at the belated winter downpour from the front door of the clinic, cocking her head to the side with a resigned sigh. Though her pocket umbrella would help, the bus stop was a long walk away, with another walk home, dooming her to wet stockings and cold feet.

Miguel had left earlier, and Eliza regretted not taking the ride he'd offered before leaving. But it hadn't been raining yet, and she had work to catch up on. In addition to her usual demands, she'd been trying to help

Lily by digging further into the causes of death, but there wasn't much information to go off of. There was something odd about this Opus, but she couldn't follow the thread. She also didn't feel entirely comfortable asking her coworkers for advice, considering Will's response last time.

Still, none of that helped her current predicament.

Opening her umbrella, she stepped out into the rain, no sense in putting off the inevitable. She tried to keep positive but hit two puddles before she reached the main sidewalk, which didn't bode well.

She barely reached the corner when a car pulled up alongside her, the window rolling down.

She frowned, glancing inside to see Will leaning across the seat. "Get in."

"No, it's okay—"

He sighed, loudly. "Just get in."

Thunder boomed and drowned out her reply, so she gave in, the awkward shuffle of trying to get in the car while closing her umbrella lasting a little longer than usual. Finally, she was seated in the car with the door closed. Tucking her wet hair behind her ear, she smiled at him. "Thank you."

"Of course," he said, his eyes on the road.

Wiping the water off her hands, she said, "The bus stop is just at this corner, if you don't mind."

"It's pouring, Clark. Let me drive you home."

The invitation wasn't new. Miguel and Will constantly offered to drive her, but she enjoyed walking. She liked to have that quiet time to herself. Miguel had given up, except for rainy or snowy days, but Will offered at least three times a week. She had given in once or twice, both because of rain. This would be no different. "Thank you."

He was good with directions and didn't ask her which way to go, not after the first time he took her home, so they fell into silence. Will didn't say anything about the other night, but Eliza began to shift slightly, guilt still niggling at her. She finally found her voice at the same time Will tried to talk.

"How's the case go—"

"I wanted to apologize—"

They both broke off, him scoffing quietly and her smiling, then he gestured for her to go first.

"I wanted to say sorry for the other day. I didn't mean anything by it. I was just…frustrated."

"You don't have to apologize for anything," he said. "I shouldn't have tried to tell you what to do. You're smart and capable, and don't need me butting in."

Though she knew he felt that way, hearing the actual words flattered her more than she expected. "I always want your advice, Will. I just didn't want you to try to talk me out of it."

He hummed quietly in agreement, and Eliza considered the other reason she had been so uncomfortable the past couple of days. Now was as good a time as any.

"Are you still…upset with me?" she asked, watching his profile.

Will frowned, cutting his eyes over at her. "I was never upset with you."

"But you were mad and then you left—"

"I…" Will interrupted her, but then paused, familiar enough with her to know that when interrupted, she would just talk louder over the interrupter—usually Miguel. Eliza waved for him to go ahead. "I wasn't mad.

I was…an idiot. Instead of offering help, I passed judgment. I'm sorry."

Eliza reached across and touched his arm. "I'm sorry, too."

He scoffed, keeping his gaze straight ahead.

"You found an employee with MDMA in your clinic, you reacted a lot better than most would, I'm sure," she said, trying to instill some humor into her voice.

"Well, if it had been Ramirez…"

She laughed, knowing he didn't mean that, and felt the tension leave him. He reached over and squeezed her hand tightly, then took his away, letting her hand slide off of his arm. Her hand seemed to tingle slightly, but she kept her eyes on him.

"But I should have offered to help from the very first. I trust your judgment far more than I trust my own."

Eliza smiled at the praise again, then bit her lip. "So, if I ask for your help with Lily's case…"

"I'm here for anything you need, Clark."

"Good, because it's been driving me crazy not bouncing theories off of you," she sighed in relief.

He chuckled, and the tension vanished. "Tell me what you have so far."

The conversation lasted long past the drive to her apartment. They sat in the car for another hour afterward, talking through what she had discovered so far and her potential theories.

Will seemed as surprised as her when she looked at the clock and realized it was almost ten.

"Oh gosh," she said, gathering her things. "I'm so sorry. I've kept you here—"

"It's not a problem," he assured her, his faint smile

still visible from the console.

The rain still flooded down, harder than before. She sighed, getting her umbrella ready.

"It's supposed to rain all week," he said.

"Great." She made a mental note to wear boots.

"Am I going to have to fight you every day?"

Eliza turned, frowning as she tried to decipher the question.

"To allow me to drive you home."

"Oh." She blushed as she realized how obvious he'd been. "I'm really fine—"

"Clark."

Had he always said her name like that? Low and dark and…maybe the rain played tricks on her ears. Or the late hour. But he stared at her and—

"I would be grateful for a ride home," she replied eventually.

"Wonderful," he said. "Then, this is goodnight, Doctor Clark."

"Goodnight, Doctor Lintz."

She hadn't meant for her voice to emulate his, dropping a little, with a tiny smile at the corner of her mouth. This almost felt like…flirting. With Will?

Escaping the car, Eliza took a deep breath, unfiltered, with no hint of his cologne. Still, the feeling in the pit of her stomach didn't fade, and as she approached the door, she glanced behind. Will still sat at the curb, making sure she got inside okay. She waved, and he smiled back, pulling away from the corner, and Eliza watched him drive off, that little smile reappearing on her lips. She shook her head the second she realized, then headed upstairs to her apartment.

She needed a glass of wine.

A big one.

****

Lily had to admit—Sebastian delivered.

Not, after reading about his past and family, that she expected anything different. But reading was one thing, seeing a completely different one.

He orchestrated the whole job, and Lily had let him take the lead, from organizing the route, to timing, to an alibi, and to dealing with the guard outside. She followed his instructions, and that's how the two of them ended up outside Southton City Morgue at eleven-thirty on a rainy Thursday.

They'd taken a circuitous path to get there, doubling back several times, and Lily silently wondered what the Galani family would have been like had he taken over. His attention to detail, his intense focus, his organization and ability to see the big picture of everything…he seemed perfectly designed to be a criminal mastermind. She doubted they'd be struggling so much if he had taken charge instead of his brother.

And instead, he chose to run a club, and that somehow made her even more impressed.

They'd changed just after leaving Tartarus, Lily exchanging her heels for a functional pair of boots and a black jacket to cover her flowered top. Sebastian had disappeared for a moment, the suit vanishing and replaced with dark jeans, boots, and a black sweater. Lily had been momentarily speechless, but fell into step behind him, the rain making conversation difficult.

They approached the back entrance of the morgue, a younger man standing sentry. Lily hesitated, but Sebastian walked right up. "Good evening, Preston."

"Good evening, Mr. Galani."

"Cameras?"

"Off for now," Preston said. "I can give you twelve minutes, but system does a check every fifteen, and they'll automatically reboot."

"More than enough time." He glanced over Preston's shoulder to the darker hallway. "Just Simon on the inside?"

"Yeah. He doesn't check inside the rooms, just waves his flashlight around in the main hallway. Make sure you're out of sight of the windows, though."

"Perfect. Thank you." He handed over an envelope which Preston pocketed.

"Thank you again, sir. For everything." Preston opened the door for them, waving them inside.

Lily stayed on Sebastian's heels as they entered the dim hallway. Hearing the door shut behind them, she whispered, "How much was the bribe?"

"Not a bribe," he answered, his voice quiet, too. "Preston's sister had some medical bills. I paid them off."

Still sounded like a bribe, but something else lingered in his tone. "When?"

"A year ago."

She frowned at his back, and he glanced over his shoulder. "I don't bribe people. I make deals."

She thought of how he bought out Jed without telling her, just to do something nice. How he let her use the club. He hadn't asked her for much, just to be a partner in something she was already involved in. "You're something else, Galani."

He glanced down at her with a smile, then went ahead into the hallway, his footsteps almost silent on the tile.

As the bodies had been incinerated weeks prior, there was no point in going into the morgue proper. They just had to reach the records room, which had far less security, according to Sebastian's information. Which made very little sense to her—people were far more likely to steal information than a body, right? The circumstances in which that might not be true were too weird to consider, so she stopped that train of thought at once.

Luckily for them, the records room was on the same floor as the autopsy room. The morgue had digital files, which were what they used more often and shared with the police and public, but paper copies of all the original autopsies and findings were kept, too.

The records room sat down one long hallway, a stressful stretch of exposed building to get through. Sebastian had told her the cameras would be off, thanks to Preston, and Simon wouldn't come down for another six minutes, which gave them enough time to get in, find the files associated with Tartarus, take the pictures, and get out.

Lily had memorized the three names she would look for—Monica Carpenter, Marcus Jimenez, Ushi Lam. Ushi had been the girl she hadn't been able to...

The sound of a file cabinet opening had her glancing over, but Sebastian moved swiftly, grabbing the two files he'd been looking for—Jason Shannon and Ira Suri.

Taking more time than she expected, Lily found what she needed. She pulled the files out and opened them up, taking pictures and skimming quickly. They could analyze more later—tonight was just about getting information and getting out.

Even just skimming, something was obviously off.

All three of her cases were deemed death by overdose, and the bags photographed were the same ones she had found, but she saw both of the things Eliza had been talking about—serotonin syndrome and cardiac arrest with muscle tears. If they were all using Opus, why were people dying in different ways?

She flipped the next page over and saw a picture of Marcus's body.

Lily inhaled, staring down at him. He looked young. Younger, in fact, than the pictures Michaela had given her made him out to be. He didn't deserve this.

"You alright?" Sebastian whispered, returning his files to the cabinets.

"Yeah." She snapped the picture, then made to close the file, noticing a note on the margin of the papers.

Injection site on left arm.

"Nehme," Sebastian hissed.

She looked up, seeing the glow from Simon's flashlight approach. Quickly, she put the files back, slid the cabinet shut as Sebastian came over and grabbed her shoulder to guide to the back corner and behind a cabinet, out of sight of the guard's sweep.

"In here," he whispered, stepping back into a shadowy corner.

A tight fit, the space was obviously meant for another file cabinet as opposed to two adults, and Sebastian had to duck slightly to be completely obscured. He looked behind her, and she resisted the urge to turn around and see what concerned him.

She saw the glow from a flashlight pass over the top of the cabinet, and Sebastian moved without warning, snagging her waist and pulling her further back into the shadows as the light, presumably, shone where she hadn't been concealed by the cabinet.

He, for lack of a better word, hugged her against him to keep them both in the shadows, his mouth next to her ear to keep his taller frame out of sight. Her hands were stuck between them, pressed against his chest.

Well aware a security guard approached who, if he discovered them, could destroy everything they'd both been working for, she could only focus on Sebastian's arms around her, the quiet, steady thud of his heartbeat beneath her fingers, and the tentative warmth of the side of her cheek as he breathed.

The guard checked the door with an abrasive rattle, and her head jerked slightly towards the sound, her nose bumping Sebastian's jaw. She reacted without thought, trying to step back to give him space, but he just held her tighter, keeping her from moving, with no other visible reaction.

Physically, however…

She felt his heart beat just a little faster.

Perhaps the urge came from a combination of everything — the months of smoldering attraction, the missed opportunities and close calls, the fact that this feeling was mutual, the adrenaline from breaking and entering, the fact that they were hiding in a dark corner, where neither one of them could speak or escape from…

Lily tilted her head slightly, then pressed her lips against his throat, just above the collar of his jacket. He inhaled audibly, and his fingers flexed on her waist.

She moved slightly closer, knowing his back was against the wall behind him, grabbing two fistfuls of his jacket as she kissed his neck again, moving a little higher. Her nose brushed his jaw again, the tickle of stubble she could feel but not see, then her lips tasted the bitter tang of his aftershave. His heart jumped again below her fingers as her teeth scraped lightly against his jaw. Whether this had been her idea or not, her own breath came a little louder now, lost in the dark around them.

One hand left her waist, moving up along her back until he cupped her cheek in his hand, tilting her face up towards his. She couldn't see much in the shadows, not really, but even in the dark, she could see how dark his eyes were, the electric blue now just a thin ring around his eyes.

"Wicked," he whispered against her lips, his thumb tracing the edge of her mouth.

She just smiled, her eyes sliding closed as he closed the short distance between them—

A slamming door made both of them jump, the guard having finishing his rounds downstairs and heading to the next floor. This was their opportunity to get out.

Slowly, she stepped back, and Sebastian, just as reluctantly, lowered his hands. Lily grinned at the image he made, slouched against the wall, eyes still blown out. "Come on. No rest for us, right?" she said, her voice not sounding quite as calm as she'd hoped.

He took a breath, pushing away from the wall and straightening his collar. "Let's go."

She grinned at his back as he took the lead again, the taste of him began to fade from her lips. For now.

****

It was several hours later before she climbed into bed.

They returned to Tartarus without further incident, closing down and cleaning up without anyone asking any questions. Lily hadn't commented when he showed up on the corner in his car. The ride had been tense, but they barely spoke, and neither of them tried to continue her overture from earlier. So, she merely grinned at him as she darted out into the rain on her doorstep, unlocking the door with alacrity and sliding in before he pulled away from the corner.

Sitting cross legged in the middle of her bed, she brushed her hair, braiding it up to keep the humidity from wreaking havoc during the night. Mid-braid, a wayward thought struck her, and before she could reconsider, she rose, crossing the dark living room and knocking on Eliza's door.

"El?" she said. She knocked again before opening the door.

Eliza stirred in her bed, frowning as she sat up on her elbows. "Lily? What's wrong?"

"On autopsies, when they're recording things and they say left, is that the subject's left or the doctor's?"

Eliza seemed completely blindsided and Lily suddenly realized it was four in the morning, but she needed to know now. She tried to explain, "If someone was shot, and they wrote the gunshot was on the left, whose left are they talking about?"

"Uhh…" Eliza rubbed her eyes, sleep disturbing her normally speedy thinking. "Uh, the doctor's left."

"So, if they say on the left arm, it would be my right?"

"Yeah. Yes."

Lily turned on her heel, heading out.

Eliza called after her, "Lily, what—what's going on?"

"What's going on," Lily said grimly, "is that Marcus was right-handed."

Chapter 13

Sebastian knew his luck would run out sooner or later.

Tartarus was thriving; they were up; without anything to hang around for, the cops had backed off; his staff worked efficiently, and Lily...

He resisted the urge to smile, keeping his face blank as he looked across the bar.

Well.

But, too many good things happened recently. He waited, breath bated, for the other shoe to drop. So far, nothing had struck. Yet.

Tonight, Tartarus's infamous Black Tie New Year's Eve party had arrived, and though stressful to put on, it remained one of the biggest and most successful parties in the city, growing bigger every year. The line started at closing the night before and grew to record levels. Marley had found a live band, Darcy streamed all worldwide coverages of the New Year to coincide with the stroke of midnight here, and Ellis had, as usual, acquired his terrifyingly large supply of fireworks to be set off above Tartarus at midnight.

Everyone dressed to the nines and then some, tuxes and suits, ball gowns and evening dresses. The band was wonderful, upbeat swing music interspersed with Marley's usual when they took breaks, keeping the crowd enthralled. Her red ball gown glittered with black belts and silver chains, her hair swept up in an impressive mohawk.

Teegan strolled through the crowd, her gold gown drawing more gazes than usual, but her eyes fixed on her tablet, focused on keeping this night successful and safe. Darcy kept checking in on her, the suit making the Boy Scout look more his age, as he darted around the floor, keeping fights from breaking out with smiles and drinks. Ellis's suit strained at his shoulders a little and Sebastian doubted he would have the jacket on any longer, but he still did his job up front, keeping the crowds soothed and moving forward. Sebastian donned his usual suit, though his cufflinks were a bit nicer and the tiepin a touch of class. And Lily was exactly what he had come to expect.

Her black, slightly sheer gown brushed the floor, and all over, from the thin straps at the top to the hem, were embroidered flowers. There were a few in her hair, but the dark hair stayed loose and flowed over her shoulders.

He had been prepared enough not to pause when seeing her this time, but it had been close.

Having staked out his seat early on, Sebastian didn't have to fight the crowds this time. His drink appeared too quickly for him to thank her, but Lily smiled when he caught her eye before refocusing on her work.

"This place is amazing, right?" a guy said to Sebastian's right.

Sebastian glanced at him, unsure if he was speaking to him.

The man to his right grinned, a large glass almost empty in front of him. "I've been here a dozen times in the past month, at least! And it's great!"

"Glad you think so," Sebastian said, sipping his

glass.

The man next to him drained his drink, putting the glass down a little too hard. His cuffs were unbuttoned and the jacket too large for him. Lily came over just a second later, a quick smile for the man. She grabbed the empty glass. "Can I get you another?"

The man leaned forward, grinning, his glasses crooked on his nose. "Yes. And you can also get me your number."

Sebastian tensed, but Lily merely smiled. "Sorry. Not interested."

"But I'm a doctor," he insisted.

"Congrats! Another?"

"Yes!" he shouted, slamming his hands on the bar.

Lily filled up a glass, placing it in front of him, and holding out her hand for his card. "That'll be—"

He snagged her hand, and Sebastian put his glass down, but Lily kept smiling, her brow arched.

"Please," the guy pleaded. "You're breaking my heart."

"Sorry." Lily pulled her hand away without a problem. "You're gonna have to find someone else. But I'll give you this drink on the house for the heartbreak."

"I won't forget you," he said, grabbing his drink and standing on unsteady legs. "I'm gonna find you at midnight."

Lily waved as he teetered off, then looked at Sebastian.

"Do you give away drinks to all the men who ask you for your numbers?" he asked.

"No," Lily grinned. "Usually just the women."

"And how many kisses have you been promised this evening?"

"A dozen or so."

The cavalier response irked him, and he frowned into his glass. When he heard her laugh, he realized the misstep he'd made.

Lily smiled. "Jealous?"

He merely took another sip of his drink, but her grin widened. She leaned on the bar top, her hair falling over her shoulder. "Because if you were, the solution is easy."

"Is it?" Sebastian asked, intrigued despite himself.

"Of course." Her grin reminded him of the records room, slow and dark, and Sebastian felt his body react to her expression alone. He arched a brow, and she took that as a question.

"You'll just have to make sure I'm busy at midnight."

What an idea.

Sebastian lowered his glass. "Well, maybe I'll see you at midnight."

"Looking forward to it." She gave him one last smile before turning back to man the bar. The grin she gave to others was very different from the one she gave him.

He hoped his luck would hold out just a little longer.

****

Lily's phone blew up with notifications from friends and family, wishing her a happy new year. She could see messages lighting up the screen below the bar: Eliza, out with Miguel, Reva and Jason, out of town for a holiday vacation, everyone sending her messages, and still a few minutes to go.

Teegan had joined her behind the bar as they poured out champagne flutes for everyone—not the great stuff, but still free, which people enjoyed. Teegan passed them out as Lily poured bottle after bottle. As Teegan started slowing down, Lily glanced around, seeing that everyone in view had a flute

"Last call before we close till the new year!".

She caught sight of Sebastian at the corner, his glass empty. She replaced his drink with the full one she had waiting and winked. He smiled, holding the side of the bar up as she and Teegan exited the latter darting off to get out of the crowd.

There were forty-five seconds to go, and Lily noticed that Sebastian lingered at her side, not touching, but definitely close enough to deter other would-be midnight kisses. She cut her eyes at him, appreciating the dark silver tie he wore and the tiepin with the jet stone.

"Happy New Year, boss," she said, as the crowd counted down from thirty.

"Happy New Year." His hand came to rest on the small of her back, and Lily began turning towards him.

The sounds of a fight broke out as they hit twenty, and Sebastian glanced over. "Dammit." He looked down at her, and she appreciated the hesitation.

"Go. You know where I'll be."

He didn't smile, but vanished into the crowd, heading towards the sounds of chaos. Even from here, she could hear Ellis's laughter, the doors having shut before the countdown so everyone within Tartarus could celebrate together.

The crowd hit five, and Lily got carried up in the fervor, counting down with them.

"Four!"

"Three!"

"Two!"

"One!"

The band broke into song, people mumbling their

way through the traditional words if their mouths weren't otherwise occupied. Lily grabbed a few empty champagne flutes dangling from the hands of preoccupied revelers before she gave up.

The crowd laughed and cheered and hugged, and for a moment, Lily forgot about drugs and dealers and dead kids and being a PI. She forgot everything except this feeling of euphoria, of a new chance, a fresh start.

Lily allowed herself to be pulled into the crowd, and laughed, floating between arms. She pecked Darcy on the cheek, laughing as he blushed. Marley grabbed her and planted a good one on her. Even Teegan gave her a kiss on the cheek and a roll of her eyes. Lily laughed, kissing friends and strangers alike on the cheek, receiving some in return, the whole crowd mixing together to share in the excitement.

Catching sight of the doctor lurking at the bar, she snuck around the corner, putting the bar between him and her. Looking over her shoulder, she was pushed off balance by a rather voracious couple and fell into someone.

He supported her, lifting her onto her feet, holding her steady as the crowd heaved around them. The lights flared and went dark, again and again. She felt the man lean down and Lily presented her cheek.

A pair of lips brushed her cheek, ghosting over the corner of mouth.

Lily inhaled sharply, a spark passing through her like a live wire pressed to her skin. She smelled sandalwood and opened her eyes.

Sebastian looked down at her, a faint smile in place. His collar was a little crooked, but his eyes were dancing, the adrenaline from the fight giving his face some color.

Lily grinned up at him, straightening his tie.

Sebastian's eyes narrowed just slightly, then he leaned down, hesitating for just a moment before he kissed her properly.

Even with just a simple kiss, Sebastian burned away memories of all other lips, freezing them in the past. The lightheartedness vanished as Lily leaned into him, the kiss turning soft and lingering.

He broke away for a moment, not very far, and Lily exhaled against his mouth shakily, her eyes darting up to his. Raw and unchecked, his expression infused with a sudden unexpected longing that Lily had never seen before. Her face must have been something similar because his arms tightened on her elbows and pulled her against him.

This time, no hint of hesitation or laughter appeared in the kiss. His mouth moved hot and insistent against hers, one hand leaving her elbow to wrap around her, pulling her against him. Lily clung to the lapels of his jacket as she willingly moved towards him, parting her lips and tasting the pomegranate she'd muddled into his drinks for him since day one. Sebastian leaned down towards her, his usual aloof and stoic demeanor peeling away, and her sarcasm and quips silenced, until they were two raw nerve endings meeting.

Lily made a sound in the back of her throat; though lost in the chaos of the club, Sebastian must have felt the noise, because she felt his hand weave into her hair and tilt her chin up, exposing more of her to his hands and his lips, and god, she wanted—

Someone bumped into them, knocking Sebastian to the side and forcing them to break the kiss.

"Happy New Year!" the person shouted.

Sebastian held her steady, but the expression didn't change, even if he didn't lean down again. Lily's breath came too quickly, her lips tingling. Exhaling shakily, she looked up at him.

His eyes were dark again, watching her recover her composure. He seemed too still, though, like he expected her to say something he didn't want to hear.

It was too crowded, too loud, too open to be honest at the moment. She couldn't tell him that she felt like she'd been waiting her whole life to kiss him. She couldn't tell him that he was worth any wait. She couldn't say that she was ready to personally tear down every building in Southton to find Oren so they could do that again, as soon as possible. She couldn't, though she wanted to.

Instead, she smiled, smoothing his jacket down again, and got on her toes so he could hear her. "Knew you were jealous."

Sebastian laughed, then retorted, "You deserve the best. We both know that's me."

His arrogance shouldn't be attractive. It really shouldn't. And yet.

She laughed in agreement as Sebastian held her. Loathe to move, she knew they were pushing their luck. Most of their interaction could be played off as an intoxicated celebration of the New Year, but they couldn't continue. Not until everyone was safe.

She pulled away gently, and Sebastian let go, his expression understanding if annoyed.

"I should get back to the bar," she said.

"And I should help Ellis."

"Give him a kiss for me."

He scoffed, shaking his head, and turned away from

her. Lily snuck back to the bar, avoiding the doctor and shutting the bar as she prepared to reopen the tabs. While the register loaded, she checked her phone, seeing two from her father, one from Eliza, and…eight from Reva? She opened up the chat with Reva and Eliza.

—*11:20 Body dropped. Call me. ASAP.—*

—*11:30 Call me.—*

—*11:45 Dad says Hughes's on the warpath. He's coming to Tartarus.—*

—*11:46 He thinks it's one of you.—*

—*11:50 He's making an arrest. Tonight!—*

—*11:51 Call me!—*

—*11:55 He's on his way! Lily, if you get arrested again, we both know it's deep shit!—*

—*11:59 CALL ME—*

Lily looked up, catching sight of Sebastian across the room. Either she or Sebastian was Hughes's target, and considering who pissed him off the most last time—

"Seb!" she shouted, trying to get his attention.

Sebastian paused, glancing back at her.

The doors to Tartarus burst open. Detective Hughes in the lead of two dozen cops. "Sebastian Galani," he announced on a bellow. "You're under arrest for murder!"

****

Eliza rubbed her aching eyes. She'd made the mistake of celebrating at a bar with Miguel, who could not hold his liquor. That meant she spent most of the night on the sidewalk as he alternated between trying to pick up girls and vomiting. Not a nice memory.

Miguel had been in bed before the New Year rang in, and she'd just been getting home when Reva's messages came through. She'd stared at her phone, waiting for a response. She didn't get one until after midnight.

—Sebastian's been arrested.—

She tried to wait up for Lily but dozed off on the couch. When her alarm went off, Eliza checked Lily's room to find her roommate curled up in bed, a frown on her face even in sleep.

Eliza started the coffee before she left, leaving Lily a note to call her when she got up. Then, she set off to work early, determined to find some answers.

Lily's question the other night had left Eliza unsettled. Though not impossible that Marcus had simply used his other arm to inject, there weren't any marks or scars on his left arm to suggest habitual use. If he hadn't injected the Opus, that meant…

"Someone injected it into him."

"Hmm?" Will asked, looking up from his computer.

"It's just…Lily's case."

He minimized his work, turning his chair to face her. "What about it?" he asked, steepling his fingers together.

"The victims of Opus have either died from serotonin syndrome or heart attack, and all of them had been at Tartarus the night of their deaths."

"Meaning the dealer was likely there."

Eliza nodded, but that wasn't the part that concerned her. "Lily noticed Marcus had a needle mark on his arm."

"Not unheard of."

"Except he was right-handed, and the site was on his right arm."

Will nodded slowly. "So, someone else did it for him. Again…doesn't rule out that he chose to indulge. Just that he had help."

Eliza sighed, blinking a couple of times to clear her

head. She opened up the pictures Lily and Sebastian had sent her, skimming through the notes. Will turned back to his computer, letting her work quietly.

Frowning, Eliza checked the causes of death against the images. "Will?"

He stared at his computer, so Eliza came over, putting the pictures over the keyboard. "Every victim who died of heart attack had injection sites. Four of the five are associated with Tartarus. Marcus, and the girl Lily tried to save, Jason, and Ira. All of them had it done to them."

Will stared at the images. "The odds of all of them asking for help are…slim."

"And Monica, the only one with serotonin syndrome, had all the signs of being a habitual user. Combine any number of drugs with MDMA, or something close, and the body will react poorly." Eliza sat on the edge of the desk. "Someone is targeting people at Tartarus."

"To what end?"

Eliza shook her head slowly, not sharing every detail of her conversation with Lily. But if Sebastian was the immovable wall keeping Oren from dealing in Tartarus, and therefore the only one standing in the way of him taking over the slums completely…that seemed like motive.

"A hell of a way to go," Will said, looking over Eliza's notes. "Injected, it would directly affect the thalamus. That would make them feel like they were in pain, theoretically for hours. Days, depending on their strength."

"Eventually the heart just gives out," she finished. "That's why they have the muscle tears. They're straining against the pain."

"If they're targeting Tartarus," Will said after a moment, "stands to reason they're watching those who work there."

"I know."

"Clark…"

"I know." She rubbed her eyes, letting her hands fall into her lap.

A large, warm hand covered hers. Eliza opened her eyes, to see Will staring at her. "I'm not going to talk you out of it. I wouldn't succeed anyway. But if you need anything…"

"I know that, too," Eliza said, turning her hand under his to entwine their fingers.

Will's eyes were concerned, but something else lingered in them that Eliza couldn't discern. Too much to think about just now, she looked away, catching sight of his computer screen.

"Are you still researching hallucinatory drugs?" she asked.

"Just theorizing." He pulled his hand from hers, collecting her papers and blacking out his screen. He stood up, walking towards the door.

Eliza stared after him, a little confused. She got to her feet, "Will—"

Her phone started to ring, and Eliza sighed, glancing at the name.

She sighed. "Hey, Lily. I have some information, but you're not going to like it."

Chapter 14

Lily had been moving since she saw Eliza's note. Unsurprised El was at work before 8 AM, the information she'd given was helpful, if terrifying.

But she had a lead.

Jason, despite his complaints, gave her all the information she needed, after confirming Sebastian was okay. With him out of town, getting information was difficult, but he still came through for her. She figured Reva had a hand in it.

A knot continued tightening in Lily's stomach with every passing hour Sebastian stayed in custody. In order to avoid thinking about that, Lily stood outside of a small apartment building in the projects before 9 AM, waiting for the brunette from the night Ushi had died.

Willow Stanley.

She'd been in the bathroom when Lily had found Ushi's body, and since Ushi had the Opus injected, Willow was probably the one to drug her. She either distributed the drugs or she knew who was. Either way, Lily needed to talk to her.

And she'd get answers.

She waited just over an hour before Willow appeared, stepping out of her apartment with a to-go coffee mug in one hand and her phone in the other. Lily crossed the street and fell into step behind her. Willow didn't notice her for the first block, but when she turned, she caught sight of Lily. She kept walking, probably just assuming Lily was another pedestrian out for a walk. Timing it carefully, Lily made sure no one saw when she grabbed Willow's arm and dragged her into an alley.

"Hey—get off of me!" Willow shouted, trying to shove Lily off.

Lily slammed her against the wall, not flinching as Willow's head smacked against the brick. "I've got some questions for you."

"Who the hell do you think you are?" Willow hissed, pushing Lily back. "Get off—"

As Lily pulled out the knife from the back of her belt, Willow's voice shrunk and disappeared. "I have questions," Lily repeated quietly. "If you scream, or lie, or don't answer, I'll assume there's no point in letting you keep your voice."

She shook beneath Lily's grip, and just nodded once, her eyes huge.

"Great. You were found with that girl who died in Tartarus, Ushi. You injected her with Opus, is that right?"

Willow's mouth opened and Lily moved the knife closer to her throat, her voice dropping low and turning cold. "Don't. Lie."

She swallowed hard and nodded. "Ye—yes."

"Who gave it to you?"

"I don't know—"

"Describe him. He must come to Tartarus often. Where does he hang out, how do people get the drug off of him?"

"They just…it could be any of them. It's always a guy, but they change who it is."

"How do you know, then?"

"They've always got a tattoo on his wrist. An O with a line through it. Like this." She lifted her arm, showing a tattoo on her wrist. The same as what was on the baggies. "They…they move around, sometimes they don't even come inside, just point out someone in line."

"Why?"

"I don't know! They tell me who and I go! I've seen what happens to people who refuse, and I don't want to be like one of them!" Willow's eyes were starting to tear up.

"Why Tartarus?"

"Oren's got a grudge against the owner. They want him gone, but they want the club."

"Why are you helping them?" Lily asked, her list of questions waiting for the moment.

Willow met her eyes, a tear spilling over. "What else am I gonna do in the slums? It's sell or be sold."

Lily refused to bend, though that hit a little closer than she wanted. "Where's the dispensary? Where's Oren making the drugs?"

"Some gym. Used to be on the wharves, but they've moved closer."

Too coincidental to be anything other than Jed's, especially with the other body nearby. "His lieutenants, how many? Where do they gather?"

"Ten or twelve, I don't—I don't know! They hang out at the gym, then get sent out to other places, but they only go a couple of nights a month to get the Opus. They don't want them there often, but I don't know anything else, please!"

Lily believed her. She knew what she needed to know. "If you tell him I spoke to you, he might kill me, but he'll definitely kill you for spreading their secrets."

"I won't, please, I don't want them to come after me," she stuttered, her face ashen.

"Who's they?" Lily asked, frowning. "Who's backing Oren?"

"Please, I don't want to die," Willow sobbed, and Lily almost felt guilty. "I don't want to end up like Marcus—"

Lily drew back, loosening her hold. "You knew Marcus?"

"He was here when I started, he dealt pills, but then the boss caught him—"

"Oren?" Lily interrupted.

"No, the asshole at Tartarus. Galani. He caught him. Marcus started asking questions. Lieutenants, about the dispensary, everything. Then Marcus wound up dead. Anyone who asks questions gets killed."

Sebastian knew Marcus? He caught him, and then Marcus started asking the questions that Sebastian had mentioned wanting to know, and then…

Lily swallowed tightly, then took a step back, lowering the knife. "Get out of town. If you don't tell anyone, if you move quickly enough, they won't find out until it's too late."

Willow stared at her, mascara streaming down her face. "You…you aren't going to kill me?"

"No. But if I see you at Tartarus again, I'm going to give this recording to the police." Lily took her phone and waved the recording screen.

Willow sobbed again, then wiped her face. "They're gonna kill you."

Lily grinned, turning her back on Willow and stalking out of the alley. "Not if I kill them first."

****

The shouting outside the door would have brought a smile to Sebastian's lips, had he not been so irritated by the situation.

"...tell me you don't have Galani in there!" A deep bellow echoed through the interrogation room door. Sebastian couldn't place the voice, but familiarity lingered in the sound.

"I—we had evidence—"

Definitely Doyle Hughes's sniveling tones. He didn't sound nearly as gleeful as when he had cuffed Sebastian in front of the entire club, making sure his announcement of the charges carried enough for all to hear. Sebastian rolled his shoulders, the restless morning at the interrogation table not helping his lack of sleep. He snuck a glance at his watch, which Hughes hadn't confiscated—idiot—the display reading 11:32 AM.

They'd kept him in the holding cell overnight. He'd dozed a little, his back against the wall, but he couldn't get comfortable enough to fall asleep completely. Not that he would have been able to sleep much, not with the taste of Lily at the forefront of his mind. Every time he closed his eyes, he saw the way she looked at him afterward, that little shocked smile on her lips. If he'd known that would be the way to get her to go speechless, he might have tried earlier.

He smiled to himself.

"You've got jack shit!" The bellow again.

"Galani is—"

"Loaded and you'll be lucky if he doesn't sue your ass for wrongful imprisonment." A thud sounded, like a heavy file folder slammed against a wall. "And if he doesn't, I might press charges for complete idiocy in the first on your sorry ass."

"At least let me talk to him! I'll break him, I promise!"

"I seriously doubt it."

The door swung open, and Detective Hughes strode in, looking slightly paler than usual. Behind him, a tall, broad-shouldered man in a thick sweater and pressed slacks followed. His badge said Detective Hall, and he carried a folder of papers.

Hall leaned against the wall, crossing his arms, looking more than a little annoyed. Hughes glanced at him briefly, then dragged out one of the metal chairs, the legs squeaking against the tile floor and made Sebastian sigh. "Do you know why you're here, Galani?"

Sebastian just stared at him.

"Another man was murdered last night. Kyle Darnet. Ring a bell?" He didn't wait for Sebastian's answer before slapping down a photograph. Sebastian didn't even look, keeping his eyes on Hughes. "You know him?"

Sebastian didn't respond.

"Of course, you do! Because he hassled your new friend, Lily Nehme!"

That got a note of interest, and Sebastian actually lowered his eyes to look at the photo. After a moment, he recognized the dead man in the photo, even with his contorted face and limbs. The guy who had grabbed Lily's arm the night she returned to work still hurting from the earlier beating. The man he'd publicly embarrassed was now dead, a Tartarus stamp on his wrist. Perfect.

"Lily Nehme?" Hall said, a frown of question on his weathered features.

"The feminist pain in the ass we've picked up a

dozen times," Hughes added. "You know, the assaulting piece of—"

"Yeah, I know who she is, jackass. Watch it."

Sebastian felt a kinship toward Detective Hall for that comment. He pushed the photograph across the table. "Lots of people come into my club and harass my staff. How am I supposed to have killed him?"

"Same way the others were killed, and we'll be looking into those again, you can be sure. The new drug, the green pills. You gave it to him." Hughes's nasty smile was only matched by the hatred in his eyes. "We know you've had it. CSI found traces in your drains."

Sebastian smiled coldly. "Because hundreds of people with access to the drains aren't walking through my club every single day."

Hughes blinked, a frown appearing. "He was in your club the night he died—"

"As were hundreds of other people," Sebastian drawled. "And my security cameras, which I'm sure you reviewed."

Hall crossed both arms over his broad chest, the police corporal badge shining. "We have."

"Then you'll have seen that I wasn't anywhere near this…Darnet person."

"Yup," Hall said.

"So," Sebastian said with a sigh, "anything you have is circumstantial at best, and you stalked into my club without a warrant, arrested me without cause, and made a scene."

Hughes's mouth opened and shut without a sound.

"Congratulations," Sebastian said, smirking.

Hughes stood, the chair screaming across the floor as he leaned across the table to get in Sebastian's face.

"You're a son of a bitch, Galani, and I'm going to take you down if it's the last thing I—"

"Go see the captain," Hall ordered.

Hughes turned on Hall, still glaring.

Hall straightened, using the eight inches he had on Hughes to his full advantage. "You've got something you want to say to me, officer?"

Hughes's jaw snapped shut, and he stalked out of the room without a backward glance.

Hall sighed, rubbing his eyes. As he approached Sebastian's side of the table, he took a key out of his pocket. "I don't suppose you accept apologies?"

"You have nothing to apologize for, Detective," Sebastian said. He rubbed his wrists once they were free, the ache fading. "Hughes is an idiot."

Hall snorted. "Well, I'm still sorry for putting you through this. We'll get your paperwork pushed through so you can get out of here as soon as possible."

"Thank you." He narrowed his eyes slightly at Hall. "You know he's taking bribes from the Mazranis, right?"

"Know? Yes. Can I prove it yet? No. Don't suppose you can help me out?"

"I'll see what I can do."

Hall pocketed the key, taking the seat across from him. "I think I should be thanking you anyway."

Sebastian, sitting back in his chair, arched a brow.

"My girl, Reva, she's close with Nehme. I heard you hired her as a bartender."

Sebastian nodded. "I did."

"Good. She's been dealt a crappy hand, but she's got a good heart. I worried when she and Reva met, that she was heading towards an early grave." Hall opened up the folder, the discharge paperwork already printed.

Apparently, he hadn't had much faith in Hughes, either.

"She can be...reckless," Sebastian said, taking the pen Hall offered.

Hall laughed, filling out one of the forms before passing it over for Sebastian to sign. "That's for damn sure. When Lily went the PI route, I knew she'd get herself into trouble."

Sebastian signed the bottom of the paper, then paused.

Hall continued. "The two of them both got involved in this drug thing and...I'm just glad Lily's got a stable job, with good people now. Reva hopes she stays at your club and gives up the whole PI thing permanently. It's good, what she does, but with cops like Hughes out there and the people she's already managed to piss off, it's just not safe."

"Right," Sebastian murmured, everything sliding into place. Her connections, her rap sheet, her almost omniscient knowledge of the drugs. All part of her plan to get information.

Not that he blamed her for trying to bring down Oren; he'd seen how far she'd go—she seemed ready to take on Oren single-handedly. He didn't think there was anything she wouldn't do to stop him.

Even including leading someone on...?

He obviously had the most information on Oren. The largest connection. The most access. She'd convinced him to work together. She'd convinced him he needed her. She'd convince him that she needed him. That she wanted him. And he'd fallen for her. Flowered bait and all.

"Just sucks she ended up right in the middle of this whole drug thing anyway. Some luck she's got, huh?"

"Yeah," he said, signing the papers without really looking at the words, his thoughts making the lines swim. "Some luck."

****

Though Tartarus wasn't quite as packed as usual, it was better than what Lily expected. Darcy had thrown together a homecoming party for Sebastian, who had been texting Ellis to let him know when he'd be released. The flyers were haphazardly created, and messages were sent out on their social media. Teegan and Lily had made a *Welcome Home* banner after nixing Marley's suggestion of *Knew You Weren't a Murderer.*

Though she knew Ellis would be driving him back from the police department, Lily couldn't help but glance up at the door every few minutes, checking to see if he'd arrived.

When she wasn't looking for Sebastian, she looked for anyone with an O tattoo and told Ellis to keep an eye out, as well. But she got nothing on either front.

Forcing a smile, she continued to serve the drinks as best she could, keeping the momentum going as Marley's music pounded through her skin. She hadn't made much effort in her ensemble tonight: just black jeans and a black tank top with her usual flowered wrap.

Suddenly, the doors slammed open, and Marley paused the music, the absence of sound making Lily feel as if she'd gone temporarily deaf. She looked up, seeing Ellis stepping through the doors. Ellis looked out over the crowd for a moment, then inhaled.

"He's back!" he roared, taking a step to the side, his words echoing over the still masses.

The crowd in front of Lily shifted, and she had to slide down the bar to see.

Sebastian stood in the open doors, fixing his cuffs and glancing out over the crowd. Like he hadn't just been in prison for a day, like he hadn't been arrested, like he hadn't been accused of murder. He straightened his jacket, his brow arched at the crowd. His gaze swept over them, lingering for a moment on Lily before he continued past. "Isn't this a party?" he asked, his voice carrying.

Marley didn't miss the moment, and the music thumped back down, as raucous cheers rose up, drinks lifting in Sebastian's honor. Lily grinned, making his usual to have ready when he came to the bar.

She knew that Willow hadn't been lying to her. Marcus and Sebastian had crossed paths, and maybe Sebastian had been using Marcus to get information on Oren and Opus. Maybe Marcus had volunteered. But she knew, undoubtedly, that Sebastian didn't have anything to do with Marcus's death. He wasn't that kind of man. He was the kind of man to try and help Marcus. To let people think the worst of him so he could protect his friends. He'd give up everything to save the people he cared about. Sebastian was so difficult to get close to, but once you did, it was impossible not to love him—

Lily had to jump back as she dropped a glass, the shattering sound drawing all nearby eyes. They gave her a cheer as she smiled ruefully, sweeping the broken glass up with the small brush they kept for just that purpose.

When she looked up, she noticed Sebastian had arrived, taking his usual seat in the corner. She smiled, putting the brush away and grabbing his drink before approaching. "Welcome back, boss" she said.

He didn't smile, but he took the drink. Lily's eyes darted over him, taking in the bruises under his eyes from not sleeping. He looked tired but fine. A knot of tension in her stomach unraveled, seeing him whole and hale. And maybe something larger than a knot unraveled somewhere in her chest, making her breath come a little easier.

She leaned over and put a hand on his wrist. "We need to talk after closing up."

Sebastian picked up his drink and stood, pulling away from her. Lily saw the shadows under his eyes, the lines of exhaustion on his face. That was nothing new to her.

The suspicion, however, the cautious stillness, was new. And hurt. "We certainly do." He walked away.

Chapter 15

With Miguel still out of town, Eliza and Will had been the only two staffing the clinic. She loved Miguel, so very much, but sometimes, just having Will around was nice, too. They could be working on completely different things, with random questions or statements tossed across the room and answered without any more interaction than that. Sometimes he would just come over and watch her work, helping, so he claimed. Sometimes she'd read through his work out loud, helping him catch any errors he might have missed on his paperwork. Sometimes they worked in utter silence for hours.

Eliza rarely worked with anyone as well as she worked with Will. He pushed her beyond what she thought she was capable of, while still acknowledging her intelligence. One of the many things she loved about him.

She frowned at her computer as that thought materialized. She knew that she and Will were friends, close friends, but that was all. She didn't care for him in that way.

He was too serious for her because Will rarely laughed, but…he smiled often, when he thought people weren't looking. He was older than her, though not ancient. He was still healthy and active, and an avid runner. More realistic than optimistic, like any good doctor, he saw what the world was coming to and still tried to help. He stood by her even when she argued with him and fought with him and pursued drug cases with illegally obtained information. And he cared about her, sometimes going overboard, but he honestly just cared, and he was definitely handsome—

"Clark? Everything okay?"

She jumped, turning in her seat and nodding. "Yeah. Yes."

"You sure?" Will asked, coming over to lean over her chair. "Something I can help with?"

He'd pushed the sleeves of his sweater up, and she'd always been a sucker for nice arms. She could see the faint five o'clock shadow on his jaw, and he pushed up the glasses he wore when using a computer, his eyes crinkling slightly just as they did every time he tried to decipher something for the first time. On his breath, she could smell the coffee she'd made for both of them earlier, his usual with three sugars and cream, unless Miguel was here, then he only drank black coffee. His hair was mussed from how many times he ran his fingers through it when he worked on a difficult problem. She hadn't realized she'd noticed so much about him. She hadn't noticed when she'd made him such a huge part of her life.

She hadn't noticed when—

Eliza tried to take a deep breath, but everything smelled like him. She rolled away and stood up. "You know, it's late, I should get going."

Will frowned at her for a moment, then glanced at the clock. "I didn't realize." He shook his head, then grabbed his bag. "I'll drive you home."

"It's really not a problem—" she said, pulling her

Eliza sighed. "Lily was tailed back to our place. Usually, when that happens, I go stay with my friend, but she's out of town—"

"Wait," Will said, his voice rising. "This has happened before?"

"I don't take her classes for fun." Eliza tried a smile she didn't quite feel. "Lily is nothing if not persistent. So, the motel—"

"I'm not bringing you to a motel," Will argued, flipping on his blinker and took another turn to take them in the opposite direction. "I wouldn't be able to sleep, not knowing if you were alright."

Feeling the flush start on her cheeks, Eliza glanced at him out of the corner of her eyes.

He cleared his throat, his hands gripping the steering wheel tighter. "You can stay with me. I've got the room. I mean, if that's okay."

"I don't want to be an imposition."

"You're never an imposition, Clark."

She smiled at her lap. "Then okay. I'd feel…safer with you, anyway."

She saw one of those rare smiles on his face.

"Just don't tell Ramirez where I live."

"Deal."

****

Sebastian unlocked his door, stepping aside to let Lily enter first. He didn't meet her eyes as she looked up at him, closing the door behind her and dropping her bag by the door. She took a seat on the couch, turning towards the empty side, but he didn't join her. He walked over to his bar, pouring himself a drink.

"Are you okay?" she asked, a slight frown appearing between her eyes.

"I'm fine. You said you had information."

"I know how they're dealing the Opus here."

That was new information. Essential information, which should be the only thing on his mind. Instead, he couldn't think of anything other than the fact she'd used him.

He was above this sort of nonsense. Certainly, he and Lily shared a connection, but that didn't excuse his distraction from the bigger problem. They'd barely even kissed, and here he was, mooning over her as if she'd broken his heart—

"Seb?" Lily asked, getting to her feet. "Did you hear me?"

He had to focus on the issue at hand. The drugs, the Opus, Oren, the seemingly unavoidable conflict that was coming. He was Sebastian Galani, master of deals and devils, one of the rare few who walked away from the family and thrived. He would focus on what mattered, and not get distracted by flowers and smiles.

"Seb?" She put a hand on his arm.

He immediately moved away, putting the glass down and facing her. "I'm curious, were you going to tell us the truth before you left? Or just vanish once this was over and go back to being a PI?"

So much for not being distracted.

She dropped her hand and took a step back.

A small part of him was disappointed that she didn't deny the truth. He killed that feeling, keeping his face impassive as she sighed and rubbed her neck, obviously collecting her thoughts.

He'd gone back, searching through her background once he heard what she was. Though there had been nothing overt—no business license registered to her, no address of her business, no pictures, or even a flyer—but he'd found the missing piece eventually. Just a second cell phone registered under a false name but paid for with her credit card. That was the only sign he'd missed, and the one that changed everything. His only consolation was Teegan had missed it, too.

"I tried to tell you...the night Oren came," Lily said quietly.

"And as we were interrupted," he responded, his voice carefully flat, "you didn't have the opportunity to tell me that night. Or in any of the weeks since then, obviously."

She looked down. "I was afraid that you'd think I had used...Tartarus."

"And I'd be right," he snapped. "You did."

"I was here just for information, at first. You're right."

He scoffed, turning away from her.

"But it's not like that anymore," she insisted.

"So, you have a few drinks with us and suddenly you care?"

"Yes."

He rolled his eyes, putting his hands on the back of the couch and looking at her.

She shrugged, anger starting to appear. "I'm sorry, but isn't that how it happens? I don't know you, I get to know you, I care about you. That's what happened."

"You lied."

"No. I didn't lie about anything. I...omitted some things, but I never lied." The anger faded, and her voice got quiet. "Not to you. Never to you."

He wanted to believe her. Foolish, but he desperately wanted to. Even though she'd used him.

Them.

"Why?" he asked. Why did she choose Tartarus? Why did she choose him? Why did she make him...care?

Lily collapsed once more to the couch, her hands wringing one another in her lap, a display of nerves that he'd never seen on her before. Automatically, he took a step toward her, before catching himself.

"A girl named Michaela found me, asking me to find her brother. I'd helped her cousin out, getting away from a bad divorce. I've never advertised my business. Sometimes I find the clients, sometimes they find me through word of mouth. I never wanted anyone to know what I looked like...kind of defeated the purpose of being a PI when everyone knows who you are."

She inhaled slowly. "Her brother had been missing for three months, and the cops had already labeled him a runaway. I did what I could, but I..." She shook her head. "They found his body. He had a Tartarus stamp on his wrist. I came here and...tasted your drinks. I talked to Teegan, and she gave me a job. I was looking for the dealer." She looked up at him. "I just wanted to make sure that whoever killed Marcus gets what's coming to them."

"Marcus?" Sebastian echoed, frowning.

"You knew him," she said quietly. "The girl who told me about the Opus, Willow, she said Marcus dealt here, and you caught him. Then he started asking questions and—"

"No." His smile felt bitter. "No. I didn't catch him." He took a seat across from her. "He came to me and asked for help."

Lily leaned towards him but didn't interrupt.

"I offered to get him out of town. Help set him up

with some connections I had." He paused, recalling Marcus's face, so full of trepidation. "I explained why he couldn't tell anyone, since Oren already had half the slums by then. He didn't realize it was that bad, so he offered to help. To get me the information I needed. I warned him to be careful with his questions." Sebastian paused. "He wasn't."

She didn't look surprised at his involvement. She just sighed and sat back against the couch. "Oren kills anyone who asks questions. That's why no one knows anything. We need—"

"We," he echoed harshly.

"Yeah, we." She leaned forward on the couch. "What do you want me to say? That I'm sorry I didn't tell you everything? I am. That I really care about Tartarus? I do."

He scoffed, shaking his head and Lily moved over, taking the seat next to him.

"I have worked with a lot of people," she said, intensely, nervously speaking. "But working here, meeting all of you, being with…you, has felt more like home than anywhere else I've ever been."

"You lied."

"I kept secrets to protect people I didn't want to get involved. To keep them safe. Does that sound familiar?"

He didn't bother answering that obvious question.

Lily put her hand on his. "I'm not keeping secrets anymore."

A deal. He could ask, and she'd tell him the truth. But asking implied he'd believe what she said. For a moment, his mind stayed blank, content to take her words at face value. But slowly, doubt began to swim toward his lips.

"The day you were hurt. Thugs nailed you when you were coming home from work?"

She hesitated, but spoke, pulling her hand away, her fingers wringing in her lap. "I was out on the streets, shaking down dealers. We needed answers, but I didn't get anything. So instead, I took the Opus I stole off of Ushi and gave it to Eliza."

"You were why the dealers were running scared?" He'd heard tales from Tanner—a dozen dealers were found half-alive, beaten to pulps. Those that could talk said they were attacked by a group, or the cops, or an accident. A good third of Reyes's men disappeared that night, leaving town, afraid to keep working. He'd been hoping for some of them to come to him for safety, but Oren had them too afraid to look to Tartarus.

She nodded, and Sebastian stared at her, reluctantly amazed. Dozens of men were beaten that night, and though she hadn't looked perfect, the injuries she'd had were minor in comparison.

It was also obvious why no one had spoken out against who attacked them—who'd want to admit that a petite woman had handed them their asses?

Sebastian stared ahead, still trying to wrap his head around this. He didn't have room to judge. She hadn't really lied. She told him the truth. But something still felt a little…off in the aftermath. He shoved that feeling to the side and nodded. "How are they dealing Opus?"

He saw her staring at him out of her peripherals, but she said, "Willow said men with the O tattoos are giving needles and Opus to people they own, pointing out who would get it. They're targeting Tartarus, and she also said Oren is holed up in a recently purchased gym in addition to the wharf."

"Your old gym?" He'd suspected after the body fell near there but had no proof.

"Best guess. He's got about a dozen lieutenants, but they do meet there a couple of times a month. If we were to get the cops there on the right night, we might've been able to get them all."

"Might have?" he asked.

Lily's jaw jumped a couple of times. "Willow said that if she told, they'd kill her. I thought that was motivation enough. But I think Oren found out."

"Which means he'll be on high alert at least, if not moving his dispensary," Sebastian finished her thought. He sighed, rubbing his eyes. "Though...if they're moving, they'll be out in the open. We might get enough to have the cops called."

"Stakeout?" Lily asked.

He nodded. "I'll have Ellis and Marley there during the day. You and I at night. Teegan will be in charge of Tartarus, and Darcy on hand for emergencies. We document everything and hope it's enough. At the least, we'll get faces." He got to his feet. "It's a step."

Lily mirrored him but didn't say anything.

He glanced at his watch, the exhaustion hitting him hard. He crossed the room to grab his keys. "It's late. Let me drive you home—"

"No, it's okay," she said, heading towards the door and grabbing her bag.

"It's even more important that you get home safely. If you think Oren is aware, then..." He trailed off, her comment sliding home as he turned to face her. "How do you know he might be aware?"

Lily hesitated, playing with the strap. "...Eliza called me, and a few of his guys are staking out my place."

Sebastian swore, running his hand over his head. "Because you asked questions?"

"I don't know. I was going to go by Teegan's on my way home to see if someone was there—"

Sebastian pulled his phone out and called Ellis.

"What?" Ellis rumbled.

"Oren has men outside Nehme's. What about you?"

"Didn't see anyone on my way in. Give me a minute."

Sebastian waited, hearing Ellis walk around. He could picture his apartment—a small window near the front east side, facing the street, and a corner window on the north side, facing the alley. The perfect vantage point and exactly why Ellis had taken the smaller place.

"Don't see anyone here. And Teegan said the usuals weren't outside Tartarus tonight. If they're targeting Nehme—"

"Yeah, thanks, Ellis."

"Be careful, boss."

"Sure. Bye."

"Bye."

Sebastian shook his head. "Just you. Not even Tartarus."

Lily frowned. "But if they knew what I was asking, they would have known you were involved...wouldn't they be watching both of us?"

Putting his phone down, he rubbed his temple, thinking. "Unless that's not why they were targeting you." The answer hit him, and he struggled to keep his voice calm. "But if any of them were here at New Year. He would've seen..."

"He saw us kiss," Lily finished quietly.

Sebastian nodded with a frown. Idiot. He should have known better. Moles or collateral, just as he'd said.

"It's fine," Lily said after a moment. "We're planning on watching the building anyway, I can lay low. I'll just go to a motel—"

She stopped and he realized he was shaking his head.

"No?" she asked.

"Stay here. If Oren is already watching you, there's nothing to be lost."

Several emotions flickered across her face before she lowered her eyes. "I can take care of myself. And I don't want you to ask me to stay because you feel responsible—"

"That's not," he stopped, then restarted. "I know you can. But I'd feel better if you stayed."

She didn't look at him, and he finally recognized her hesitation.

"I don't care that you're a PI. I don't care that you…omitted the truth. I would care, very much, if something happened to you. So, stay here." She looked up and he knew he'd been right. Carefully, quietly, he said, "Stay with me."

Lily watched him for a long, long moment.

Then she put her bag down.

Chapter 16

Lily expected awkwardness.

Sebastian's couches clearly weren't exactly made for sleeping. They were too modern and fancy. The armchair in his office would be too small for her, let alone him, as she pointed out when he tried to say that's where he would sleep. So that left only the bed.

The massive, satin-sheet bedecked, black and grey bed.

"I really don't mind taking the couch," Lily lied.

"Don't be ridiculous. It's big enough for both of us."

"I don't want to make you uncomfortable."

His faint smile soothed her leftover worries about her job. "I think that's inevitable, though not for the reasons you seem to believe."

He had offered to let her get ready for bed first. She'd thought, for a moment, that she'd have to ask him for something to wear, but she remembered her gym bag had a couple of changes of clothes. She pulled out a tank top and shorts that were a little too small for class, but that had fallen to the bottom of her bag and never resurfaced until now.

She brushed her hair with the comb she had, and her teeth with her fingers as best she could, stealing his toothpaste. Figuring that was as good as she'd get, she went back into the bedroom as he went into the bathroom. Though they'd been around each other partially clothed before, and there had been some delicious tension, it was different now that they'd kissed. She knew both of them wanted more, but acting on it now, with all her secrets so recently exposed, didn't seem likely.

He had turned out the lights in the hall and kitchen, leaving just the lamp on one side of the bed on. From the book and glasses, which she very much wanted to see him in, she figured he preferred that side of the massive, king-sized monstrosity. She went to the other side, sliding between the smooth sheets and plugging in her phone with her extra cord. She sent a quick text to Eliza, hoping she didn't wake her, just letting her know where she was in case she needed to get in touch.

Sebastian's phone pinged from where he'd tossed it on the comforter. Automatically looking, she couldn't help but read the words *Movement: Side Alley.*

His security app for Tartarus.

She hesitated, pulling her lip between her teeth. As she wavered, another notification came up. *Door: Side Alley.*

She got out of bed, grabbed the knife at the bottom of her bag, and crossed to the bathroom. She turned the handle to crack the door just barely and kept her voice low. "Did you call Ellis to come over?"

She couldn't see him, but his voice matched hers as he answered. "No. Why?"

"Someone's inside."

He opened the door fully, his shirt half-buttoned and his shoes off. "I'll—"

"I've got him," Lily said. "Just come down in a minute."

His focus darted from the set of her mouth to the

knife in her hand. "Don't kill him. Unless he tries to kill you first."

"No promises."

Familiar with the layout of his apartment, she didn't need to turn on any lights. The door was quiet enough to blend in with the hum of the air conditioning. She locked it behind her, just in case, then gliding down the stairs, her bare feet silent and her breath coming slowly and noiselessly.

The hallway from the side door stood empty, though the chill on her feet said the door had been opened recently. She cocked her head to the side as she stepped back into the shadows, listening for her quarry. For a few moments, there was nothing.

A scuff of a shoe.

She followed the noises to the employee lounge. She didn't open the door, just peered through the crack to see a man, shoulders hunched, as he rifled through one of the lockers. Her locker.

He didn't know she was there until the tip of her knife pressed against his ribs. He inhaled loudly, a squeak left his throat, and Lily leaned in close. "Surprise."

****

This had been a very long day. A long couple of days. All Sebastian wanted was to go to sleep.

First, he'd been arrested, then discovered his bartender was a PI. After he was released, he came back and had an open conversation with said bartender. He found out how Opus was being dealt in his club and then offered up his bed to his bartender. His bartender caught a drug dealer. The drug dealer was now tied to a chair in his employee lounge, where they were questioning him.

Sometimes he wondered how taking on the family business would have gone. Would living as a crime kingpin really have been so different? This is what he got for trying to be an upstanding businessman: an inquisition in the floor just below his apartment.

He'd come down to see Lily lashing the dealer to a chair with what looked like his own shoelaces. Resourceful as always.

She'd seen him entering and smiled briefly. "Boss."

"A friend of Oren's, I assume," Sebastian said, coming in to lean on the door frame. In the two minutes she had asked him to wait, he'd done up his shirt and put on his jacket again, refusing to meet with whoever she'd caught in anything less than his normal wardrobe.

She tightened the shoelaces and the man winced. She stood, pleased with her handiwork, and then went to her locker. He was about to ask what she was doing when she stepped back with bags of Opus and syringes in her hands.

"Let me guess," Sebastian said lowly. "Officer Hughes was going to receive an anonymous tip?"

"Would I have even made it to the station?" she asked, dropping the items on the table.

The man pulled at his bonds, but they held. "This isn't what it looks like."

"Enlighten me." Sebastian stalked into the room, letting the door shut behind him.

"I'm not even involved in this, I swear! This is all a misunderstanding!"

"What's your name?" Sebastian asked.

"Jaime," he blubbered.

"Jaime. Pleasure. I see you have a tattoo on your arm."

Jaime tried to turn his wrist, but the laces were tight enough that his skin turned white against them.

"Don't lie," Sebastian said, keeping his voice calm. "Was your plan to have Miss Nehme arrested?"

Jaime glanced at her, standing somewhat behind Sebastian, the knife flipping over her fingers. He gave them a jerky nod.

"Was she going to arrive at the police station?" Her comment had sparked a flare of anger in him, and he wanted to justify it. He wanted to know just how badly he'd have to burn Oren to the ground.

Jaime shook his head, his face pale.

"And you would have used her for...what? Motivation to get me to sign over Tartarus?"

Out of the corner of his eye, he saw Lily glance at him, the knife stilling in her hand.

"That's what he wants, yes," Jaime said, drawing his attention again.

"And where might he and his lieutenants be?" Sebastian asked. No sense in letting a good source go to waste.

"I—I can't tell you. I can't!"

"Pity," Sebastian said lowly.

Jaime winced, squeezing his eyes shut, but Sebastian merely pulled out his phone.

"Since you're not cooperating," his fingers danced over his phone, "I suppose we'll have to call the police."

Lily grabbed his arm, the knife out of sight. "No, wait. That would put him in so much trouble."

His eyes narrowed. She wasn't stupid—that's what they wanted. So why—

She turned to Jaime, her smile sympathetic and kind and completely fake. "If we call the police, he might be under investigation. They might track him, put bugs in his house, and maybe even arrest him. He might have a police presence for years."

She let go of Sebastian's arm and walked slowly towards the captive. Her smile in place, Sebastian heard the shift in her voice. That dangerously threatening tone warned him to run even as he realized he couldn't force himself to move away. "We should let him spend the night here, with our thanks. Then tomorrow, we'll send him out of Tartarus with a car and maybe some cash." She nodded as she spoke, and Jaime mirrored her unintentionally.

"And then, we'll make our move with what we already know," Lily continued. "We'll bring down his operation, but at least Oren will have back his faithful servant, in perfect health, and Tartarus's obvious thanks. I'm sure he'll be…grateful."

The blood leeched out of Jaime's face. "Wait, no, please—"

"How long do you think someone who has the ire of Oren can survive on the streets?" Lily glanced back at Sebastian. "Two days?"

He liked the way she thought. "If they're lucky."

Her hand brushed against Jaime's shoulder. "I've only heard of a few people surviving after defecting on Oren. Do you know where they are?"

"Prison," Sebastian answered as Jaime continued to panic, his breath coming rapidly.

"Alive and well. A few are approaching parole. Which would mean so much more if Oren was behind bars for the rest of his life."

"But, since you don't have information, we won't call the police. We'll just let you go."

"And we'll see how far you get," Lily finished.

"You...you don't have anything, that's why you're questioning me!" Jaime said, spittle flying from the corner of his mouth.

"You broke into our club," Lily said, stepping away from him and toward Sebastian. He liked the way she said 'our' club when he definitely should not. "We didn't go looking for you. Who says we need anything from you besides inconsequential details?"

"But—"

Lily smiled up at Sebastian, ignoring Jaime completely. "Do you feel like a midnight snack? I could go for some pizza."

"How about Chinese?" he suggested, gesturing toward the door.

"Wait!"

Lily continued toward the door, Sebastian on her heels.

"I can tell you things, I can...I can..."

Lily met Sebastian's eyes, a smile hidden under her expression. He turned around to face Jaime. "Such as?"

"Th—they plan to make a move."

"Against whom?"

"Reyes."

"When?"

"Tomorrow."

That was worth knowing. He glanced down at Lily; she still faced the door, her back to Jaime, but she looked up at him, brows raised.

She whispered, "If we keep him, we risk Oren coming back. But if we just let him go now, he might change his plans. We lose our leverage."

"Other options?" he murmured, well aware Jaime

was listening.

Lily pulled her lip between her teeth, then looked at the table.

Sebastian watched her walk back, picking up the drugs Jaime wanted to pin on her. She didn't go for the needles, but the green pills.

"Ecstasy usually lasts for what…six hours?" she said, her voice emotionless.

Jaime's eyes widened as Lily opened the bag.

"And dealers don't trust those who don't indulge." She looked at Jaime, her amber eyes cold.

Sebastian pulled out his phone, summoning a car about two miles away from Tartarus. He nodded to her.

What they were doing wasn't nice, but their options were limited. They couldn't keep him, they couldn't call the cops, they couldn't just let him go, and Sebastian didn't want to kill him. So, they'd have to…incapacitate him for a while.

"Based on what I've seen, I'd guess you've got about ten minutes before it kicks in," he said, arching a brow. "If you can make it to the car, it'll take you to the wharves." Made no sense to show their full hand about knowing the gym. Could lure them into a false sense of security. Might make Oren overconfident. "You'll come through just fine."

"I wouldn't tell anyone you spoke with us if you value your life. Not only did you fail," she reminded him as she emptied the bag into her hand, "but you were made, caught, and broken."

Sebastian stepped up beside her, grabbing Jaime's jaw to hold it open as she placed the pills on the back of his tongue. They held him still until he swallowed, then Lily cut the laces tying him to the chair. Sebastian helped him to the door, but before releasing him into the alley, he took the opportunity to hiss in his ear. "Don't ever come to my club again."

They threw him into the alley and locked the door behind him.

****

Eliza paced in the guest room, tugging at the neck of her shirt.

No, Will's shirt.

A T-shirt she'd never seen him wear, in a blue that would make his eyes look amazing. A giant compared to her, his shirt hit her mid-thigh and covered more than some of her usual pajamas. But she still felt awkward moving around Will's apartment in just this, even if she was dying of thirst.

For water.

Obviously.

Giving in, she cracked the door open, seeing the tiled hallway was empty, with no light coming from beneath the door at the end of the hall, which would be Will's room. The guest room she stayed in stood between his room and a spare bathroom. He'd shown her the bathroom and given her a shirt to sleep in when she told him she had nothing else. She caught a glimpse of his bedroom when he got her the shirt, with a large bed, and unmade grey comforter half on the floor. That little bit of messiness seemed so personal, so unlike his work persona, that she'd looked away until he came back.

She walked quietly across the floor, not tiptoeing, per se, just trying not to disturb him. The faint light in the kitchen was enough for her to see the cabinets where he'd pulled a glass from earlier. She turned on the tap, took a sip to quench her ridiculous thirst, and turned toward the table.

Where a figure suddenly moved.

Eliza squeaked and dropped the glass. It shattered against the tile floor, and she jumped back, her foot landing on a jagged piece and slicing deeply. She reached down, but the glass tore against her fingers, and she cursed quietly, tears springing to her eyes.

"Clark, don't move."

Will, because it was obviously him, stood from the kitchen table where he'd been working on the tablet, the glow subtle enough that she hadn't seen him. "I'm sorry," he said. "Give me a minute."

So, she stood there, an inelegant flamingo of disaster, one foot off the ground while he disappeared for a moment, coming back wearing shoes and carrying a broom. Eyeing the situation, he huffed and put the broom to the side.

He crossed over to her, the glass crunching beneath his shoes, and grabbed her waist. She steadied herself on his forearms automatically, the slightest lift of his brows the only warning she got before he hoisted her onto the counter and out of harm's way.

"I didn't mean to scare you," he said, his tone as apologetic as he got, which was only barely so.

"I was stupid for being scared of you. In your own apartment."

He smiled at her as he swept up the glass. Eliza made a face at him, then winced as her hand throbbed.

"Here," he said, resting the broom on the side and handing her a paper towel.

She thanked him, pressing it against the cut. Though not very deep, it kept bleeding.

He finished cleaning the glass, discarding the

shards. Turning to her, he opened a drawer and pulled out a bandage.

"Let's see the damage," he murmured. He grabbed her ankle, his hands rasping over her skin. She yelped and put her good hand on the counter to stabilize herself. With an unrepentant grin, his hands stayed gentle as he put pressure on the sole of her foot.

Eliza sat up again, glancing at her hand. The bleeding had stopped.

"Sorry about your cup," she said.

"You can buy me a new one."

"Are you serious?"

Will smiled wider. "Yes."

"You're a jerk."

"I know." He finished with her foot and stepped between her legs, taking her hand. His eyes were lowered to her palm, focused on her cut the same way he focused on his work. He grabbed another bandage without looking and smoothed it over her palm.

"What's the prognosis, Dr. Lintz?" she asked. "Am I going to live?"

He smiled at her palm. "I believe so. Might scar a little."

She shrugged. "Not my first and I'm sure not my last."

He went very still, and she felt suddenly aware of her lack of clothing, and how close he stood. His hands were warm on her wrist as he finished placing the bandage, then turned her arm over, the tips of his fingers running up her arm to her elbow.

"Funny, because I don't see any scars here." He continued the examination up to where the sleeve of his overlarge shirt began, then did the same thing on the other side.

"And none here, either."

Her stomach swooped in her middle, her breath coming a little faster, but she fought to keep quiet. His fingers left her for a moment, then reappeared at the neck of the shirt, running up her neck so lightly she didn't know if she imagined it. She tipped her head back as he touched her chin, his thumb hovering above the hollow in her throat, where she knew he could feel her pulse fluttering without any sense of decorum.

"None here either," he said, stepping even nearer, not touching her except for his fingers, but she could feel the heat of his body between her legs and up her chest.

"Will," she whispered, her eyes fighting to slip closed, but she refused to let them.

He stared down at her with a flicker of a smile in his dark eyes, his thumb moving along her cheek. "I had to see if this was even possible. I had to try. But say the word and I'll stop."

Eliza leaned into his hand, not taking her eyes away from his. "Don't stop."

He leaned down, slowly, stopping a breath away from her lips, like he was waiting for something or trying to figure something out.

Figure out how this worked. It was simple, actually. They fit together perfectly. And for once, Eliza beat him to the answer. She lifted up just slightly, brushing her lips against his. Will inhaled sharply, and she broke away for a moment.

He followed her, his arm sliding around the small of her back and tugging her forward against him. She gasped against his mouth, her legs hooking behind his knees. His other hand threaded through her hair, tilting her head up towards his. She wrapped her arms around his neck, and he took the unspoken command, his arm lowering enough to hoist her up.

He could lift her one-handed. Why the hell was that a turn-on? She rolled her hips slightly, and he used a word she'd never heard him use before. "You do that again and we aren't going to make it to the bedroom," he whispered against her lips.

Grinning up at him, Eliza licked her lips, tasting scotch and coffee and something ionized. Will's breath came shorter as he watched her. She rocked her hips again.

They did not make it to the bedroom.

Chapter 17

Lily woke up slowly, suddenly alert despite the late—early?—hour. Getting her bearings, she exhaled slowly, her arm curled under the pillow beneath her head and the blankets tangled around her hips.

Despite her preferences, both she and Sebastian had been exhausted when they got upstairs. After they wedged the side door closed—Jaime had to pick the lock—and disposed of the rest of the Opus, they'd trudged upstairs. She'd used the bathroom after Sebastian had changed, but when she came back out, he'd already fallen asleep, his phone next to his hand. She smiled tiredly, knowing better than to take it personally. She plugged his phone in and got into the other side of the bed, falling asleep almost at once.

From the angle of the light, it was late. At least noon, even if the dark curtains blocked out most of the sun. She stretched to grab her phone to confirm, but he shifted behind her, and she stopped.

"Everything okay?" Sebastian murmured behind her. His voice sounded, if possible, lower than usual, sleep hovering at the edges of his words. He moved again, and she could feel his breath on her shoulders.

"Fine," she whispered, not wanting to disturb the early hour just yet.

"You sure?"

"Yeah. Didn't mean to wake you."

"You didn't." His hand brushed her arm, apparently as a soothing gesture, but the second he touched her, it felt like the kiss all over again—her nerves were alight, her heart stuttered, and her eyes closed, at just such a simple touch.

He must have felt something because he removed his hand from her skin immediately. "Sorry, I—"

"No," she said, still barely above a whisper, still not turning around to look at him, because some things were easier to say without having to stare into his eyes when she said them. She meant to say something like 'Don't be sorry' or 'Don't apologize,' but instead, what came out was—

"Don't stop."

In the beat of heavy silence that followed, she considered retracting her words. But she kept her mouth shut, knowing that she wanted this. Now he had to decide.

Sebastian inhaled almost silently, but she heard it, nonetheless. The touch of his palm along her shoulder, running slowly down her arm, the wide hand covering her skin completely, the tips of his fingers brushing along her ribs and waist, all so innocent, but Lily felt her heart beating in her throat, her stomach tightened with anticipation.

He continued, dipping below the blanket and reaching her hip, the shorts not an obstacle, and his fingers tightened briefly, before smoothing down her thigh and back up slightly, blunt nails scraping gently across her skin. The noise that Lily made was technically too quiet to be called a moan, but Sebastian heard.

"Fuck," he exhaled, still pulling his hand back up, nails dragging across her thigh, her hip, her stomach, pushing the scant tank top up with his journey until he reached the curve of her breast, his fingers dancing along the swell, coaxing another quiet, not-quite moan out of her, as he gently tugged and twisted.

Anxious for some relief, Lily rolled her hips, her eyes still closed. Sebastian's free arm slipped under her shoulders, taking over, and pulling her against his chest, as his hand returned to her hip, running along her briefs to the center where she was already wet, just from those slight touches.

Sebastian groaned loudly in the quiet, and his hips pressed against hers, hard and just the right amount of friction against his hand. His fingers slipped beneath the elastic cotton, pressing firmly against her, and Lily couldn't keep her voice down any longer.

"Seb," she moaned, pressing against his hands, his hips, desperate and needing him. Her arm reached back, her nails scraping against his short hair, and eliciting another muffled curse from him, the other followed his hand down, giving him the slight guidance he needed.

"Jesus, Lily," he hissed in her ear. "Yes, my Lily..."

His mouth pressed against her shoulder, alternating kisses with gentle bites, his arm a vise around her chest, keeping her molded against him, and making it impossible not to feel how his body reacted. His hips rolled against hers in time with his hand, and Lily's grip tightened as she held on, the edge approaching faster than she expected.

"Come on, Lily-love, come on," he kept up the murmuring in her ear, his teeth pulling at her as she pressed against him as tightly as she possibly could, hanging onto him until she worried she'd leave bruises. "Fuck, come on, Lily..."

She fell, his name lost amid the sighs and moans of her climax. Sebastian held her against him as she shuddered and shook, his words not registering in her ears until a good few seconds later.

Exhaling slowly, she rolled onto her back, and Sebastian lifted himself up, leaning over her and pushing her hair out of her face. She could see a thousand thoughts rampaging through his head, the desire to talk about what had happened, and the pros and cons list she knew he was already making. Talking would maybe answer some things, but would complicate everything else, and right now, she knew all she needed to know.

So, before he could say a single word, she looped her hand around the back of his neck and pulled him down to her lips.

God, kissing him would never get old. His mouth, clever in his speech, kissed exactly the same. Lily's tongue darted in, tasting whatever words made it to his mouth and replacing them with obscenities and only thoughts of her in this bed, right now. He grabbed her hips with both hands, holding her steady beneath him as he rolled against her repeatedly, until Lily was nearly senseless with want, her greedy hands tracing over every defined muscle, and she knew she could draw each line perfectly, so ingrained in her mind.

Her hands reached the sweatpants he'd worn to bed, and she started to push them down, when his phone went off, the loud ringing startling both of them.

Sebastian pulled back slightly, his breath coming shorter. Any other day, she might have told him to ignore it, but considering everything that happened last night, he had to answer. She jerked her head towards the phone, her own breath coming short.

Leaning to the side, he grabbed his phone. "What?"

"Good morning to you, too, boss."

Ellis's voice was loud and distinct enough that Lily could hear him just fine. She grinned, half in frustration, half in actual humor that they'd wasted their night in sleep. She leaned her head back and Sebastian bent down, pressing his lips to her exposed throat, his tongue darting against her skin. She kept the noises she wanted to make trapped behind her lips, closing her eyes.

"Just calling to give you a heads up we're downstairs."

Sebastian stilled. "We?"

"Staff meeting. You're gonna fill us in."

Lily knew Ellis wasn't messing around, and they wouldn't get out of this. Time for everybody to know.

"So, you and Nehme put on some pants and get down here, or I'll send Darcy up."

Squeezing his eyes shut, Sebastian said, "We'll be down in five," and hung up. After a breath, he looked at her.

Their friends were downstairs, waiting. So, she ignored the way she was panting and how her hips arched to meet his, and met his eyes, the dark nearly swallowing her as he stared.

"I'm going to kill him," Sebastian murmured.

Lily laughed, drawing a reluctant smile out of him. "We have five minutes. I can get dressed very quickly."

She saw him consider the possibility for a half second, but he shook his head and rolled off of her. "Not a chance. I want to take my time with you. Five minutes is not nearly enough for what I have planned."

"Promises, promises," Lily said, running her fingers through her hair to get herself back into a semblance of control.

Sebastian grabbed her hand before she could roll out of bed, catching her eye. "Not a promise, Nehme. A deal. And I always keep my end of a deal."

A shiver went down her spine and Lily couldn't breathe until Sebastian looked away, shutting the bathroom door behind him. Swinging her legs off the bed, Lily exhaled slowly, her blood still singing in her veins.

Now she kind of wanted to kill Ellis, too.

****

Eliza felt sore.

She'd not been with anyone for a while. There had been a few dotted here and there, but no one she felt comfortable enough to keep a relationship with, not with her work and her schedule. Getting close to anyone was hard. No one understood why she chose this life.

She rolled onto her side, smiling into the faint aches and sleeping face of William Lintz.

Almost no one.

Last night had been what felt like a grand finale to the overtures of the past few weeks. Maybe Lily had been correct in guessing he'd been jealous of the lawyers dogging her for her number. She didn't know what had gotten him to make his move, but she was thrilled.

She slipped out of bed, ignoring the late hour, and decided to make coffee. Finding the shirt Will had loaned her took longer than expected. Eventually, she found it in the hallway, left where Will had nearly torn it before he…she pressed her hands to her warm face and went into the kitchen.

As the coffee began to brew, she stared out the window, her chin in her hand as she leaned over the counter, her thoughts not nearly as jumbled as she would have expected. She and Will made sense. Work wouldn't change, other than Miguel tormenting both of them. She knew Will well enough to know that he wouldn't have initiated this if he wasn't serious. One-night stands were fine, but they were friends and colleagues and worth more than one night together.

Though even just one night had been spectacular.

She heard him shifting in the bedroom several minutes before he came out. The coffee finished and she had two cups waiting by the time he appeared, his feet stomping louder than normal. She eyed him, amusement and irritation in equal measures as he approached.

"I didn't want to startle you again," he said in lieu of a good morning. "You already owe me enough for the first glass and the use of my shirt."

Eliza rolled her eyes at him, and he grinned, reaching for the other cup of coffee. She moved it out of his grasp. "No, coffee isn't for jerks."

He chuckled, leaning down and placing his hands on either side of the counter next to her, his thumbs brushing her sides. "Come on, Clark. I'll be good."

"I don't think you know the meaning of the word."

"Sure, I do." He moved closer, his chest brushing against the mug she held between them as if such an ineffective shield would keep him at bay.

"Good. Adjective." The smirk became invisible as he bent down, his breath brushing her ear and neck. "Favorable. Suitable. Pleasant. Of a noticeably large size—"

She gaped and pushed him back. He allowed himself to rock back, the other mug of coffee in his hands.

"You're terrible."

"True. But all the best things are terrible for you, in too large a quantity. Drugs, alcohol, rich food, mind-blowing orgas—"

"Do you ever stop?" she laughed. She hadn't seen him quite this happy in a long time.

"Not as of yet." He smiled, sipping his sweetened coffee and the energy seemed to redirect. "What are the plans for today?"

She finished her coffee, taking a moment to think. She went to the sink and rinsed it, reaching up to grab the small towel hanging off a cabinet. "I can't go back to the apartment until Lily deals with these guys, and I don't really want to go back to work until I have clean clothes."

"There's nothing wrong with what you're wearing now."

She arched a brow at him, realizing the shirt had ridden up a bit higher than she'd expected. His eyes were dark again as he watched her move around the kitchen, and she decided staying on the opposite side of the counter might be in her best interest for the moment.

"There is if I want to go to work."

"Take a few days off."

"Will—"

"Eliza."

The shiver was unintentional, though she knew his use of her name wasn't. She couldn't remember the last time he'd used her first name, until last night, when she'd been on top of him, moving too slowly for his liking and he'd grabbed her hips and—

She cleared her throat, but he spoke first.

"Take a couple of days off. You can't go home yet, we shouldn't go to work during the holidays, and I would much rather have you in my bed right now. Or the couch. Maybe the shower. I'm not picky." He moved around the counter, but she circled with him, staying on the opposite side.

"I have things I need to get—" she said, but they both knew she had lost this argument, even if she hadn't conceded defeat.

"I'll go in tomorrow and pick them up for you." He dumped his coffee in the sink and turned back to her.

"Why not today?" she asked, knowing the answer and trying not to smile.

"There are a lot of untested surfaces in this apartment," he said, his voice dropping lower as he stared at her, "and we both know I am all about being thorough."

She arched a brow, then heaved an exasperated sigh she didn't feel. "Fine. But I'm getting all my clothes washed today."

His grin was entirely wicked as she quirked her mouth at him. "Deal."

"*All* of them," Eliza repeated, before pulling the shirt she wore off in one smooth move, rewarded with the sight of Will's jaw dropping before she turned and started back to the bedroom.

The couch was almost as comfortable as the bed.

****

Sebastian shrugged. "And that's it."

Teegan, Marley, Ellis, and Darcy all stared at him, their eyes darting over to Lily periodically, clearly trying to come to terms with everything they'd just told them over the past forty-five minutes. Everything he'd done over the past year to make sure that Tartarus remained as safe as possible, what he'd discovered, who he'd had to become to protect them. Lily had told them everything, too. Her real job, her encounters with Oren and his men, the fact that she was being targeted, and, slightly glossed over, why.

"So," Darcy said slowly, resting his elbows on the table in the employee's lounge, "you're saying that...you're together?"

"That's all you're taking from this?" he asked dryly, ignoring Lily's laughter next to him.

"When exactly did you get together?" Marley pressed. "Because if it was the New Year party, Teegan owes me twenty bucks."

"You're all fired."

Teegan rolled her eyes at him, her smile tugging at her lips. "Not a chance, boss. So, what's the plan?"

"Starting tonight, we stake out Oren's place. I want two of us at the gym at all times. Movements change every day, teams mixing up, so Oren can't get a bead on who's where." Sending Jaime back to the wharfs all but guaranteed they'd abandon whatever they had left over there and cut their work in half.

"Leaves us short-handed here," Darcy observed.

"I've called in some backup," Ellis grumbled. "We'll be covered."

Darcy had a huge grin on his face. "You called Alex?!"

Marley sighed in annoyance, but Sebastian didn't miss the faint tinge of color that spread across Teegan's cheeks.

"Alex, Toby, and John. They'll be here tonight."

"Everyone is on guard," Sebastian reminded them, lowering the excitement. "No one walks home. If you're not here, you check in every fifteen minutes. And if you think, even for a second, you're being watched or followed, call Lily."

Ellis looked outraged for all of a half second, then begrudgingly nodded.

"Any questions?" Sebastian looked around at his friends, and they all looked right back at him, unafraid. "Good. Then let's get ready for tonight. Teegan and Darcy, you're heading out to the gym just before we open. Lily will give you the address. I have to make a call."

He nodded once at Ellis, silently thanking him for taking the steps he had. Everyone knowing was better, especially now.

When he got back to his office, he slumped into the chair by the window, closing his eyes for just a moment. He didn't feel physically tired—his ill-timed night of sleep had done away with his exhaustion—but he felt tired of this nonsense. He didn't want to have to constantly look over his shoulder and he wanted time to himself.

The only thing worse than not having any time with Lily was having just enough to get him addicted. All he could think about was how she tasted and sounded, her lips on his, and—

Exhaling slowly, he got himself to focus and picked up his phone.

"Hello?" A rough, accented voice answered, familiar enough to Sebastian to know who he spoke to.

"Hello, Reyes." His voice dropped lower, colder.

"Galani…to what do I owe the pleasure?"

He and Reyes had a complicated relationship. While he didn't approve of what Reyes dealt with, he respected the man's code of honor, even if it differed from his. That code was what he was betting on now.

"I've come into some information, and I'm willing to make a deal."

He could hear Reyes's smile. *"Oh? What kind of deal?"*

"The kind where I save your ass, and you keep drugs out of my club."

"You want out? Scared to deal with criminals? Or too good for us?"

"I'm tired of the cops at my doorstep, Reyes. I'm tired of getting rid of bugs almost weekly." He sat back. "I've made my mark on this town, and I'm done clawing among the dogs in the pits."

"No, you'd rather be a king in your club."

"Better a king than a rival. You know I don't deal, so there's no need to worry about a competitor."

"Another gang—"

"I didn't say just your drugs."

Reyes went quiet for a moment, long enough to consider it. Taking Tartarus out of his territory would be detrimental to Reyes's income, but they both knew the club wasn't significant enough to get into a war over.

"So, you want me to keep all gangs out of Tartarus? All drugs?" Reyes scoffed, and Sebastian knew they'd entered the bargaining. *"What do I get out of this?"*

"You get to survive."

Reyes fell silent again, and he waited.

"If your information is good and worthwhile, we have a deal."

"Oren is making a move against you," Sebastian said without further ado. "Today. Him and his dozen or so lieutenants. They have two safe houses, one at the wharves and one at a place formally called Jed's Gym in the slums."

"Bastard."

"You know I have no love for dealers, but I prefer you over Oren. Take the warning. If I'm right, if they come after you, you'll honor your side. If I'm not, keep Tartarus."

"How'd you hear this?"

"I had an uninvited guest last night."

"Idiots." Reyes laughed. *"I'll let you know what happens, one way or another. Goodbye."*

"Reyes," Sebastian said, the name coming out before he stopped himself.

There was no answer, but no dial tone, either.

"Oren's drug. If any of your men get hit by it, get them to a hospital. It'll kill them."

With a hint of reluctance in his voice, Reyes said, *"If Oren is sending men to your door, then I'm not the only one on his list."*

"I'm aware. Goodbye."

"Goodbye."

Sebastian lowered the phone, and a mug of coffee landed next to him. He looked up, not entirely surprised to see that Lily had snuck in without his noticing. She wore a skirt that he'd seen Marley wear a few times, and a black shirt that could have come from anyone, but her usual flowered wrap hung over her shoulders.

"Is he going to take the warning?" she asked, obviously aware of what he had done.

"Reyes is a criminal, but he's not stupid. There's a chance we won't have to deal with Oren at all, depending on how hard he strikes back."

She hummed quietly, sipping her coffee and looking out the window. Sebastian followed her gaze, relishing the calm.

"Would it have worked?" she asked after a few minutes.

He looked at her, resting against his desk and lifting the mug of coffee to her lips. "Would what have worked?"

"Oren's plan. Would you have signed Tartarus over?" The question sounded casual, but she didn't meet his eyes entirely, they kept sliding down his face, or past him to the view outside. He took too long in responding, the hesitation so out of character for her. She started talking again, that nervousness rearing its head.

"I just…if that was all it took, taking someone from here, why wouldn't they have done that months ago?" she clarified, taking another sip.

"I've been careful," he answered, watching her place the mug down on the desk. "Kept a distance. Kept my reputation. They believe that I wouldn't have signed over for anyone."

"What about Ellis?"

Her tongue darted out, and that seemed to be all he could focus on for a minute. He took a breath, placed his mug on the small table next to him, and got to his feet. "God help the poor soul who tried to take Ellis anywhere."

She tensed, straightening slightly, her fingers wrapping around the lip of the desk. Without her usual heels, she was shorter than he expected. "Then why would they think it would work with me?"

"Because it's different with you." He hadn't meant for his voice to sound like that. Soft. He hadn't meant for his feet to guide him forward to her, but suddenly he stood inches from her, staring down at her, her hair over her shoulder in loose, soft curls.

She blinked, chewing on her lip.

"Ask me," he murmured, tucking her hair behind her ear.

"Why is it different with me?"

"Because you saw me, even when I gave you every excuse to look away."

Such an insignificant thing, but more than any stranger had ever given to him—the benefit of the doubt. Teegan, Marley, and Darcy, even they believed the worst at the beginning, but had nowhere else to go. Lily had seen the worst possible thing and still stayed, still hoping for him. Though not his style, he wanted to live up to her expectations, because they didn't involve changing him—just becoming the best possible version.

Her mouth tilted up. "Maybe I just really love your club."

"I know you do."

She did love Tartarus, the same way he did. The past it stood on, the people he helped here, those who worked here, what it had become—a symbol that dark didn't always mean bad. And that even the bad parts could create worthwhile. Tartarus's name carried everything he gave up and everything he achieved to get here. That's why he would never give it up. Not for anything.

Except for Lily, everything Tartarus represented and more.

Sebastian leaned down the scant inch between them, kissing her softly, the way their first kiss should have gone. Gentle and slow, full of the promises he was too realistic to make, just in case. He kept his hand on her jaw, not letting it wander. When he pulled away, she breathed out shakily and opened her eyes to reveal the blue nearly swallowed by black.

"I love you, Galani," she whispered.

He smiled, constantly amazed and surprised by this woman. And for once, the words didn't seem to get caught in his throat. "I love you, too."

Chapter 18

At the bar, Sebastian kept his gaze steady as he stared Lily down. She glared right back at him, her blue eyes sparking. "You aren't serious," she said, her voice and fists tight.

"You aren't going to take a shift watching Oren," Sebastian repeated, doing his best to keep his tone calm. "They're already going after you. I'm not about to leave you on their doorstep."

Darcy and Marley shifted awkwardly as they watched Lily glare at their boss, Teegan was in the back, speaking with the extra help, letting them know what they would handle in the coming days.

"I'm the best choice to watch them. Literally my job," she insisted, with a wave of her hand. Sebastian noted the scars on her hands and arms and knew she was right. But so was he.

Ellis, surprisingly, leaned forward. "If Oren is looking for you, and you ain't here, he's going to look a little harder. Be safer for the rest of us if you're here, keeping their eye on the club and Galani, rather than looking for us."

"A distraction," Marley murmured. "Not a bad plan."

Sebastian saw Lily weighing the idea. Finally, she sighed and nodded. "Fine."

Letting out a silent breath of relief, Sebastian turned

to Ellis. "You ready?"

"I'm off. See you later." He shook Sebastian's hand a little too tightly, then grabbed his jacket and headed out the side door, taking the first night watching Oren's place.

Darcy watched Ellis as he left, then looked back at the others. "Right. Now what?"

"We open in an hour," Sebastian reminded him, walking towards his office. "Get ready."

****

Several hours later, while Tartarus was its usual bombastic self, Sebastian lurked, making sure John and Toby handled the crowd. Alex had been chatting with Teegan as they walked the crowds and was set to relieve Lily for a break a little later. Marley grinned a little more wildly than usual, but the music hit perfectly, and the crowd responded.

The bar was packed, and before Sebastian took a seat, he made the rounds, checking wrists for tattoos and knowing Lily and Teegan were doing the same. As far as he could tell, there weren't any of Oren's cronies here tonight, at least not yet. Or at least not ones with tattoos.

As he sat at his usual spot at the bar, he checked his phone again. Reyes still hadn't called back, He began to wonder if Oren had changed his mind.

Lily placed a drink in front of him, a faint smile on her lips. He nodded at her, unable to muster up a similar smile, but appreciated her efforts. She cocked her head, a skeptical look crossed her face. Leaning slightly, she put her hand on his wrist. "We're gonna get him."

Sebastian scoffed faintly, with a faint nod.

"Seb," she repeated. "We going to get him."

He smiled, turning his hand beneath hers and ran his

fingertips along her palm. "I know."

Lily squeezed his hand, then returned to her work, a quick smile on her face, confident and at ease.

He knew she was right. They would get him, one way or another. Either before Oren made his move, and everyone would be walking away just fine. Or after Oren made his move, and Sebastian would make certain Oren wouldn't walk away at all.

He sipped his drink and kept watch over his club and his people.

****

Teegan smiled at Lily as she entered the bar; a tall man with impressive hair followed behind her. "Have you met Alex Harris?" Teegan said.

Lily shook her head. "No, I haven't. Hi. Lily Nehme."

Grinning, he shook her hand. "Nice to meet you."

"I thought you were Sebastian's investor or something."

"I am." His smile was wide and his eyes kind. "But I used to be a bartender here when Tartarus first opened. Galani helped me out and when I took over my dad's business, I didn't forget that."

Lily smiled back at him, then cast a knowing look at Teegan.

She blushed and spoke quickly, "Well, we're taking over for you while you take your break. Go away."

Lily laughed, waving at them as she grabbed her glass and wove her way through the crowd to the employee's door. She sighed in relief at the cool air in the hallway as the door closed behind her. There must have been more bodies than usual in the club because it felt hot in there. She didn't feel tired, or hungry, despite the late hour. She felt she was waiting for something, she didn't know what. Skipping dinner, she made her way up the stairs, bypassing Sebastian's door and heading toward the catwalk above the club.

As the music washed over her, she sighed in relief. The air was cooler up here, but the sound still rumbled through her bones, working at the edge of her nerves. She rested her hands on the railing, watching the masses below. She could see Marley rocking out on the stage and Darcy taking over the tablet for Teegan. The bar was packed, and she saw Alex and Teegan working well together. Despite Ellis's absence, the crowd seemed well-managed. Though she wasn't really looking for him, not entirely, she couldn't find Sebastian.

The catwalk door opened, the sound swallowed up by the music. Lily glanced over just enough to confirm Sebastian was a short distance away from the door, walking toward her. Then she turned her eyes back to the crowd with a smile, anticipation sliding into her belly.

She felt the heat of him before he put his hands on her hips, pressing up behind her. Rolling her neck to the side, she grinned as he took advantage of the exposed skin, his teeth scraping across the muscle at her shoulder. She rocked her hips slightly, maybe in an attempt at dancing, and he anchored her hips to his, his fingers tight on her.

Twisting away, she turned to face him, her back pressing against the railing. He let go of her, his hands grabbing the railing on either side of her. His features were shadowed up here, silhouetted by the stars around them, but she could read the expression that mirrored her own—the want, the love, the damn impatience. They didn't need any more words at this point. Everything important had already been said.

Lily kissed him, her tongue pressing against his lips, and he parted them at once. She tasted everything uniquely him on her tongue, ignoring the faint discomfort from the railing behind her as he stepped nearer to her, sealing everything from ankles to lips together, not an inch of space to separate them and still far too much. One of his hands in her hair, the other fell to her hip, edging beneath the shirt she wore. The music swept around them, silencing any noises they might be making and forcing them to feel the sounds instead, the rumble in his chest as she bit his lip, the staccato of her breath as he pulled her hair slightly, exposing more of her to his wandering lips, the vibration beneath her fingers as she hooked her fingers in his belt loops and pulled—

They shifted down the walkway, towards the door of the catwalk, but as Sebastian went to open the door, to lead her somewhere private, she shook her head, flipping the faint light above the catwalk off and locking the door. Here, against the wall next to the door, with the light off, no one would see them, and she wanted him here, among the music, amid the stars.

Backing her against the wall, he kissed her until she was dizzy, his mouth so unfairly talented. Her breath came short, but she returned the favor undoing the button on his slacks and slipping her hand down and around him.

Even with the music, she heard him swear.

She stroked up and down slowly, her hand seeming cool in comparison until Sebastian grabbed her thighs in both hands and lifted her up. It was an awkward few moments as they shifted, and he pulled her underwear to the side while she moved to the left and—

They both went still as he slid in slowly, holding their breath until he filled her completely. Lily took in a shallow breath, catching his eyes, even in the dark. He smiled, wonder in his gaze, and kissed her gently.

She had never felt like this before. Not with anyone.

Marley dropped the bass, and the vibrations slid through both of them in a new and unexpected way. They moved together, her arms around his shoulders and his hips pinning her to the wall, slowly at first, but rising and falling with the music around them. It was fast, both of them approaching the edge they'd been dancing around the past few weeks. He seemed to grow harder within her, obviously close, but he gave up the momentum long enough to slide a hand between them, his thumb finding the same spot he'd driven her insane with this morning. Stars, literal and imagined, danced in her eyes, but she focused on Sebastian, unable to hear him, but wanting to see and feel him.

He came first, the groan inaudible, but she saw the way his eyes blew out, and felt him shudder within her. He pressed harder against her, and the combination was enough to send her falling, the stars winking out temporarily.

Once her legs weren't jelly, she slid off him, took the tissue he'd pulled out of his pocket, and cleaned up. He tucked himself away, letting out a long breath. Lily unlocked the door and they both went onto the stairs, the quiet sudden and strange.

Before she could get back to the bar, he grabbed her arm, pulling her back against him and kissing her so thoroughly she wondered if they'd have enough time for round two. When he pulled away, he exhaled against her lips and said, "Tonight, I'm gonna pay you back for that."

"You didn't have fun?"

The glare was scathing, but she just grinned.

"Payback's a bitch, Nehme," he said, letting go of her arm.

"It's a deal, Galani."

****

Sebastian locked up the side door, relieved beyond measure to say goodbye to John. His old coworker had been giving him dirty looks all night, obviously blaming him for everything that was going on. Having decided long ago not to waste his breath on explaining things to the man, Sebastian dealt with the looks and hustled him out the door as quickly as possible.

Ellis had checked in several times throughout the night, reporting movement from Oren's place and sending tons of pictures of faces. Sebastian sent them to Lily and the others, so they could keep an eye out for them. He didn't recognize any of them offhand, which wasn't entirely surprising, but he sent copies to himself, too.

However, he didn't worry until he and Lily were getting ready for bed, and his phone went off. Recognizing Reyes's name, Sebastian picked up, taking a seat on the edge of the bed. "Reyes. How are—"

"He fucking did it."

"What?" he asked, leaning forward. Lily came out of the bathroom, a frown on her face at his tone.

"He killed fifteen of my men. Eight more are in the hospital from that Opus shit."

"How the hell did he manage that?" Sebastian said. He had expected Reyes to crush Oren, or at the very least survive to damage him, but this…

"I don't know. Half my guys were knocked unconscious, and Oren swept in. I'm at a place in the financial district." Reyes's voice had never sounded this frantic.

"You're hiding?"

"He threatened my wife."

Sebastian rubbed his eyes. "Jesus…"

"I know. But I couldn't…"

Looking up, he met Lily's eyes, and quietly said, "I don't blame you."

"Take this bastard down, and I'll keep everything out of your club. Hell, I'll keep it out of the slums." Reyes sighed into the receiver. *"I'll do what I can, but you have to get rid of him."*

"I will." He hung up and looked at Lily.

"Oren succeeded?" she asked, taking a seat next to him.

"Apparently," he muttered.

"Shit. So much for making our jobs easier." She leaned her head on his shoulder. "Oh, well."

Sebastian scoffed, looking down at her, tucking her hair behind her ear. "Oh well? That's all you have to say?"

"What else would I say?" she asked, tilting her head to look up at him, she pressed her thumb to his chin. "That we're done? Screwed?" She arched her brow. "Forget that. If Reyes had taken him out, that would've been nice, but that doesn't stop us. If you want something done right, you've gotta do it yourself, right?"

He chuckled, her optimism and confidence catching. "You are…insane."

Lily grinned up at him.

"I like it," he admitted quietly.

"Good." She turned and straddled him, her arms over his shoulders, and a filthy smirk on her face. God, he wanted her. She was all he wanted, but the looming threat of death from a threatening drug dealer kept distracting him for some reason.

"Ellis is—"

"Ellis can take care of himself, and we'll leave your phone on loud," Lily murmured, her lips brushing across his face. "We keep going with the plan. And for now, our place in the plan is right here, all night." She kissed him slowly. "You've got somewhere else to be, boss?"

"I do not," he murmured, letting her push him back onto the bed.

"Now," Lily said, leaning over him, her hair falling over her shoulder. "You said something about a deal."

****

Hours later, Lily watched the sunrise through the curtains, Sebastian's arm rested over her side, and his body tucked in behind hers. His breath tickled the back of her neck, but she didn't mind. Her phone lit up, and a message appeared on her screen. Moving slowly, she grabbed her phone off the nightstand, pulling it back over to her.

She hadn't lied to him last night. She fully believed that they'd be able to stop Oren. But that didn't mean there wouldn't be consequences. She'd reached out to Eliza after he'd fallen asleep, the lines disappearing from his eyes as he'd pulled her close against him.

Unlocking her phone, Lily read the message.

—I checked in on the men at the county hospital. Five died during the night. Two are still in ICU. They're struggling to keep them stable.—

Lily chewed her lip. *—Do you have an idea of how to cure this?—*

—It's synthetic. I've been trying to develop something, but I won't have the results until later today.—

—Okay. Anything else?— Like her day couldn't get worse.

—There weren't needle marks on the arms. They looked bigger. Like darts. And the coma levels haven't been explained either.—

Great. So now they were weaponizing Opus, along with another drug. She would bet they used Reyes as a practice before Tartarus, and it clearly went well. She sent one last text to Eliza. *—Find a cure. I think we're running on borrowed time.—*

—Be careful.—

She returned her phone to the nightstand, curling up a little closer to Sebastian. His arm tightened around her in his sleep, and she tangled her fingers with his. She could feel it in her bones—Oren would make a move on Tartarus, and soon. He'd do whatever he had to in order to get Sebastian to sign Tartarus over.

She watched the sun light up the room, her resolution growing with the dawn. Oren wasn't going to get anywhere near Sebastian, even if she had to kill every single one of his men herself.

Chapter 19

Eliza woke up slowly, still sore, but not as much as the day before. It had been a…different kind of day yesterday.

She and Will had a late start yesterday, not that she minded. Only once they'd really started to starve did Will finally deign to leave the bed, puttering around in the kitchen and returning with coffee, eggs, and toast, even though it was already after noon.

The rest of their day had been spent in a mix of things…the expected activities in bed, chatting, and more laughter than she'd ever heard from Will in a single day. They made dinner together, watching a movie on the couch before getting distracted, and Eliza could easily see how this could be her life. They just worked so well.

The next morning had gone in a similar way, with the addition of her conversation with Lily. Afterward, she'd started voicing her concerns to Will, who seemed very worried, but only until she mentioned her own feeling of helplessness—the possible antidote sitting there and not ready until later. He seemed bound and determined to distract her by exhausting her completely. Not until she shut her eyes for a nap did he mention heading into the clinic for a while.

"I'll go with you," she insisted, starting to sit up.

He laughed, kissing her forehead. "I won't be long.

I'll check on your antidote while I'm there. Text me what you want for dinner, and I'll pick it up before I get home."

She liked the sound of that. Home.

Not entirely reluctantly, Eliza settled back into her sheets, the texts from Lily forgotten until she woke up as the sun went down. Guilt slammed into her—here she was, fooling around with Will while people were dying. She appreciated the gesture, but she needed to go down to the lab herself and deal with this. Even if it meant staying there all night—with or without Will.

She got dressed in her clean clothes, feeling more like herself as she went downstairs and caught a cab, the rain that had been threatening all day seeming imminent. It was completely dark by the time she got dropped off at the corner of the clinic, heading toward the employee door.

Low conversation stopped her, that instinct Lily encouraged her to trust cautioning silence. She held her breath, not making the turn around the corner, and listened.

"...know better than to go back on a deal with us."

She didn't recognize the voice, but his tone made her nerves jangle nervously.

"I did what your boss asked." Will's voice sounded cold, unlike how he'd spoken to her just a few hours ago. "There was nothing about additional services. Hold up your side of the deal."

The other man laughed, not at all a mirthful sound. "You're brave, doctor. Fine. Our work is done, for now, and we'll do as we promised."

"You'd better."

"Come tomorrow, every gang in the slums will

either be working for me or dead."

Will went quiet, and she heard footsteps starting to head around the other side of the building, leaving. Holding her breath, she waited for them to go, but—

"Oren!" Will called.

Eliza covered her mouth with her hand, stifling the gasp.

"Yes, doctor?"

"What are you going to do to Tartarus?"

Oren laughed. "It's already done."

****

Tartarus was packed, almost to the same level as New Year's Eve. With Teegan on lookout, Lily slung drinks to the best of her ability. Alex helped Darcy and Toby deal with the crowd with Ellis, John, and Sebastian at the door. With Marley in her usual spot, there wasn't time to catch a breath. Sebastian hadn't even made it to the bar to pick up his drink.

Lily chugged her water when she could, the club seeming hotter than normal as the minutes ticked on, and it was only shortly after opening.

Some sort of celebration echoed down at the end of the bar, a tall woman in a beautiful dress talking about some kind of promotion at her work. "Drinks all around!" she shouted, much to the pleasure of all other ears. She leaned toward Lily, her card on her fingers, "But just make it the cheap beer, if that's okay." She leaned toward Lily, her card on her fingers, "But just make it the cheap beer, if that's okay."

Lily grinned. "Congratulations."

The woman blushed and returned to her guests as Lily began tapping the most reasonably priced keg they had, giving a discount, nonetheless.

Lily downed the rest of her water, her throat parched as she passed out the generous gift to everyone who passed, until most people had a drink in hand. With a lull in the crowd, she leaned against the bar, exhausted.

She spied Sebastian coming in the doors, his own face pulled in a tired expression that he smoothed away almost instantly. His eyes sought hers in the crowd, and she gave him a small smile. A shout from the side of the bar reached her ears and she turned, expecting an irate college kid.

Instead, she saw a group gathered around a girl on the ground, concern on their faces as one of them knelt down next to her—

Before falling himself and collapsing beside her.

Screams rose up as people began stumbling, falling, dropping like stones—dozens of them. Glass shattered and the music paused as Marley noticed.

"I need everyone to calm down and sit down now!"

Lily looked around, Marley's words having no effect as the panic began to set in, people were rushing for the doors, pushing past one another, stepping on those who had already collapsed or dropping unexpectedly themselves.

"Calm the fuck down!" Marley said, stepping out from behind the stage. A group surged past her, and she stumbled, nearly landing in the middle of them.

Lily moved toward her, pushing past a girl as she stepped in the way.

The brown hair was familiar. She froze as Willow looked up at her, her eyes red and filling with silver.

"I'm sorry," she mouthed. Oren's tattoo was visible on her wrist.

With a glare, Lily made to push past her, but Willow

lunged to the right—

No, Lily listed to the left.

Her head spun and she blinked against the haze—how?

She looked back at the bar, her phone lighting up next to her glass of water.

Praying Marley could fend for herself, Lily turned, heading to the employee door, fighting against the masses and her own swimming vision, whatever drug had been dumped in her water—and the beer, apparently—acting faster with her accelerated heart rate.

But she was okay, if she could make it there, she could hole up away from Oren's men, and she would be okay, she could see the door now—

The lights went out.

****

Eliza slammed the door to the lounge open, the wood crashing against the wall. Will jumped, spinning around to face her and—

And she read everything on his face.

First, surprise, then relief—that faded into a look of dawning realization, then resigned acceptance.

She hated that she knew him so well. She hated that she hadn't known him at all. "How could you?" she asked.

This was why Will had been researching. The hypotheticals weren't hypothetical at all, and she felt like a fool for believing that. All those attempts to be at work when she wasn't, because they both knew that she could have fought against this tooth and nail. Selling his soul to a piece of garbage like Oren while knowing what he did to the people in the city? To their people? And for what?

"Clark," he said softly, like he could convince her she hadn't seen what she had. "It's complicated—"

"Bullshit." She stepped in, keeping the table between the two of them, because she couldn't bear it if he tried to touch her now, not after this. "You helped design drugs for Oren, even though you knew—you *know* what he's been doing!"

"I designed one aspect of a non-lethal pill," he argued. "A minor addition that won't hurt anyone."

"So, him threatening to kill people doesn't bother you at all?" Her heart stuttered. "What about Lily? What about Tartarus? What's he going to do?"

"I don't know," Will said reluctantly. "I didn't even know I was working for him, at first, not until he came to collect. But they promised…"

"What?" What could possibly be worth this betrayal?

"He promised you'd be safe. The clinic. We'd be under his protection."

Eliza laughed bitterly, and she ran her fingers through her hair, unable to believe any of this. "Oren's protection? You've seen his kind of protection. He's killing people, why would we ever trust—"

"Not Oren," he interrupted. "He came to collect the drug, but the one I was working for originally, he has the power and pull to do what he promised."

She stared at him, something hovering at the very edge of her knowledge. Some missing piece that she hadn't realized they'd failed to notice.

Who would have had the money to back Oren, to provide him with lieutenants? This type of drug wasn't a cheap creation, especially when she factored in Will's involvement. Who benefitted from running down Reyes and other dealers?

Why was Oren targeting Tartarus…unless it had never been Oren's decision?

Eliza stared at him, fear choking her words to a whisper. "You're working for Daniel Galani."

He didn't nod, but she read the answer on his face.

Turning away from him, she fumbled for her phone. If Oren felt confident to say that everyone would be working for him, he'd be going after Tartarus tonight. She pressed Lily's contact, and the phone rang.

And rang.

And rang.

Sirens began to echo down the streets, rising and fading as the call went to voicemail.

****

Lily stumbled through the crowd, looking for anyone she recognized, but her vision blurred together, doubles and triples of everyone. With only the emergency lights, she could barely see anything, and the screaming didn't help.

"Seb?!" She tried calling out, but the chaos drowned out her voice. She stumbled again, and fell to the ground, someone stepping on her fingers almost immediately. Forcing herself up, she grabbed whatever was near to get upright, and her palm scraped across something metallic and heavy—

The employee's door.

Fumbling for her key card, she brushed it over the sensor, but the power was out. She pulled, a noise of anger escaping her lips, and the door slid open—the locks disengaged in an emergency. No one else knew that.

She shut the door behind her, resting against the

wall, her body wanting to give in and collapse. She'd never made the trek up to Sebastian's apartment, but maybe she could get to the lounge and manually lock the door...

The employee door creaked open, and Lily looked up to see a man standing there. "Hello, Lily."

She knew him...she'd seen his picture somewhere, but she couldn't...she blinked hard, trying to shake away the blur, but his face swam in front of her eyes, his dark hair and jaw familiar, beyond the picture...the tattoo on his arm, the O with a line—

No, not an O.

G.

"Galani," she mumbled, hanging onto the wall.

Daniel Galani smiled, so similar and so different than his older brother. "At your service. And it is a pleasure to meet you, Ms. Nehme."

He reached out to grab her, but she backed away. Her vision was fading fast, but if she could just buy herself some time...

Shaking his head, he merely looked amused, staring down a slightly crooked nose at her. "You've got ten more seconds of consciousness, max. I can wait."

No, no, she would not go out like this.

She turned, heading for the side alley door with a speed that surprised both of them. Daniel swore, coming after her, getting close—too close—

She stumbled on unsteady legs, falling to her knee. He laughed behind her, and it almost sounded like Seb. Grabbing the back of her wrap, he hauled her up as she reached down to her boot. She whirled, her knife slicing across his face—it would have been his throat, but her aim was off. Still, he shouted, throwing her to the ground. The knife skittered across the ground, and as her vision went black, she saw his face, covered with red and still streaming.

Her last thought before unconsciousness claimed her was that at least she'd gone down fighting.

****

Sebastian took a girl's arm, helping her towards the door. As far as he could tell, the rest of the city still had power, and outside in the moonlight would be better than in his close club.

Ellis lunged back into the crowd, trying to protect those that had passed out, and John and Toby were stationed at the door, helping people get out and into the street. Sebastian had texted Teegan, checking in on her, but the message kept saying error and not going through.

"Galani!" Darcy shouted, fighting against the crowd.

"Did you see Lily and Marley?" Sebastian asked, snatching his arm to keep him from getting lost as the crowd pushed and screamed against him. The emergency power cast a silky orange glow on him and the club, making shadows extend.

"Marley was helping drag the unconscious people to the wall. Alex and Ellis helped her. Lily was at the bar last I saw her, but…"

Sebastian's hand tightened on his arm as Darcy hesitated.

"…I haven't seen her since."

The last few screaming people had been removed from the club, and Sebastian heard the doors locking behind them. Ellis straightened from in front of the stage, Marley with him, though her skirt was torn.

"Everyone okay?" Ellis asked.

"Lily?" Darcy shouted.

Sebastian spun in a circle, not seeing her among the unconscious bodies. He leaned over the bar, his nerves rising as he saw her phone and nothing else.

"Maybe the lounge?" Marley suggested.

"Toby, Alex, and John," Sebastian ordered, "Stay out here and keep trying to get through to emergency services." He went for the employee door, noting that it wasn't locked in the disaster. He had his phone out, the flashlight function adding some more light to the emergency ones in the hall. A step in and he paused.

The hallway was a mess. Boxes that had once been neatly stacked were thrown on the ground, the glass inside of them shattered and liquid seeping out onto the tile.

"What the hell happened?" Marley whispered, coming in behind him.

A pit opened up in Sebastian's stomach. "Lily?" He took a few steps up the stairs, maybe she was in his apartment…

"Is this…is this blood?" Darcy's tremulous question came from near the side door.

Turning back, Sebastian got to Darcy's side, seeing a spray of crimson on the wall and floor—not enough to kill someone, but enough to leave a mark. A small blade lay by the back door. One that he recognized from his nightstand just this morning.

The side door was ajar, and he stepped outside, as Ellis came out of the employee lounge, shaking his head. They all went into the alley, searching for anything. Ellis bent over some tire marks in the middle of the alley, and Sebastian turned, trying to find any sign that Lily—

He stopped, facing the door. Something was nailed

into the wood. He took two steps forward, his heart thundering in his ears. He pulled the nail out, the sheer, flowered fabric already wrinkled and torn, but he recognized it all the same.

"Oh, god," Marley whispered, covering her mouth.

Sebastian spread out Lily's wrap, a piece of paper fluttering out from between the folds. Ellis picked it up, reading in as close to a monotone as he could at the moment. "'Ready to make another deal? -G'"

It clicked into place, too late. The one who would benefit most from destroying Tartarus and, by extension, Sebastian himself.

There were no other threats. No promises of violence, because they already delivered those. By taking Lily, from the middle of Tartarus, right from his home, Daniel had shown that he was helpless to stop him.

His brother only ever played games he knew he could win.

Sirens sounded from several blocks away, getting closer. Ellis cursed. "You gotta go, boss."

"If he runs, they'll think he's responsible for this," Darcy said, his face pale.

"They think that already," Marley said, heading to the fire escape of the next building and looking up, testing the ladder. "If they get him, that just means Lily'll be…"

"Where are you going to go?" Darcy asked, watching Ellis head toward the ladder.

"Away from here," Ellis snapped. "Get Teegan back and tell her she's in charge. Keep everything under control. We'll be in touch soon as the phones work again. Let's go, boss."

Sebastian stared at the flowers.

"Galani!" Ellis snarled. "Move your ass! You get arrested, and you know what'll happen."

He knew what would happen. What might already be happening.

He fell into step behind the Ellis, the wrap clutched tightly in his fingers as he left Tartarus behind. Despite the fact that he hadn't signed it over, not yet, Sebastian couldn't stop the thought from running through his mind.

Daniel had already won.

Chapter 20

Eliza rubbed her eyes, the ache of exhaustion, and fear from unanswered phone calls not exactly conducive to sleep. She heard a cup of coffee placed on the table to the left of her but didn't open her eyes. Leather creaked, and the couch depressed next to her.

"Police have cordoned off Tartarus," Will said, his voice detached. "Emergency services are there, but they'll likely tell us to handle to overflow of people."

She sighed. Miguel had managed to get through to the clinic, telling them that he was on his way in. She hadn't gotten through to Lily or Reva yet, and the number for Tartarus went straight to voicemail. Will had sent messages out to the other RNs they had on staff, but she didn't know if they'd get here in time to handle the rush.

"Clark," Will said quietly, putting his hand on her arm.

She got to her feet, pulling away from him. "Stop. I can't right now. We need to fix this."

"I know, and we will, but I did this for—"

"If you say you did this for me, I might punch you," Eliza interrupted, putting her coffee back down a little too hard.

He rose to his feet, his coffee left on the table behind him. His brows were drawn together, and Eliza should have found it imposing or threatening. Instead, she only found it irritating. "We could have been happy," she said, spreading her hands wide. "It wouldn't have been perfect, but we could have been close."

"Clark—"

"And then you had to go and try to play the hero, even knowing that I would never—" She stopped as her voice caught, and she hated that she couldn't even be properly angry without crying.

They had been discovering something amazing between the two of them. And now they… The betrayal and the lying, that was something she'd never expected from Will, despite his love of privacy. At best, they were on hold, put on the back burner, because work was more important and it was, honestly.

At worst…

"We need to fix this," she said, her shoulders sagging. "Everything else can wait."

Will crossed the room and got in front of her. He didn't take her hand or hold her, but his hands flexed at his side. "I'm sorry."

Taking a deep breath, Eliza turned away from him. "I've been using a variant of naloxone to try and develop something that would stabilize the victims long enough to get them to care. You need to look and see if your additions would react."

"I already have been. When you started, I…I ran some tests, too."

Eliza gritted her teeth. Another lie, even if this one might be more useful. "We need to reach out to emergency services, too, and tell them what we know."

"I'll do that. You—"

"What the hell is going on, guys? I leave for a week, and you blow up the city?"

Miguel's voice was a welcome sound, and she turned, a smile on her face. She ran up and hugged him tightly. "It is so good to see you," she said, squeezing him again before letting him go.

He grinned. "I got you. Now, where should the magic be done?"

Will stepped up, and she backed off, heading back to her computer. They would need to pull the supplies from the utility closet on the second floor, and they might need to convert their lounge depending on the number of people they brought in.

"See if you can get in touch with Joyce," Will said, his voice completely calm. "I'm heading out to the hospital to see if—" He stopped abruptly, and despite herself, Eliza turned to see what was wrong.

Two men stood in the doors behind Miguel, who turned and yelped, backing up until he stood in line with Will.

Eliza recognized both of them. "Sebastian?" she asked, coming back down towards the door.

His face looked like a mask as he glanced at her. None of the easy, arrogant charm, or drawling humor she'd seen the last time they'd met. He looked empty, which frightened her more than whatever could have been there.

"Doctor," he said quietly, the affected tone gone.

"El, that's Galani," Miguel hissed.

Eliza waved her hand at Miguel to shut him up, her heart pounding in her chest. "What's wrong?"

Sebastian swallowed, the movement looking painful, and the other man—Ellis, she remembered—spoke instead. "Oren and Galani hit Tartarus. They drugged half the club, knocking them out."

"Opus?" Will asked, stepping up.

"No," he said, shaking his head. "Just unconscious. Most of them woke up fine. Just some bruises from falling."

Something was terribly, terribly wrong for them to be here. Eliza's fists clenched.

Will said, "Then why are—"

"Where's Lily?" Eliza interrupted, her voice quavering as she stepped in front of Will and Miguel.

Sebastian had yet to look away from Eliza, and she saw something in his eyes shattered.

"Where's Lily?" she repeated, though she already knew the answer.

Sebastian's eyes lowered, and she followed his gaze, seeing the flowered shawl Lily had worn to work so many times, laughing as she did, because Sebastian hated the flowers.

He clutched it like a lifeline.

****

Lily slowly came to consciousness, keeping her breathing steady and her eyes shut. Her head still felt fuzzy and ached, but bits and pieces of the abduction came back to her, and she pieced it together, her ears alert to any sounds.

No movement or inertia, so she wasn't moving. No hint of gasoline or rumble of an engine to be found, and the ground below her felt too hard to be a vehicle of some kind. She could hear the drip of water, but echoing strangely—a bathroom, maybe. Metallic smells, with plastic and the scent of old sweat.

It tugged on her memory, but her head spun, keeping her from focusing.

Slight tensing of her muscles revealed that her hands

were tied to something strong, and her legs were tied, but not attached to anything. It felt cold and clinked slightly. Handcuffs. Her arms ached and she shook, which said that she'd been here for a while.

A door creaked open, and Lily remained still, her breathing steady. Two sets of shoes on a tiled floor.

"Jesus," said a familiar voice. Oren's voice echoed strangely in the room, like a large bathroom or something. "How much did you give her?"

"The same amount I'd give anyone who stabbed me in the face," another voice snapped, his words bouncing back harder. That was familiar, too. The man who'd taken her—Daniel Galani. "It's fine. We'll forego the video message and just call. He'll meet you at the wharves with the deed ready. I'll stay here to make sure he comes through."

"And if he doesn't?" Oren asked.

"Then you'll have given me bad information. If she's not the leverage we need, I'll kill her."

"And…if he does come through?"

Lily didn't expect the boot to hit her squarely in the ribs, so her gasp of pain was genuine. Opening her eyes, she made sure to blink multiple times, twisting her head as if trying to place herself. Eyes open and head a little clearer from the pain and adrenaline, she finally recognized Jed's Gym. She was in the locker room, handcuffs zip-tied to one of the benches between the rows of lockers. Her old locker faced her, and the absurdity almost made her laugh.

She met Daniel's gaze, though, and the hatred that pulsed from his eyes was enough to give up on looking at her surroundings and keep her eyes on him.

"Accidents happen," he said, a long cut on his face

still red and raw. "As long as we get Tartarus, I really don't give a shit."

She laughed at him, then. "Do you really think people will still come to Tartarus if you're running the place?"

"Shut up," Daniel snapped.

Never. "All you'll get from Tartarus is the reminder that even when he's not in the game, Sebastian can still grind you into the ground." She chuckled, shrugging, and ignored the pain in her arms. "How does it feel for the mob boss to be taken down by the club owner? Must sting."

Daniel crouched down, his dark eyes flatter and colder than Sebastian's ever could be. "It does sting. Years of my brother flaunting his successes, while my family name has slowly lost every bit of power it once held."

She stared back at him, refusing to blink first.

"So, you can imagine, it will be so satisfying to build my family back up on the ashes of his life."

She shifted until she sat up as best she could. No breaks or pains, other than in her chest right now. "And you think drugs that kill people will be the way to do that? You know he can't get it right." She jerked her chin at Oren. "The two of you together couldn't even get rid of Reyes. How the hell are you going to run a criminal empire when you can't even deal properly?"

Oren flushed with fury, but his phone rang and cut him off. He glanced at the screen, then looked to Daniel. "It's time.

"You've got the new product?"

"What?" Oren stared at him for a breath. "I mean, yes, but it's untested. I haven't been able to stabilize—"

leave Sebastian and Tartarus alone.

Sebastian had held up his side of the deal.

Ellis spoke on the clinic's phone, his voice hushed. Miguel Ramirez, who'd gotten over the fact that this Galani wasn't looking to shake him down, directed EMTs in the hallway, as more and more people came in. Almost none of them were suffering from Opus; these were the people who'd been hurt during the attack or suffering from concussions from falling.

Eliza and William were bent over the computers, conferring almost constantly, and William juggled a couple of phones at the same time, speaking with nurses and other staff. They didn't look at Sebastian, but he felt the weight of their attention, nonetheless.

He stared at the burner phone in front of him, that Ellis had handed over once they got settled here. It wasn't anything special, just an older phone, but one that Teegan had the number to—

It rang.

He picked up, noticing Ellis going still and watching him, and Eliza following suit. "Yeah?"

"Daniel got in touch," Teegan said, no hello or small talk. *"He said to bring over the signed deed to the wharves at nine tonight, and they'll release Lily."*

"Did you speak to her?"

Ellis came over, and Sebastian put the phone on speaker, knowing better than to try to hide anything from this group at this point. They knew everything that mattered already, and he might need their insight.

"No. And they didn't say in what condition they'd release her. Or where." She didn't say out loud what they were thinking, and no one else did, either.

"Send the paperwork over to Dr. Clark's clinic," he

said after a moment.

"You're not seriously going to sign, are you?" Miguel asked. "Galani is a monster. If you give him Tartarus, he's going to kill more people."

"And if he doesn't," Ellis jumped in, "Nehme's gonna die."

"I don't know who the hell is there, and feeling a little annoyed about that," Teegan began.

"Oh, I'm Miguel Ramirez, from—"

"I don't care. Boss, Daniel is never going to let you walk out of there, deed or not. And...and Lily may already be—"

"I know," he interrupted. "And I don't plan on letting him take Tartarus, but I'm not going to take it off the table. Not when they have her."

Eliza's eyes lit up. "You're going to get Lily before the meeting."

"During, actually," he said, his mind filling in the gaps of the plan he'd been working on since the shock of Lily's abduction wore off. "Can you get everyone over there on speaker?"

"Sure, give me a second."

William's eyes were narrowed, but he glanced at Eliza, then said, "Whatever you need, Mr. Galani. We're in."

"Alright, boss," Teegan said. *"We're all here. What's the plan?"*

"Ellis, Teegan, me, and the deed will go to the wharves, while the rest of us head to Jed's Gym. Daniel has no intention of handing her over. He won't bring her anywhere near the meeting. We get into Jed's Gym, get Lily, then get Oren, Daniel, and the wharves arrested in the process."

A beat of silence.

"There are like, a thousand things wrong with that plan," Miguel said.

"Explain."

Miguel didn't balk. "How the hell are you going to get into the gym? Daniel Galani's got connections and none of us are like…" He mimed finger guns.

"True. But I also have connections." Sebastian looked at Ellis. "Reyes?"

"He's in. Got some of his guys waiting. I also know that Ben and Jonesy are still on the family's payroll."

"Good. Have a few of Reyes's men go to Tartarus and meet with the wharf group. Rest come here."

"Here?" Miguel asked, sounding a little nervous. "More gangs?"

"We're not a gang."

"Might as well be," he muttered.

"Another thought?" Darcy said hesitantly over the phone. *"You seemed to have said that you'll be at the wharves and the gym at the same time."*

"I'll appear to be. John is about my height and can pass for me from a distance. Grab a suit out of my closet and stay back enough. I doubt Oren will wait all that long to try and make a move, and if he recognizes a few others from Tartarus, he'll assume."

"And bonus if he gets shot," Ellis muttered.

"I heard that."

"Good."

"How exactly do you expect to arrest Oren and his men at the wharves?" William spoke up.

"We call the cops and tell them."

"How are you going to get them there?" William said, his words blunt, but not cruel. "You have no evidence, no proof, no warrant, and they're running thin right now. No cop in his right mind would help you."

Sebastian smiled tightly. "Good thing I know one not in his right mind. Marley, how would you like to get me arrested?"

"I mean, sometimes, sure. But what for?"

"You call Officer Hughes or go to the station and get him. Tell him that Sebastian Galani is making a deal with Oren at midnight at the wharves, and it doesn't matter what else is going on, Hughes will be there with bells on. Mention Lily is involved, and he'll be chomping at the bit."

"Then how are we getting out?" Teegan asked.

"I imagine Reyes's men will be able to come up with something." Sebastian glanced over at Ellis. "And Ellis is always good at making a scene."

Ellis grinned. "I am."

Eliza stepped forward. "What can I do?"

This was the most dangerous part, because even if everything else worked perfectly, it might not matter. "Doc, you're with me."

William opened his mouth to speak, but shut it quickly, glancing at Eliza. She frowned slightly. "Why?"

"If I know my brother, we're going to need that antidote," he said quietly.

Her eyes widened. "I don't know if it's ready."

"It has to be."

She nodded after a moment, going back to the computer she had been working on earlier, her shoulders straight. Sebastian glanced at the phone. "Get me the papers to sign. Be ready to move by seven. Everyone needs to be in place by eleven. Make the call at 11:30."

the human body couldn't be endured. Beneath the flames that licked along her skin, she could feel the sharp crack of joints and tendons giving way.

Oren's drug killed people and there was no cure.

Tears began to spill, noiselessly, but she couldn't stop them from coming. Every rolling drop that slid down her cheeks left a trail of fire on her face.

She felt cold hands on her pulse point, and Daniel's face became clearer as he leaned over her. She tried to strike out at him, but the cuffs still held her. He patted her head, sending a blast of pain through her skull, then walked away.

She rolled onto her side, clenched her fists, and ignored the sound of Daniel's shoes on the ground, Reva's whispers, Ellis's cursing, and Sebastian saying her name over and over again.

No. Only one of those things was real. She pushed aside every noise but that of Daniel's pacing. She tracked him, her eyes watering, but her head starting to clear. She had a lodestone. Something to keep her grounded. She began to pull at her cuffs, a distraction as she pulled her thumb down into her fist and pressed and pressed and pressed—

She heard Sebastian's voice and the sounds of shouting but pushed those away, hearing Daniel go to the door. He faced away from her.

She might be dying, but not yet.

The job wasn't done.

****

Sebastian checked his phone one more last time. "You ready, doc?"

At his side, Eliza nodded once, her face pale.

They were just outside Jed's gym, across the street.

Most of Daniel's men had been pulled back to the wharves, obviously expecting him to come there. He hoped Hughes had fallen for the bait. He hoped Teegan had been convincing enough to get them in the door. He hoped Ellis was ready with the distraction.

The panic from earlier had abated. It wouldn't help.

"Stay back, until I call you in. Don't take stupid chances, and don't drop that vial," he said.

"I won't," Eliza said, clutching the antidote she'd created. "Don't get yourself killed."

Sebastian smiled tightly, then walked across the street.

There were a dozen ways he could play this. He could have snuck in the back, grabbed Lily, and tried a quiet rescue, but that meant people coming after them, and Lily would need time to recover somewhere safe. He could have staked out the gym for a few hours, taking out men one by one, but that gave Daniel too much time to move Lily or to decide she wasn't worth the risk.

The one way they wouldn't expect him to take was the front door. So, he walked up to the front door.

Ben, a familiar face from his childhood, straightened upon seeing him approach. His hand went to his hip, but Sebastian showed his empty palms, clearly unarmed.

"Evening, Ben."

"M—Mr. Galani," he stuttered. "You're supposed to be at the wharf."

Sebastian continued to move forward. "Actually, I'm supposed to be making a deal with my brother. Do you mind?"

The other man at the front door cut his eyes at Ben, but the older man nodded, opening the door. "Sure. Go on."

"Thanks." He entered the gym, aware that Ben and the other sentry had followed him inside, the door shutting behind them.

It was dark inside, and Sebastian needed a moment to adjust. Details began appearing: the boxing ring in the center was covered with boxes, the move clearly ongoing. There were bags of pills and vials stacked in a corner by men playing cards. Guns were against the wall, different types and quality, but enough to be concerning.

His brother always had high aspirations. Running all the crime in Southton would be a bit beyond his reach.

There were eight or so men loitering in the center of the gym, one vanishing into the offices along the right wall. Sebastian waited, unconcerned and enjoying the looks of confusion and discomfort on the men around him.

He hid the fear that he couldn't see Lily anywhere.

The office door slammed open, and he saw Jonesy, another old acquaintance, and Daniel.

The years hadn't been kind to his brother. The once youthful face looked gaunt, his hair sweat-flopped and unkempt. His clothes, still too big to fill out properly, hung at strange angles as if he'd lost more weight than when he'd bought them. Sebastian eyed the red-rimmed eyes and cracked lips in disgust. Apparently, his brother had more in common with Oren than he expected.

"Sebastian." Daniel's voice was as sharp as it had been, despite the wear on his body. "What are you doing here? You're supposed to be—"

"I don't make deals with henchmen," Sebastian said, glancing around the room. "Figured I'd come right to the top."

Unprepared, Daniel just stared at him for a second.

"Then…the deed?"

He patted his chest pocket. "Ready to be signed, barring a few details."

"By all means," Daniel gestured to a folding table occupied by a few of his men. They got up as Daniel looked at them. "Let's do business."

Taking a seat, he noted the last set of closed doors that read 'Locker Room.' He doubted Daniel kept her in the office, not if he knew anything about how easily she could piss off anybody in her proximity. His brother's temper wouldn't do well under Lily's needling, and he bit down on worry as to how he might have reacted to her smart mouth.

"So, Tartarus?" he started, taking out the folded piece of paper. "I'm assuming that, in addition to the deed of the building, you want me to step down as owner, as well?"

"That was implied," Daniel said, his smile more like a baring of teeth.

"Nuances are important in a deal."

"Obviously."

He didn't blink. "My employees will be out of a job, I'm guessing. You'll be covering their severance pay?"

Daniel stared at him. "No."

"It's also my personal residence. Take some time for me to move out—"

"No," Daniel interrupted, his temper snapping. "No, the deal is this: you will sign Tartarus over to me, and leave, effective immediately. You and anyone now or formerly under your employ will not set foot in the building, you will make no claim to the property, and you will never question the legality of this deal."

The room went quiet, tension wafting from the

people around them as they watched the conversation.

"And in exchange?" Sebastian asked.

"In exchange, I'll return your girlfriend. You can walk out of here with her and I will never speak to you again."

He noticed what Daniel didn't say, and though terror rose up, he kept his voice calm and quiet. "I'd like to see her first."

"She's at the wharf."

"Don't lie to me."

The room held its breath while Daniel stared back at him. Finally, he snapped his fingers, and Jonesy went to the locker room door, swinging it open. No one spoke, the rattle of metal clear even through the door. It swung open, and Jonesy reappeared with Lily.

He supported her to keep her upright, her dark hair plastered to her neck and face, and her eyes hollow. Bloodshot amber eyes swept over him without recognition. Handcuffs dangling from her wrists as she shook from head to toe.

She was alive, but for how long…?

He might not have looked away, he might have ruined their desperate plan, had his phone not buzzed in his pocket. He took a breath, refocusing.

"Do we have a deal?" Daniel asked.

Tearing his eyes away from her, he leveled his stare at his brother. "No."

"No?" Daniel sputtered. "Why not? I've—"

"Because I made a deal with you once before," Sebastian said. "When I stepped down from the family and allowed you to take over."

Quiet murmurs broke out from those who worked for the family; though rumors had abounded when he left, he doubted Daniel would have ever admitted Sebastian chose to walk away. It would have made him lose face.

"I promised to never question your authority or ask for anything from you, in exchange for you to leave me and my club alone." He tucked the paper away, not breaking eye contact with his brother. "You broke that deal."

"So what? You're a club owner." Daniel got to his feet, shouting down at Sebastian, "I will take what I want from you, and from anyone else who gets in my way, and there's nothing you can do to stop me! You're not a member of the Galani family, for all you flaunt the name!"

Sebastian didn't stand, looking up at his desperate little brother. "You're right. I'm not. I'm just a man who keeps his end of a deal."

He didn't look away from Daniel as he raised his voice, just slightly. "Ben."

Footsteps approached, and he heard Ben's voice, resigned, as if he already knew what he would say. "Mr. Galani."

"I'd like for you to take your men and leave."

Daniel scoffed, but as Ben began issuing quiet orders, he spun on him. "What the hell are you doing?"

Ben ignored him, heading toward the door with a majority of the men in the room.

"What are you doing?!"

"Keeping his side of the deal, since I helped his mother keep their house." Sebastian watched Daniel panic for a moment, then said, "Jonesy."

"Mr. Galani?"

"Release Ms. Nehme and leave."

"Jonesy, don't you fucking dare!" Daniel turned toward him, and Sebastian finally got to his feet.

Jonesy gently lowered Lily to the ground, stepping away from her. "I'm sorry, Mr. Galani, but he—"

"I don't give a fuck what he did for you!" He strode toward Jonesy, who moved with alacrity to the door. "I am Daniel Galani, and I am the head of this family!"

Sebastian pressed a button on his phone. "You don't know the meaning of the word."

Daniel spun toward him, spittle flying from his lips. "You—I am the one in charge here!"

"Of what, exactly?"

Daniel let out a howl of rage, taking two steps toward Sebastian. He'd been counting on the anger, ready to hit him with the move Lily had taught him during his one and only class with her when—

Changing direction mid-stride, Daniel went for Lily, still lying on the ground.

"Daniel!" Sebastian warned, worry finally breaking through. "It's over—"

He grabbed Lily's arm, hauling her up and pulling her toward the side door with him. "I will not lose to you! I am—"

Sebastian's panic choked his voice, and he thought he was imagining things when he saw the handcuffs fall off of her left wrist, her thumb bent unnaturally.

The door slammed open behind Sebastian.

"Don't move, asshole," Reyes warned, with more footsteps heralding what remained of his gang.

The moment of hesitation seemed to be all Lily was waiting for. With the last bit of her strength, she swung her hips back and her torso forward, making Daniel lose his grip. With a pained breath, she turned, decked Daniel, and stumbled away from him.

A gunshot shattered the quiet, and Daniel dropped. Sebastian didn't flinch, knowing the price of his deal with Reyes. Revenge in exchange for Lily.

Sebastian ignored the body of a man who had never been his brother, stepping closer to where Lily stood, breathing heavily. She didn't even seem to see him, her eyes staring over his shoulder. She shuddered in pain, her eyes unfocused, and shoulders rounded in exhaustion.

"Lily," he said quietly, coming nearer to her.

She flinched, her eyes closing, and took a step closer to him. Then she collapsed.

Sebastian lunged forward, catching her head before she hit the ground, cradling her. "Doctor!" he shouted. "Doc!"

He heard running footsteps, pushing through Reyes's crew as they destroyed what remained in the gym, but his entire focus stayed with Lily.

"Stay with me, Nehme," he murmured, pillowing her head on his lap.

Her right hand, still cuffed, reached up, as if she wanted to touch him, but hesitated. He took her hand in his, bringing it up to his lips.

"Lily, look at me."

Her skin felt warm, too warm, and he could see blood crusting at her ear. But she'd made it this long, she was still alive, and that meant she would be okay. She had to be okay.

"Lily."

Her eyes opened, glassy and out of focus, but she looked up at him, and a bloodied smile tilted one side of her mouth.

"…real?" she whispered.

Sebastian nodded, hearing Eliza kneeling next to him, pulling Lily's other arm straight and taking the cork off the syringe. She cried silently, tears pouring down her face as she looked over her friend.

"Yeah," Sebastian said, struggling to keep his voice calm. "Real. We're here. Eliza and I are here."

"'M sorry…"

"Don't be sorry," he said, holding her closer as Eliza depressed the plunger filled with the antidote. "You're fine. Nothing to be sorry for."

She shuddered in his arms, her back arching off the floor, and he tried to hold her still.

"Doc?!" he asked, looking over at her.

She sobbed openly, checking Lily's pulse with her fingers, "I don't—I don't know!"

"Lily," Sebastian said, gathering her near. "Stay awake, okay? Keep your eyes open, look at me."

"We have to get her back to the clinic, it's the only place close enough to stabilize her," Eliza said through tears.

Beyond her, he could see Reyes watching, something like sympathy on his face.

Her broken hand grabbed at his arm, but she didn't seem to register any more pain. "Don't leave…please."

"I'm not going anywhere." He tucked her head into his shoulder, getting to his feet and cradling her in his arms. "I'm staying with you. I'm not going anywhere."

****

Eliza's fingers began to burn, and she started, lowering the mug she'd been holding thoughtlessly, and picking it up by the handle. She inhaled slowly, keeping her composure, and returned to her vigil.

Sebastian and Eliza had gotten Lily back to the

clinic, but she'd dropped into unconsciousness just before arrival. Eliza had her stabilized in one of the private rooms. Her vitals were all heading back to normal, which was a good sign, but she had yet to wake up. Though she smiled and told Sebastian that it looked promising, she wasn't positive, and she knew he could see through her white lies.

He had yet to leave her side, uncomfortably straight in one of the chairs, her unbroken hand clasped between his. It had been an hour since they'd gotten back, and he showed no signs of going anywhere.

Will kept glancing at Eliza from across the room, obviously checking in on her. Part of her wanted to go over and wrap herself around him, keep everything else at bay for a few more minutes, while the other part of her knew she couldn't. They needed to talk, and she couldn't yet.

Miguel stayed uncharacteristically quiet, working silently on his computer, and only looking up when Eliza went to check in on Lily, waiting for the shake of her head to show nothing had changed before returning to his work. The clinic had been mostly cleared out, emergency services cleaning up and transporting the rest to nearby hospitals with the cure Will had provided. It seemed to work on most of the victims if they got it quickly enough.

She didn't know if they'd been quick enough for Lily.

Eliza heard the footsteps coming down the hall and tensed, turning to face the newcomers.

Ellis, Teegan, and another man entered the room, soot-streaked and smiling.

Eliza opened her mouth, but no words came out.

Miguel came to her rescue, "Well?"

"Oren's entire operation was just arrested," Teegan said, sounding exhausted, but pleased. "And Oren squealed on Jed's Gym, too. So, anything left there is bound to help out. Opus has been confiscated, and all the lieutenants are turning on one another. It's not completely over, but with Oren in custody, it should slow down."

"And the club?" William asked.

"The transfer deed was caught in a fire," John said, glaring slightly at Ellis. "Meaning it is still owned by Mr. Galani."

Eliza let out a sigh of relief. Opus was gone. Oren was gone. And Daniel was…

"Nehme?" Ellis asked.

Eliza looked over her shoulder at the door hiding Sebastian and Lily. "She's been given the antidote. We'll know more when she wakes up."

"But she will wake up, right?" Teegan asked.

"I hope so," Eliza said quietly.

Miguel forced a smile, "Of course she will, El's the best doc we know, and she's getting the best possible care. You got a dealer off the street, you kept your club, this is going to turn into a whole happily ever after scenario, just you wait."

Miguel's optimism almost made Eliza smile, but she looked back at the room that held Sebastian and Lily and found it hard to do so. Chatter started up behind her, and she ignored it until she heard someone come up next to her.

"It'll be okay," Ellis said, his eyes on the door. "Nehme's too stubborn to die. Boss is too stubborn to quit."

Eliza nodded once, forcing herself to look away. "We have room here, if you want to stay until she wakes up."

"Yeah," he said, watching the door. "Gotta look out for each other."

She stayed next to him, no longer feeling alone in her vigil.

****

Despite his exhaustion, Sebastian refused to sleep. He'd heard Ellis and the others come in and discerned enough of their conversation to know they wouldn't have to worry about Oren or the Galani family again. He wanted to thank them for what they'd done, what they'd risked in helping him, but remained in his seat instead, knowing that Ellis and Eliza would understand.

His elbow on Lily's bed, he rubbed his eyes, trying to push the tension away, and only served to make it worse. His other hand wrapped around Lily's cool one, where it had been since they'd gotten her into this bed, and where it would be until she woke up.

She'd asked him not to leave her. He never broke a deal.

Eliza said everything would be okay, but he saw in her expression that she wasn't sure. Lily was stable, but that didn't mean she was okay. They wouldn't know until she woke, and that was only if—

No. She would wake up. He hadn't fought every step of his life to lose the one thing that mattered most.

He squeezed his eyes shut for a long moment, then opened them, staring at her so still on the bed. Eliza had suggested talking to her, but he had no idea what to say. Everything he thought of sounded too much like giving up or saying goodbye. And he damn well refused to give up. Not now. But as he looked at her, her hair clean and loose, the medical gown so unlike her with its severe simplicity, and the tubes and wires coming off of her limbs, he decided he'd try anything.

"How about a deal?" he said quietly. "You wake up, and you can wear flowers for the rest of your life. I won't complain ever again."

He shook his head at the futility, his eyes sliding shut and burning slightly. He couldn't leave to sleep, because that felt too much like giving up, and if he gave up, he'd have to face that what happened was his fault, that he'd lost her, that she'd died because of—

"I like your complaining."

Even cracked and rough, her voice was unmistakable.

He opened his eyes, braced for hallucinated disappointment, but met a bloodshot amber. Her lips were split and red but turned into a small smile as he stared.

"The whole reason for the flowers is to get you to complain," she continued in a broken whisper, which sounded like the most beautiful thing in the world to him.

"Then I'll complain as much as possible," he finally answered, both of them ignoring the crack in his voice as his grip tightened around her hand.

She squeezed back, the pain still clear in her weak grip. "You stayed."

"For as long as you want me."

The tiny smile flared again, and she closed her eyes. "How about forever?"

"Deal."

The easiest deal he'd ever made.

Epilogue

Lily hefted the last box onto her hip and shut the door of her empty office.

"Is that it?"

She turned, seeing Eliza standing behind her, a mug in her hand, and a wistful smile on her face. "That's it. P.I. Nehme's office is officially closed." Lily stacked the box next to the door. There were multiple piles, some to shred, some to donate, and the smallest pile to move.

It was several weeks after the incident with Daniel, and Lily was mostly healed. The spica cast on her hand itched like a sonofabitch, and she still had three more weeks of the fun. She was grateful that Eliza helped with the muscle sprains and physical therapy. Her physical prowess had always been a point of pride, so to have to work to get back to baseline was embarrassing. At least only Eliza saw her sweating and cursing over the most basic of exercises to rebuild her muscles after the strain.

"The end of an era." Eliza put her mug down on the coffee table. It was still early, only mid-morning, but Lily was packed up. There hadn't been much, once she shut down her business. And considering how many of her clothes and bathroom things had already migrated over to Tartarus.

"Whatever will you do without me?" Lily asked, arching her brow.

Eliza snorted. "Yes, without the stalkers and odd

hours and weird questions in the middle of the night. And it's not like you've been sleeping here recently anyway." She waggled her eyebrows at Lily.

Lily rolled her eyes but couldn't dispute that. She had been spending every night at Tartarus, curled up against Sebastian, who didn't seem to mind that the nightmares woke her screaming. Sometimes he was already awake and at the bar next to the living room. Sometimes he pulled her out of them, his own nightmares keeping him from sleep. Every time, he talked her down, reminding her where she was. A work in progress, at least she didn't have nightmares every single night now.

Lily laughed shortly. "I'm sorry I was a terrible roommate."

Eliza crossed the room and hugged her tightly. "You're amazing, and I'm happy for you. I'm going to miss you."

Lily hugged her back. "I'm going to miss you, too. But Tartarus's not far."

"Oh, Galani's already promised me free drinks for life for saving you, so you'll be seeing me often."

Lily's smile stuttered for a moment, still not entirely prepared for jokes about her near demise, at least without notice. Ellis made them constantly, but Eliza's were rarer, and all the most startling. But she recovered. "You deserve it."

Eliza drew back, her brows drawing together. "You called that doctor I recommended?"

"Yeah," Lily answered. She'd folded and refolded the card with the psychiatrist's number several dozen times before finally dialing. "We meet next week."

"Good. It'll help."

"Sure you'll be good here all alone?"

Eliza rolled her eyes. "I'll be fine. What about you, Miss I-Don't-Do-Commitment? Moving in after a few months?"

Knowing that the skepticism was justified, Lily just smiled. "I'll be fine."

"You sure?" Eliza asked.

"This the last of them?"

Both Eliza and Lily turned, seeing Sebastian in the door. His moving attire was far different from his club clothes, the tight jeans and sweater having even made Eliza speechless for a moment. His sleeves were rolled up after an hour of moving Lily out of her apartment and into the truck he and Ellis brought over.

"Yeah," Lily said, unable to help the smile that spread across her face at his voice. "That's it."

"Finally," Ellis groaned. "If I have to move another damn box of boxing shit—"

"Complain any more, and she'll use them on you," Sebastian interrupted, with a faint smile. He picked up one of the final boxes, Ellis grabbing the last two, and said to Lily over his shoulder. "We'll see you downstairs, Nehme. See you around, Doc."

"See you," Eliza called. She waited until the door shut behind them. "I do like him."

"Me too. I'll see you at Tartarus tonight?" Lily said, grabbing her jacket and working it over her cast.

Eliza hesitated. "Um. Tomorrow night. I have a…date."

Lily froze, her eyes lifting to Eliza, who was blushing now. "Really?"

"Yes."

"Can I ask—"

"No," she said firmly.

"Fine," Lily huffed. "But know, if he hurts you, I can kill him, even if I only have one hand."

"I have no doubt." Eliza laughed after a moment, then helped Lily pull the coat on over her shoulders. "I love you."

"I love you, too." Lily hugged her once more. She handed Eliza her mail key and extra set, keeping one for the apartment in case of emergencies, grabbed her bag, and shut the door behind her.

The February air bit at her face, but it was a short walk to the pickup truck Sebastian had rented. Ellis and he were just tying off the last of her boxes, and Sebastian gestured towards the cab. She didn't bother trying to argue with him. They'd already had several arguments about her working at the bar while she recovered, and she'd won those, so she decided to let him have this one.

Ellis and Sebastian piled in on either side of her after another couple of minutes, the heat still lukewarm. She leaned a little into Sebastian as he put the truck into gear and started back toward Tartarus.

"You okay?" Sebastian asked as Ellis fiddled with the radio.

"I'm okay." Lily leaned her head on his shoulder. "Let's go home."

She felt Sebastian smile, and he wrapped his fingers over her knee, driving them all back to Tartarus.

****

Eliza checked her reflection in the window, adjusting a wayward curl before she stepped into the restaurant. A classy Greek restaurant, it was family run so as to be small and intimate while upscale enough to serve as excellent first date material. Hanging her coat on the rack by the door, she caught sight of Will getting to his feet. She smiled briefly at the hostess, then crossed the carpeted floor.

"Hi," she said. "I hope you weren't waiting long."

"Not at all. I'm glad you made it." He pulled out her chair, and Eliza took her seat. He returned to his chair and settled in.

The server came to take their drink orders, and their conversation spilled over to food and wine for a few minutes, but that awkward pause came in again, and Eliza had to work not to apologize.

The past few weeks hadn't given them much opportunity to talk. First, Lily's recovery and rehabilitation, then working with the new hires. A fair number of them had tattoos of a line through an O, some of which had been scarred over or covered. She made sure to smile at all of them, and they did their part in helping out.

But, in the quiet moments after they closed the clinic down and cleaned up from the day, when Miguel begged off early because he got in before them, and it was just the two of them…neither of them broached the subject of their relationship. Eliza had returned to her apartment, and William seemed to keep his distance.

Until the day she snapped at one of Reyes's men for getting in a fight not two days after she patched him up, reprimanding him until he gave a sheepish apology. William had stared at her for a good twenty seconds before abruptly saying, "Will you go to dinner with me?"

And Eliza, adrenaline pumping through her and eager to finally have a discussion with him, had said, "Yes."

Which led them here. Still awkward silences, but

progress.

Will cleared his throat, "How's Lily?"

"Moved out today, actually. She's all settled in at Tartarus now, full-time bartender."

"That's good. Galani seems like...he can keep up with her."

Eliza laughed. "Yeah, he does."

"And the apartment, are you able to afford it on your own?"

"Yeah. My lease is up in April, though, so I'm looking to get out of there. Something smaller."

She knew him well enough to see that he had something he really wanted to say, but she was impressed that he kept quiet. "I hope you find something a little closer to the clinic," he said instead, taking a sip of his wine.

"Me, too."

Work carried the conversation through most of the meal and the bottle of wine, and into a second one. It wasn't until dessert that he put his fork aside and leaned in slightly.

"I want to apologize. You were right, and I know I was trying to keep you safe, but I should have talked to you."

She saw the lines around his eyes and mouth, but said, "Yes, you should have."

His smile was self-deprecating. "I can't promise that I won't make a stupid decision like that again, because we both know I will. But I want you to know that I would never do anything to intentionally hurt you or anyone else."

She opened her mouth, but Will took her hand.

"I know there's a long list of examples of how my

words and deeds haven't lined up. I know that my lying to you while trying to build this," he gestured between the two of them, "could have broken it completely, and I'm only here through some kind of miracle—"

"And my infinite patience," she added dryly.

He inclined his head, acknowledging that. "But I want this to work. I fucked it up, and I have no greater regret. I know you don't believe me, but if I had to do everything over again, I…I thought I knew better. That I had my priorities straight. I was wrong."

Eliza smiled faintly, appreciating the words, even if she didn't entirely believe him. She wanted to, though.

They broke apart as the server came back to clear their plates and left the bill, and they returned to lighter topics. They paid and William helped her put on her coat as they walked to the sidewalk. Eliza summoned a car, pretending not to see William's faint frown as the offer for him to drive her home remained unvoiced. As she tapped at the screen, he pulled his own phone out, pressed a button and the screen lit up.

It buzzed two, three, seven, eighteen, twenty-six, thirty-four, forty-two times before finally stopping, notification after notification appearing on the screen.

"What the hell was that about?" Eliza asked, watching him start to pocket it.

He huffed quietly, "Everything catching up. I turned it off."

"You what?" Eliza asked, frowning.

"I turned it off."

"You never turn off your phone," Eliza said. "Technology was made to be used and the idiots who don't think so should be quarantined until they've seen the artificial light of day. You say that. Often and loudly."

He merely shrugged. "We were on a date."

For a moment, she just stared at him as he pocketed his phone.

Then, Eliza grabbed his jacket and tugged him down towards her, using her heels and his sudden lack of height to her advantage as she pressed her lips to his. William froze for a heartbeat before one arm wrapped around her back, the other tilting her face up slightly as he returned the kiss. His lips were soft, tasting like the baklava they'd had for dessert, and almost hesitant. She kept it short, breaking away just far enough to breathe. Her eyes opened, catching William's open as well, dazed and surprised, but hopeful. He closed the distance the second time, slow and sweet, taking his time.

A car horn honked next to them, and they broke apart, his hand still on her back. Eliza waved at the taxi driver, then glanced up at Will.

"See you tomorrow." She got into the car, letting Will close the door behind her. As the driver put on his signal to get back into traffic, Eliza rolled down her window.

"Will?"

He hadn't moved from his spot on the sidewalk, the same hopeful look on his face as he looked at her.

"I want this to work, too."

Her car pulled into the street, but Eliza could have sworn that she could still see Will's smile from two blocks away.

****

Sebastian sipped his drink, leaning against one of the walls and watching his bustling club. Business was booming, but it wasn't the numbers that made him smother his smile behind his glass.

Ellis grinned at the doors, yelling at someone out of Sebastian's sight, obviously denying him entrance. Teegan walked through the crowd, the now-familiar form of Alex dogging her feet. Both of them wore smiles and Teegan seemed to spend more time than usual with her eyes up. Marley stayed the same, her indefatigable grin and energy pulling the crowd with her as she jumped and sang to her own music. Darcy laughed, a crowd around him, and Sebastian had seen Alex popping back and forth between Darcy and Teegan.

And Lily—

"Galani."

Sebastian closed his eyes briefly, that voice immediately sparking a tension headache, before turning to face Officer Hughes, in civilian clothes for once.

Sebastian hadn't seen nor heard of Hughes since the successful raid of the wharves. And he'd hoped to keep it that way. Apparently, he had used up all of his luck.

This particular area had been built in such a way that it wasn't as loud here, thanks to some fancy design. Hughes didn't have to raise his voice for Sebastian to hear him, but he did take a step closer.

It was silent for a moment, then Hughes huffed out, running his hand through his hair. "Look, I know you don't like me, and I don't care for you, either, but…I know you only called me because you knew I'd go to the wharves. So…I just wanted to say thanks for calling at all."

Sebastian frowned. "Your mistake is thinking you're the only one in this city who cares about what happens."

"I get it." Hughes's eyes darted over to the bar,

where Lily slung drinks, if without her usual flair and techniques. "She got pulled into it, too?"

It wasn't a real question, so Sebastian didn't bother answering.

"I saw the hospital," Hughes said next. "Reyes's crew."

Sebastian's poker face had never been so useful.

"I also saw the gym. Daniel Galani's body." Hughes ran his eyes over the club slowly, like he actually noticed it for the first time. "Saw evidence of a prisoner who'd escaped. We also found vials of what the techs are saying are a new, terrifying drug."

Sebastian's jaw jumped, well aware of what the drug did.

"I've pegged it as a power struggle, between the Galani and Oren." He met Sebastian's eyes squarely. "Case closed. Good riddance."

"Thank you." The words didn't taste quite as bad as he thought they would.

"The Mazrani's have one less person on their payroll," Hughes continued quietly. "The captain wasn't thrilled, but after everything…he didn't want morale to fall. Written warning and door duty for months, but…it's good."

"Glad to hear."

Hughes stuck out his hand to Sebastian. "Thank you. For making the call. For saying what you did. For doing what you did."

Sebastian shook his hand. "I look forward to…an effective working relationship."

Hughes almost smiled. "Sounds good to me."

Sebastian released his hand and pulled a card out of his pocket. "Drinks are on the house tonight, Officer

Hughes. Enjoy. Goodnight."

"Goodnight, Mr. Galani."

Hughes vanished back into the crowd, and Sebastian took the cue to return to the bar.

He didn't slide into his usual seat, choosing instead to stay back and watch Lily in action. Despite her arguments to the contrary, he knew her hand hurt by the end of each night. But he knew better than to try and win that fight. He'd at least gotten her to agree to him and Ellis moving her.

Yes, that was a change.

Living together, though not entirely smooth, hadn't been as difficult as he'd thought it would be. He wanted her here, in Tartarus, not just for himself, but because this is where she belonged.

Though, he did enjoy waking up with her. Even on the nights when one or both of them had nightmares, Sebastian with her in his arms. On the nights she didn't have nightmares, he woke to kisses on his face and neck, slow and warm, leading to more. The nights he couldn't sleep, it might have been a variety of nightmares. Some were older scars that were still healing, but most were newer. Him getting to the gym too late, Lily unable to recognize him, Daniel making good on his threat…

Sebastian wasn't usually a physically affectionate person, but Lily seemed to be an exception. Recently, he needed to be near her, brief small touches to reassure himself that she was safe. Still here with him.

Everyone was still recovering, but they were getting back to their new normal.

He saw Lily pour a beer and add a twist of lime to another drink, placing both down in front of a couple with a quick smile. Then her eyes darted over to him, and she cast him a wink, obviously knowing he was watching.

Giving up on the pretense, he came forward and claimed his seat. Lily stood in front of him in moments. "Hey," she said, refreshing his drink.

"Busy night?" he asked.

"Busy enough." She glanced over at the wall, where a man leaned, as he had been for the past two weeks. "I see Reyes's keeping his word."

"Technically Tartarus is in his turf now, but the understanding is in place."

"Good to be the King, huh?" she teased.

Sebastian nearly rolled his eyes. Reyes's nickname had become infamous among the men he'd sent to patrol the place, and his beloved employees had taken to it quickly. Within a few weeks, the constant presence of Reyes's men wouldn't be necessary, but it helped now.

Lily laughed, running her fingers over the back of his hand. Sebastian caught them at the edge of his grasp, squeezing gently before letting her go. She smiled, then turned back to her work.

As they closed down that night, Marley kept the music going, just quieter. Sebastian helped Darcy sweep up, as Alex and Ellis collected the glasses left around the club. Teegan and Lily were cleaning behind the bar, singing to themselves while Marley checked her equipment for the next night.

As he gathered a bag of trash, he saw Lily hauling one out to the dumpster, and quickly fell into step with her. Holding the door open for her, he followed her into the alley. They tossed the bags into the dumpster and Lily brushed off her hands. She grinned at him, and Sebastian took advantage of the quiet moment to cup her cheek and kiss her.

He felt her quiet laugh before she wrapped her arms around his neck, the cast an uncomfortable weight for both of them, but sliding into the kiss all the same. Time for just the two of them had been rare, not that the cleaning and reopening of the club hadn't been important. Sebastian had just...reprioritized.

Lily stepped a little closer, and Sebastian wrapped his arms around her waist, leaning down to deepen the kiss.

"Um, I do hate to interrupt," a voice called from the end of the alley.

Sebastian and Lily immediately broke apart, turning to face the alley mouth. Her hand went to her waist and Sebastian stepped in front of her bad arm.

A man stood by the street, the glow of a lit cigarette faintly illuminating the planes of a haggard face. "I take it you two are the supposed King and Queen of the Underworld?"

Reyes's title had caught on everywhere. He didn't know how he felt about that.

Lily muttered next to him, "Queen, huh?"

"What of it?" Sebastian asked, ignoring her.

The man wore a rumpled white shirt and suit pants, with a worn coat over his shoulders. His eyes were sunken in and the smile on his face was hard. "If you are, then I'd tell you that my name's Smith and I want to make a deal."

"What kind of deal?"

He came within sight of the emergency light by their door, and now Sebastian could pick out the shadows under his eyes, the growth of an untended beard, and the familiar look of desperation. "I'm looking for someone."

"Who?"

"An eight-year-old girl. Name of Ophelia. She was taken by some less-than-pleasant folk, and I lost the trail here. I hoped you could help me find her and get her back home to her mother."

"Who took her?" Sebastian asked.

"A rival of her father. Trying to use her as leverage for her dear old daddy to step down. He overestimated her father's interest, and he'd got her here now. Rumor was he planned to join up with a bloke named Daniel Galani, but it appears you messed with that plan. Last I heard she was still in the city. You help me find her, and in exchange, I'd tell you that Opus shit is still being dealt uptown. I have names."

He heard Lily's inhale and glanced at her. She met his gaze.

He knew what she would say. Of course, he did, because it's what he wanted to say, too. But the smaller, more selfish part of him wanted to tell Smith to find someone else.

Turning, she slid her good hand into Sebastian's, squeezing in silent encouragement. She smiled up at Sebastian and he gave her an arched brow in return.

"It'll be fun," she said quietly.

"It'll be dangerous."

"That makes it fun."

"Lily," he said, exasperated.

"You know you want to."

"No, what I want is to—"

She interrupted him with a quick, hard kiss. "I love you, too."

"Are you always going to be this much trouble?"

"Absolutely." She grinned, unrepentant.

"So, do we have a deal?" Smith asked, sounding a little annoyed.

Lily and Sebastian turned to him, joined at the hand, mirrored smirks on their faces.

"Deal."

A word about the author...

Michele Leech is a teacher by day and a writer by night. She recently received a degree in library sciences, which just allowed her to find more books to read. When she's not wrangling her daughter, or watching movies with her husband, she enjoys reading, playing video games, and daydreaming about her next book.

Thank you for purchasing
this publication of The Wild Rose Press, Inc.

For questions or more information
contact us at
info@thewildrosepress.com.

The Wild Rose Press, Inc.
www.thewildrosepress.com

Milton Keynes UK
Ingram Content Group UK Ltd.
UKHW022052110624
443988UK00015B/639